COVERED BRIDGES

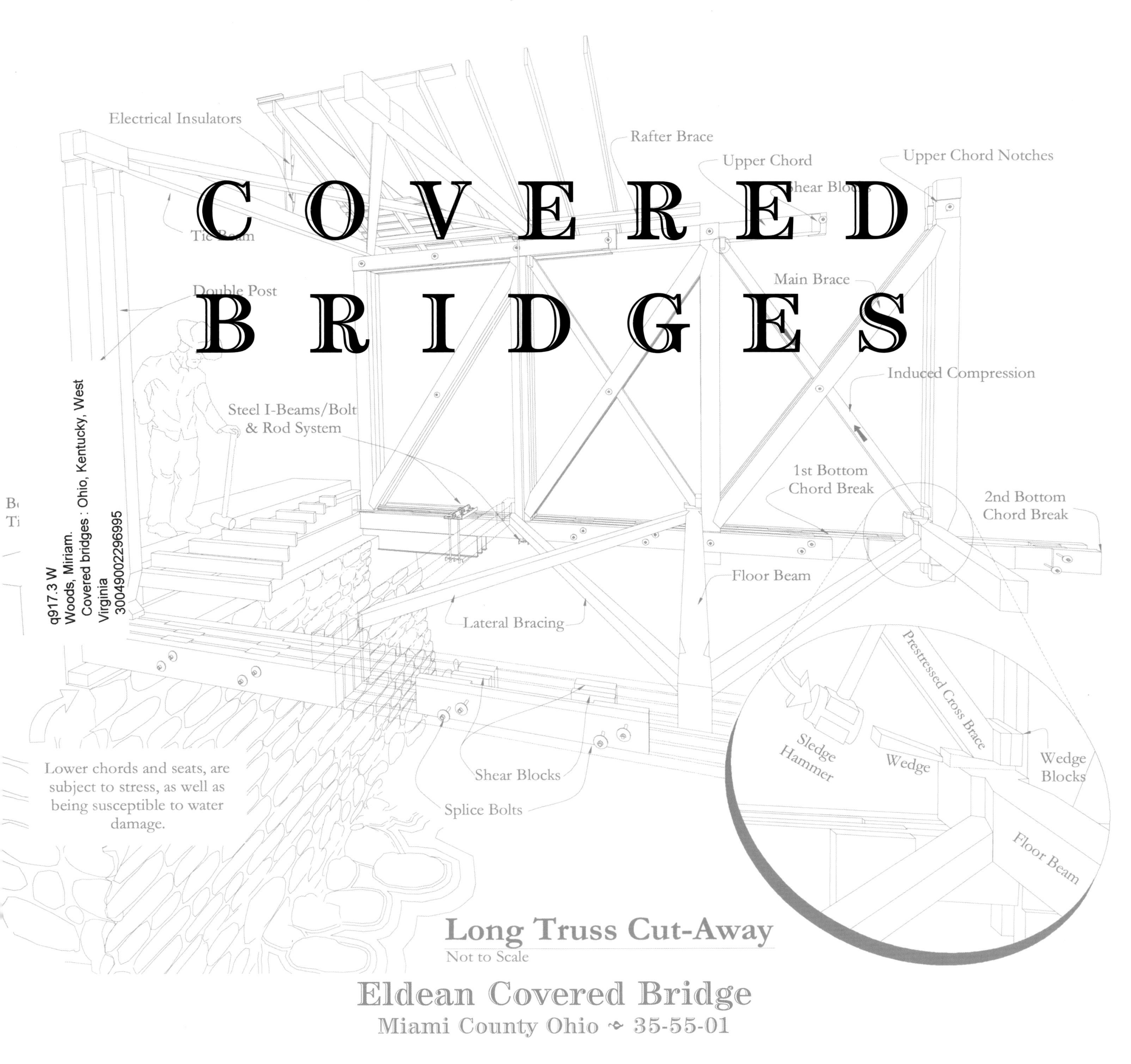

also from

The Wooster Book Company

Ohio's Bicentennial Barns

Text by Beth Gorczyca
Photographs by B. Miller

COVERED BRIDGES

OHIO • KENTUCKY • WEST VIRGINIA

text by Miriam F. Wood
and David A. Simmons

photography by B. Miller

The Wooster Book Company
Wooster Ohio ~ 2007

205 West Liberty Street
Wooster Ohio ~ 44691
800-WUBOOK-1
www.woosterbook.com

Harshman Covered Bridge
Preble County Ohio ~ 35-68-03

Printed in China.

ISBN: 1-59098-035-2

Historic American Engineering Record (HAER) drawings courtesy of the U.S. Department of the Interior • National Park Service
MAP SOURCES: *www.oardc.ohio-state.edu* and *www.nationalatlas.gov*

Library of Congress Publication Data

Wood, Miriam F.
Covered bridges : Ohio, Kentucky & West Virginia /
text by Miriam F. Wood & David A. Simmons ; photographs by B. Miller.
ISBN 1-59098-035-2 (alk. paper)

LCCN 2005276336

∞ This book is printed on acid free paper and sewn in signatures for permanence.

Table of Contents

Ohio

NORTHEASTERN OHIO

Bridge *descriptions* are in bridge-number order • Bridge *directions* are in alphabetical order by county

Southeastern Ohio

Bridge *descriptions* are in bridge-number order • Bridge *directions* are in alphabetical order by county

Southwestern Ohio

Bridge *descriptions* are in bridge-number order • Bridge *directions* are in alphabetical order by county

Northwestern Ohio

DIRECTIONS

Bridge *descriptions* are in bridge-number order • Bridge *directions* are in alphabetical order by county

Central Ohio

Bridge *descriptions* are in bridge-number order • Bridge *directions* are in alphabetical order by county

Kentucky

Boone
Kenton
Campbell
Gallatin
Trimble
Carroll
Grant
Pendleton
Bracken
Mason
Lewis
Greenup
Owen
Robertson
Harrison
Henry
Oldham
Fleming
Carter
Boyd
Nicholas
Franklin
Scott
Bourbon
Jefferson
Shelby
Rowan
Elliott
Lawrence
Bath
Fayette
Montgomery
Bullitt
Spencer
Anderson
Woodford
Clark
Menifee
Morgan
Jessamine
Meade
Powell
Johnson
Martin
Nelson
Mercer
Washington
Henderson
Daviess
Hancock
Breckinridge
Hardin
Madison
Estill
Wolfe
Magoffin
Union
Boyle
Garrard
Lee
Breathitt
Floyd
Pike
Webster
McLean
Ohio
Grayson
Larue
Marion
Lincoln
Jackson
Owsley
Crittenden
Hopkins
Taylor
Casey
Rockcastle
Knott
Livingston
Caldwell
Muhlenberg
Butler
Edmonson
Hart
Green
Perry
Clay
Ballard
McCracken
Adair
Pulaski
Laurel
Leslie
Letcher
Lyon
Christian
Warren
Barren
Metcalfe
Russell
Carlisle
Marshall
Knox
Harlan
Graves
Trigg
Todd
Logan
Allen
Cumberland
Wayne
Hickman
Simpson
Monroe
Clinton
McCreary
Whitley
Bell
Calloway
Fulton

West Virginia

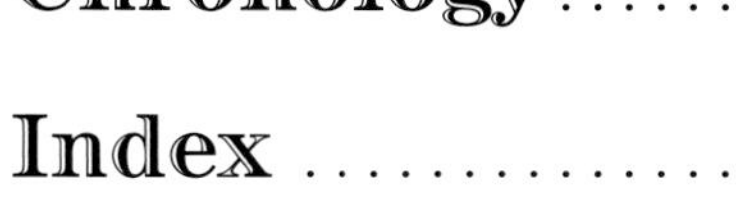

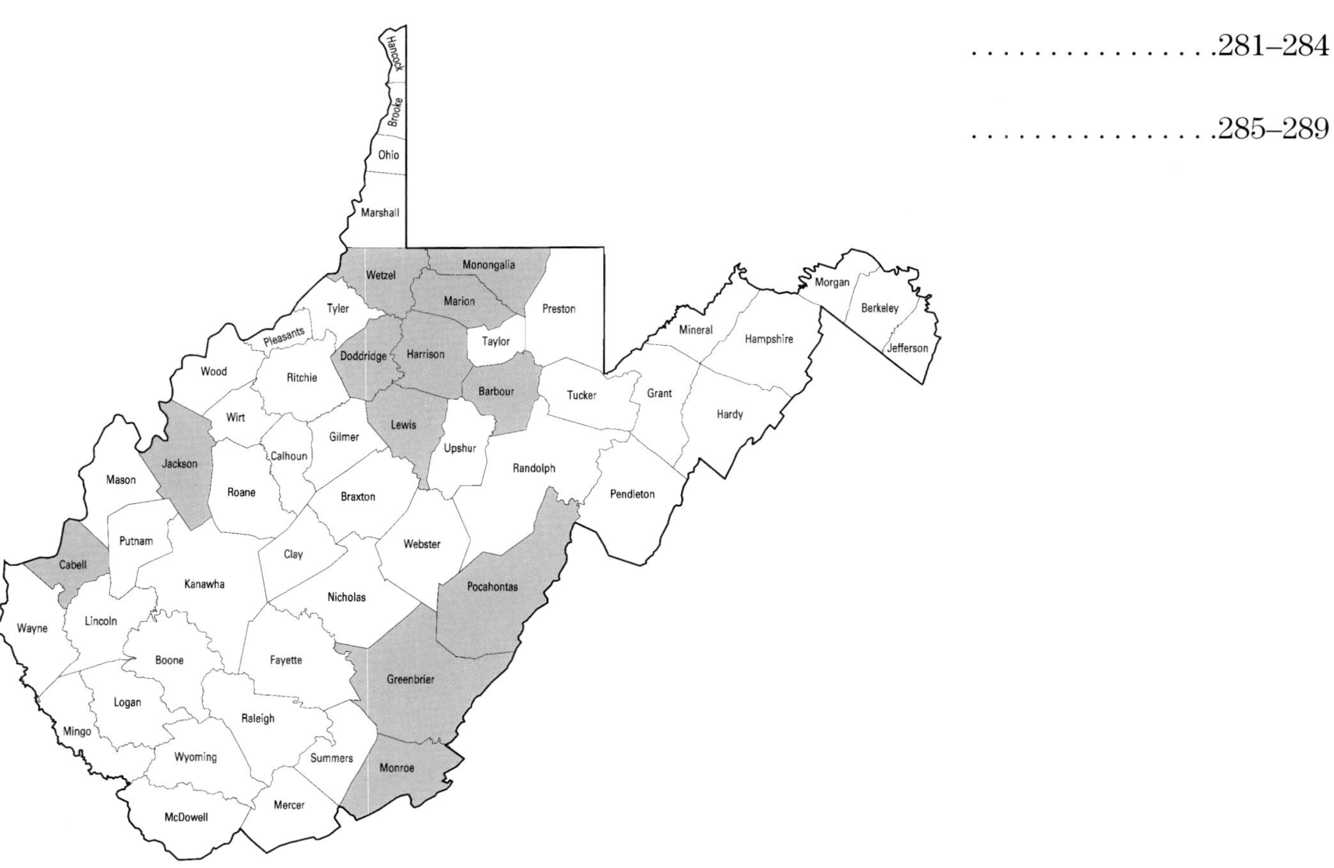

Bridge *descriptions* are in bridge-number order • Bridge *directions* are in alphabetical order by county

DIRECTIONS

Covered bridges in the United States are numbered according to a system devised in the 1940s by John Diehl, a history-minded engineer from Cincinnati, Ohio. In an effort to keep the records for each bridge straight, he came up with a numerical system in which the first number indicates the alphabetical listing of the state, the second number denotes the county, while the third is a number assigned to individual bridges within each county. Kentucky is the 17th state alphabetically, Ohio is the 35th, and West Virginia the 48th.

Reflections on Covered Bridges

Covered bridges are sought out by tourists and recorded by shutterbugs. They serve as the thematic centerpieces for numerous historical associations, and they are studied by civil engineers. Even the United States Congress has been caught up in the enthusiasm for covered bridges, passing legislation in 2000 to fund restoration projects, studies of special preservation techniques, and educational programs. Why do covered bridges hold such a special place in people's hearts?

Covered bridges seem romantic. Stories of stolen kisses and hopeful hugs within the privacy of an enclosed bridge helped popularize them in a generation that had no direct link with horses and buggies. But such visions of innocent love pale in light of the central role they played in Robert Waller's steamy 1992 bestselling novel, *The Bridges of Madison County*.

But the appeal of covered bridges runs deeper than just having a connection to sentiment and love. They appear old. And as aging artifacts, among certain parts of the populace, they earn a degree of respect.

Along with age is an assumption of rarity. In fact, some scholars suggest that Ohio once led the nation in the number of standing covered bridges. In recent years, Ohio's 141 bridges have fallen to second place behind Pennsylvania's 222. Recent research, however, has revealed that well over two thousand covered bridge spans were built in Ohio,

Wooden Railroad Bridge
Now a thing of the past, wooden bridges were once common on Midwestern railroads. Companies concerned about the long-term maintenance of their wooden bridges were quick to erect roofs to cover over the roadway surface.
Ohio Historical Society

22

Permanent Bridge
Timothy Palmer built the Permanent Bridge over the Schuylkill River at Philadelphia, which is believed to be America's first covered bridge, between 1801 and 1805. *Ohio Historical Society*

Bridge Street Bridge
Historians debate the location and date of Ohio's first covered bridge. Some give credit to a bridge across the Little Beaver Creek recorded in Columbiana County in 1809. Others recognize the Bridge Street Bridge over the Scioto River in Chillicothe, erected by Eli Fox in 1816. Regardless, the Chillicothe bridge was a remarkable and early structure. A photograph taken in 1886 during its demolition showed the large wooden arches and vertical iron rods that supported the bridge roadway. These suggest to historians that this bridge was copied from a famous arch bridge at Trenton, New Jersey. *Ross County Historical Society*

which is a survival rate of under ten percent. West Virginia now has seventeen bridges remaining and Kentucky numbers only thirteen. Rarity is, indeed, a relative thing.

The use of wood resonates with even the superficial observer. In a country renowned for its forested landscapes, what could be more natural than large wooden structures? Obviously these bridges were not created from materials that can today be purchased at the local building supply store. Nor were those who fabricated them, men knowledgeable in the techniques of timber framing, the standard modern contractor. Because they were assembled from tree-sized timbers by skillful artisans, it is assumed that they provide a special link to our nation's heritage, which, in fact, many do.

Perhaps most of all, covered bridges provide a striking visual imagery. Viewed from the side, they appear like barns—another venerated structural type—projected out and suspended over water. Among the most common photo donations to historical societies are collections of amateur covered bridge pictures. There seems to be no end of interest in these picturesque vistas.

Of equal importance to an auto-oriented society such as we have today, covered bridges can be the perfect drive-through link with history. Anyone can drive to one of the numerous examples still open to traffic, roll the windows down and study the structure as they slowly drive across—all without ever leaving the car.

Our political leaders long ago suggested that a close relationship with nature gave Americans an important edge over other, more city-bound European societies. In an age of back-to-nature products and advertising, covered bridges, found in predominately rural settings, can represent a tangible connection with nature and the bucolic American landscape.

Many covered bridges were, of course, designed to carry horse-drawn vehicles. With the exception of members of the Amish community, most of the last generation that worked and lived with horse-powered transportation is now gone. With the passage of that generation went an understanding of how truly laborious that life could be. So we can be forgiven today for having nostalgic feelings for a time that is seen as slower and less complicated. Covered bridges become the perfect representative of a nostalgic life that few have actually experienced.

Piqua Trestle Bridge
Many of the earliest wooden bridges in Kentucky, Ohio, and western West Virginia were not covered at all but open, trestle-type structures. Artist and popular historian Henry Howe included a drawing of one in Piqua Ohio, built in 1838 over the Great Miami River in his *Historical Collections of Ohio*.

Ohio Valley Origins

How American is the covered bridge? Covered bridges trace their history back to fourteenth-century central Europe. In 1570, Andrea Palladio, an architect from northern Italy, prepared drawings of wooden trusses similar to the basic types later used in North America, but he admitted to copying them from examples in Germany. It is thought that the idea of covering wooden stream crossings originated in Switzerland.

If the concept of covered bridges was borrowed from Europe, it was up to North Americans to completely develop it. Historians have identified late-eighteenth and early-nineteenth century America as the "wooden age." And what better place to foster wooden bridge building than in a country that abounded in inexpensive timber and innumerable experienced carpenters?

While materials and craftsmen were plentiful, it was the vast need that made America such a fertile ground for covered bridges. Countless streams and valleys had to be bridged to create a modern transportation system capable of sustaining a productive economy. Statewide populations in Kentucky, Ohio, and West Virginia prior to 1920 provide a rough indicator of the size of the state economies that supported bridge projects. Throughout this period, Ohio's population towered over the other two states. West Virginia's population was never more than one-fifth that of Ohio's, and there were only about half as many Kentuckians as there were Buckeyes. Not surprisingly, the covered bridges built in Ohio numbered in the thousands. In the other two states put together, they numbered, at best, in the hundreds. But in terms of covered bridges that actually survived into the middle of the twentieth century, West Virginia had twice that of Kentucky.

Virtually all of the earliest efforts at constructing wooden bridges were what we now call trestles: uncovered, wharf-like structures. We know that by 1804 such a bridge existed on Zane's Trace in Cambridge, Ohio. A traveler in southwestern Ohio in 1820 described a trestle as nothing more than two long trees thrown over the stream and covered with planks. While uncovered, not all these bridges were crude. Specifications promulgated by the Virginia Board of Public Works before the Civil War for trestle bridges on the turnpikes in the western part of the state (now West Virginia) insisted on precisely placed uprights and bracing and roadways of the highest-quality materials and workmanship.

Timothy Palmer, a Massachusetts housewright and inventor, is given credit with completing America's first covered bridge, the three-span Permanent Bridge over the Schuylkill River at Philadelphia, in 1805. Later that same year, another covered bridge was erected over the Delaware River at Trenton, New Jersey, by the celebrated bridge architect, Theodore Burr.

Burr is today viewed as such an important figure in early American covered bridges that a leading bridge preservation group in his adopted state of Pennsylvania has taken his name for their group. This Trenton bridge seems to have a close link with what some feel is the earliest documented covered bridge in Ohio. It was built in Chillicothe in 1816 under the direction of Eli Fox, a Connecticut-born millwright, and duplicated the massive laminated arch design of the Trenton structure. Although this pioneer structure was removed in 1886, the significance of this crossing of the Scioto River in what was then the state capital is still recognized in the street name: Bridge Street.

This brings us to a fundamental question. Why are these bridges covered? Despite a wealth of creative folklore explanations, there is really only one reason: to protect the essential timber framing. Left exposed to the elements, a wooden bridge might last a decade. With a covering, many are over one-hundred-years old, and there are some that are well on their way to a second century.

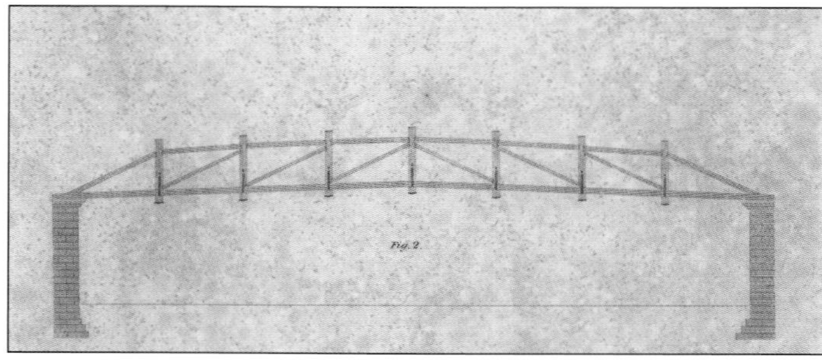

Multiple Kingpost

The multiple kingpost was the most common of all covered bridge trusses. It featured vertical tension members—which are correctly shown passing through the upper and lower horizontal members, or chords—and a series of diagonal compression beams leaning towards the center of the bridge. *Ohio Historical Society*

If covering wooden bridges was such a practical idea, why weren't they all covered? The most basic reason was cost. Simply creating an adequate stream crossing was the first order of business, especially in a cash-starved frontier environment, and a roof could seem like an unnecessary frill. In some cases, the installation of a roof might be delayed several years while financial coffers were replenished. A one-hundred-foot wooden bridge was built over Cross Creek in Jefferson County southwest of Steubenville in 1817, but it was not covered until the following year.

But what about wooden bridges built after an economy was firmly established? Was there a downside to putting a roof and siding on a wooden bridge? Indeed there was. Wind was a primary concern, especially after a major covered railroad bridge near Cincinnati was totally destroyed in an 1861 tornado. This reinforced the concern by some bridge builders that "a skeleton bridge" would allow strong winds to blow through a bridge instead of pushing it over. The sizeable cross bracing seen overhead in covered bridges was specifically designed to help counteract strong wind loads.

Many railroad bridges were left uncovered so that sparks from passing locomotives would rise into the air instead of setting a wooden roof—and the bridge—on fire. If railroad bridges were roofed, barrels of sand were placed nearby and individuals were often hired, at yet another expense, to serve as fire watchmen.

During the Civil War, Union strategists removed the roofs from some major highway bridges to reduce the chances of Rebel sabotage. Finally, the long dark tunnel of a covered bridge, particularly in an urban setting, created concern that they might harbor criminals. In some communities this issue actually helped bring about the demise of covered bridges. Citizens of Dayton, Ohio, petitioned city council in 1871 against "any kind of enclosed wooden bridge," instead preferring, "a good substantial Iron Bridge" for just this reason.

Zanesville Y-Bridge

Zanesville's Y-Bridge, built at the junction of two major rivers, was among Ohio's most famous. The use of multiple kingpost trusses by its builders, Ebenezer and Catharinius Buckingham, led many to later refer to this truss type as a "Buckingham truss." It is said of Zanesville's Y-Bridge, that it is the only bridge in the world you can cross and still be on the same side of the river. *Ohio Historical Society*

An Era of Covered Bridges

The first covered bridges in Kentucky, Ohio, and West Virginia were built by private stock corporations and were toll bridges.

In West Virginia, the legislative basis for bridges was established with Virginia's passage of the General Turnpike Act in 1817. Nonetheless, little attention was initially paid to the western counties that would later become West Virginia. Not until the establishment of the Northwestern Turnpike that ran east from Parkersburg in the 1830s did covered bridge construction in these counties begin in earnest.

Roberts Bridge
The Roberts Covered Bridge, built in Preble County, Ohio, in 1829, is a classic example of a Burr truss. This image was taken when the bridge was on its original site. *Photographers' Collection • Wm. G. Keener/C. S. Duckworth, Photographers*

Kentucky's early history was remarkably similar. The legislature put highways into the hands of private stock companies in 1817. While periodic depressions made the operations of these companies difficult, the system predominated throughout the nineteenth century. Covered bridge construction began with the completion of the Maysville-to-Lexington turnpike in the 1830s.

The most common highways built in nineteenth-century Kentucky were toll roads known as turnpikes. As late as 1890, fully three-quarters of the improved highways in the state levied tolls. The hold of these road companies was, however, broken by the so-called Tollgate Wars in the 1890s. An outcry arose among the lower classes for free roads and bridges, and tollhouses and gatekeepers were assaulted. Eventually, turnpike companies were forced to sell or abandon their roads to public entities.

Ohio's era of covered toll bridges began in 1816 on Chillicothe's Bridge Street, already mentioned. In contrast to the turnpike firms that erected bridges in the other two states, separate bridge companies built most of Ohio's early toll structures. They were initially built in communities like Dayton and Hamilton where company officials could anticipate the highest toll revenue. Petitions to the Ohio legislature by these stock companies continued to be made into the 1850s. Their bridges were erected over the Great Miami, Maumee, Scioto, Hocking, Cuyahoga, and Tuscarawas Rivers.

The Civil War changed the outlook of many Ohioans towards government. They were more accepting, perhaps even expectant, that governments take a role in large public projects. In 1869, the Ohio legislature authorized county commissioners to purchase—raising funds through taxation or bond sales—existing toll bridges in order to make them free. Taking this another step further, counties now felt more at liberty to erect their own covered bridges. In fact, the majority of extant covered bridges in the state were built in the aftermath of this legislation.

The federal government had helped point the way. The National Road was completed to Wheeling by 1820 and began a steady progression across the Buckeye state during the following two decades. While civilian contractors did the work, including bridge construction, it was under the close supervision of the West Point-trained military engineers who represented the government's interest. The quality of the work these young officers demanded set a high standard for the covered bridges erected in Bridgeport, Cambridge, Zanesville, and Columbus, and provided a model for other builders to follow.

The expansion of railroad lines in the 1850s accelerated the construction of covered bridges in all three states. Railroads' requirement for miles of uninterrupted and comparatively level right-of-way created an unprecedented demand for bridging of all kinds. During initial construction, economic concerns did not permit the creation of highly durable, but excessively expensive, stone bridges, so wooden structures predominated. Railroads also brought standardization and industrialization to the world of covered bridges.

Under pressure for rapid construction so that rail lines might begin producing revenue, railroads used bridge designs whose parts could be mass-produced and stockpiled, ready for quick assembly by semi-skilled laborers. Several Ohio-based firms were especially important in this early railroad construction: Thatcher & Burt and McNairy, Claflen & Company both from Cleveland; and the McCallum Bridge Company in Cincinnati. While the period of rapid growth fostered an era of experimentation

Town Truss

The Town truss of 1820 resembles a garden lattice and, because it simplified bridge construction, quickly became very popular especially in areas influenced by New Englanders. The Town truss also was a favorite of the military-trained engineers who supervised construction of the National Road. *National Archives, Cartographic and Architectural Branch*

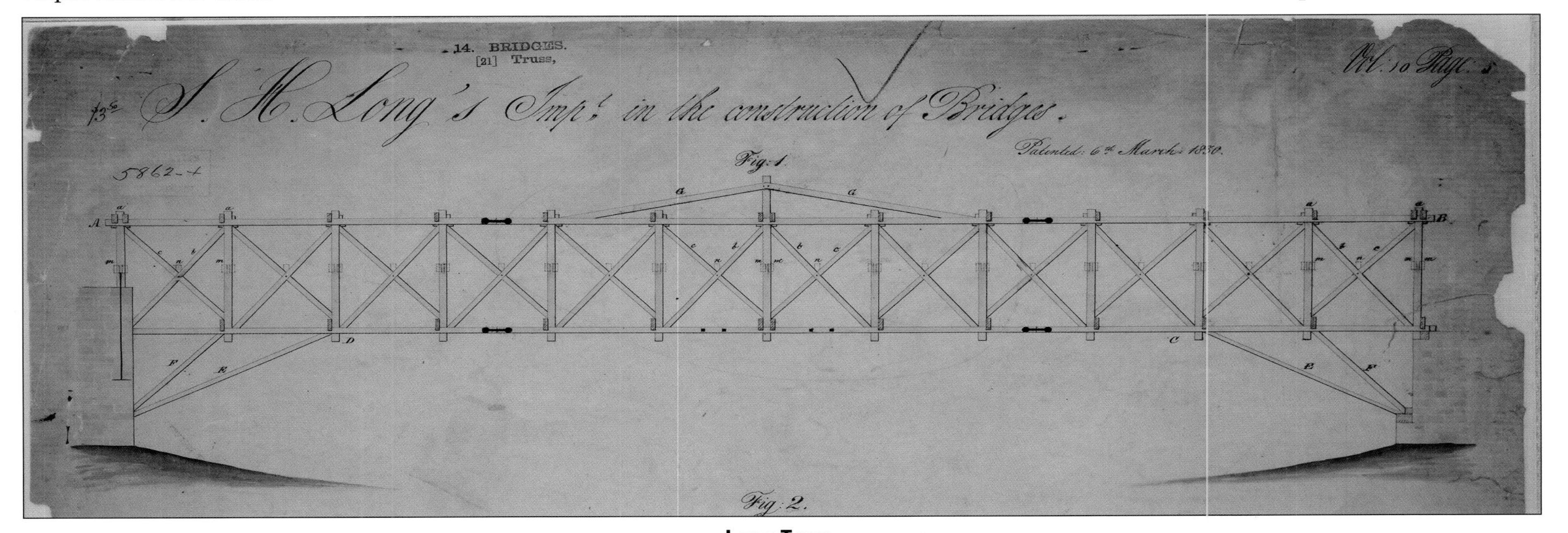

Long Truss

The Long truss was America's first scientific bridge design. Particularly popular in West Virginia, its diagonal compression and vertical tension members led it to be also called a scissor truss. *National Archives, Cartographic and Architectural Branch*

among all bridge builders, unfortunately no covered wooden railroad bridges survive in these states.

The initial period of covered bridge construction lasted in these three states as long as it made economic sense, allowing a contractor to make a reasonable profit and providing an option for public entities that was not too costly. But as early as 1880, there were signs that the wooden bridge building trend was slowing. Supplies of hardwoods, such as the white oak often used for bridge work, were starting to dwindle. Ohio builders were already shipping structural timber from the pine and hardwood forests of Great Lakes states such as Michigan. Obviously rail transport was critical for utilizing these forests, and fortunately much of Michigan's Lower Peninsula was crisscrossed by railroads that also ran through Ohio. Although both Kentucky and West Virginia retained significant supplies of hardwoods in 1880, they were not located in areas largely accessible by rail or near major rivers that would allow rafting.

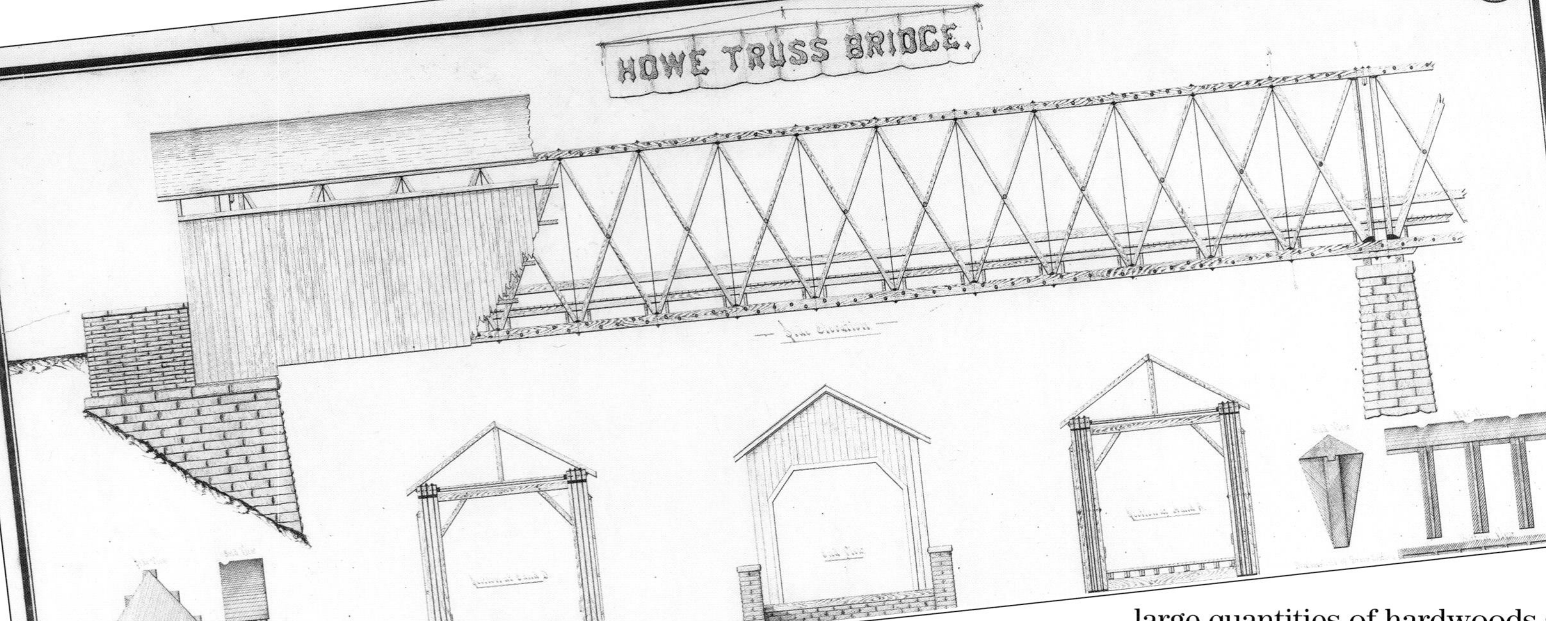

Howe Truss

The Howe truss eliminated much of the meticulous, and more expensive, labor necessary with older, framed bridge trusses. It replaced the vertical tension members of a Long truss with an adjustable iron rod. Because it could be assembled rapidly, it was a favorite with railroad companies. The Columbia Bridge Works of Dayton, Ohio, built this example in the 1870s. *Ohio Historical Society*

By the turn of the twentieth century, additional economic factors further reduced the use of structural wood. Steel progressively superceded heavy timber framing even as wood prices were steadily rising. The labor involved in harvesting hardwoods used in bridges was, in fact, considerably higher than other, softer woods. Coincident with the famous era of trust busting, political accusations that timber company monopolies lay at the root of these cost increases, led to Congressional investigations.

But there was also competition for the hardwoods used for bridges. The popularity of Arts and Crafts cabinetry, furniture, and flooring drained the supplies of oak that might have gone into bridge use.

The final blow came from the federal government's vast appropriation of wood during World War I to produce cantonments, ships, weapons, and airplanes. Restrictions were placed on uses considered non-essential for the war effort.

In an effort to insure a steady supply of timber, the government was forced to drive prices up. Between 1914 and the Armistice in November 1918, average lumber prices rose ninety percent. With the war's end, long delayed maintenance created an even greater demand, and, along with large quantities of hardwoods shipped to Europe for the reconstruction effort, prices were forced even higher.

In this context, large dimensional timbers became scarce. It is not difficult to see why Ohio's last state-sponsored covered bridge was completed in 1919. In Kentucky, it came a few years later, in 1924.

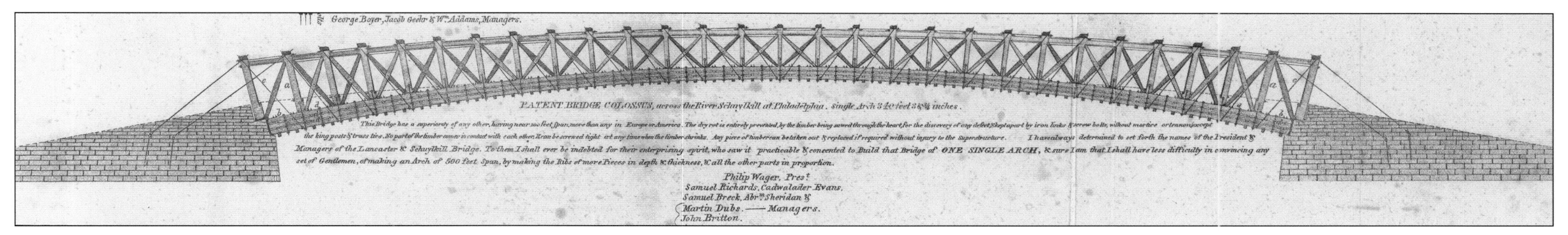

Colossus Bridge

The Colossus Bridge over the Schuylkill River in Philadelphia was an unprecedented 340-foot span. Built in 1812 by the legendary Lewis Wernweg, it was one of America's greatest engineering achievements. It was destroyed by fire in 1838. *Ohio Historical Society*

What Holds Them Up?

Covered bridges depend on trusses to stand. A triangle is the geometric form most resistant to change, and an analysis of any truss reveals arrangements of triangles. In this case, the triangles are made up of massive wooden timbers that are connected by specialized joinery techniques.

Each triangular component in a bridge truss functions in one of two ways: they are pressed together—said to be in compression—or they are pulled apart—meaning they are in tension. The arrangement of the compression and tension members of a truss defines its type. A compression member might be held in place through the simple truss action inherent in the structure without the use of any pins or bolts. But the true skill of a wooden bridge builder was defined by the connections in the tension members—fabricating a means to keep two adjacent pieces of large structural timbers from pulling apart. A whole host of simple to complex tension connections were devised and, in some cases, patented.

The earliest covered bridges were built long before scientific principles had been developed to enable builders to define the strength of a bridge truss. It was an era of empiricism, when bridge builders learned their craft on the job from their predecessors. An understanding of how large to make bridge components was based on the fact that an earlier bridge had been made with those dimensions and techniques and it had been successful. If it didn't stand up over time in this system of trial and error, then adjustments were made.

The most basic truss was a simple triangle and was called a kingpost. To erect a longer bridge, builders simply kept adding verticals and diagonals on both ends of a central vertical and pair of diagonals. This was called a multiple kingpost. The famous Y-Bridge in Zanesville, Ohio, used a multiple kingpost design. Its unique Y configuration, crossing at the junction of two rivers, attracted wide attention and made its father-and-son builders, Ebenezer and Catharinus Buckingham, renowned. Their design became so popular that in many parts of Ohio, a multiple kingpost was routinely termed a Buckingham truss.

The structural strength of arches had long been established by the era of covered bridge building, and one of the earliest and most widely popular forms incorporated a wooden arch in combination with a multiple kingpost. Theodore Burr, the pioneer builder mentioned before, is given credit for first patenting this design in America in 1804, and it was appropriately called a Burr truss. The Burr truss was especially popular in West Virginia.

In 1820, a Connecticut architect named Ithiel Town patented a simplified truss that could be fabricated by the average carpenter's crew. He based it on the common lattice. The Town lattice eliminated all elaborate joinery requiring skilled craftsmen and was pinned together from ordinary planks, thereby reducing both labor and material costs. While some derisively labeled the design a "garden trellis fence," it became highly successful and was used extensively in areas like northeastern Ohio where a New England influence was strong. It was also viewed favorably by the military engineers that supervised the National Road construction and was often specified for these contracts.

Stephen H. Long is given credit for introducing scientific design to the world of covered bridges. This New Hampshire-born and West Point-trained member of the U. S. Army's Topographical Engineers devised his truss while working for the Baltimore & Ohio Railroad, thereby helping illustrate how influential American railroads were in expanding the world of covered bridges. Long added a second diagonal, along with a wooden wedge, to the multiple kingpost truss. A few well-directed taps on the wedges in the truss would stiffen the entire bridge, a bridge-building concept that was literally centuries ahead of its time. The first example of this design, the Jackson Bridge, was named after Long's commander-in-chief and was completed in 1829. Long vigorously promoted his new concept, publishing a book on it and arranging with a small army of agents to act on his behalf throughout the East and Midwest. Five of Long's agents operated in Ohio and one in Kentucky during the 1830s.

Small quantities of strap iron had long been used in building roof trusses. William Howe, a Massachusetts millwright, is credited with being the first to incorporate, and in 1840 to patent, iron rods in a bridge truss. He replaced the vertical tension members in Long's truss with threaded iron rods that could be tightened by turning nuts on the threaded ends with a wrench. This "combination" truss—the name used for a structure that combines the use of wood and iron—rapidly became the bridge of choice on American railroads for the next four decades. With its standardized components, the Howe truss facilitated the industrialization of bridge building. Purchase of its patent rights for use on highways as well as on railroads by several Cleveland-based builders, proved a highly lucrative investment.

Many other trusses were developed and used in the three states, some quite successfully, but few as widely as these five.

Lemuel Chenoweth
Lemuel Chenoweth was born near Beverly in western Virginia in 1811. Largely self-taught, he was renowned for his mathematical skills and was a gifted wagon-maker and carpenter. Chenoweth built some of West Virginia's most impressive covered bridges; two still survive. *University of West Virginia Library, West Virginia Collection*

Legendary Bridge Builders

The stories of three bridge builders represent the transformation from the empirical craftsman to the more industrialized manufacturer and from immigrant to native-born talent in the three states.

Lewis Wernweg, born in Riedlingen, Germany, in 1769, was one of America's most important early wooden bridge builders, earning the title "Pontifex Maximus of these United States." His daring design and sophisticated erection of the so-called "Colossus Bridge" over the Schuylkill River at a site known as Philadelphia's Upper Ferry in 1812–13—an unprecedented 340' span—was one of the truly great achievements of nineteenth-century engineering. More importantly for our story, Wernweg had a hand in important early covered bridges in all three states.

Wernweg came to America in 1786 when he was fifteen and in 1790 he began work as a millwright and building contractor in the Philadelphia area. Around 1810, he began building bridges. All his designs incorporated laminated arches; large wooden ribs assembled from four smaller curved timbers. Each of the four components, held together by bolts, had iron spacers that allowed air to circulate around the timbers to reduce the chances of rot. Wernweg would also not compromise in the quality of the timbers he used, routinely sawing into the heart of every timber to guarantee its soundness.

Between 1827 and 1830, he and his son built a bridge in Cambridge, Ohio, on the National Road. While this may have been the only time the master himself worked in Ohio, other bridges were built in the state that credited him as inspiration or designer. A large two-barreled Wernweg-type design was built near Bainbridge Ohio in 1840 by John Slee, and two similar bridges in southwestern Ohio were erected by Chillicothe engineer John S. Williams. Williams was also responsible for several Wernweg-inspired bridges in Kentucky, near Maysville and Lexington, in the 1830s.

In West Virginia, Wernweg is given credit for designing bridges at Romney and Erwin on the Northwestern Turnpike in the early 1830s. Lewis V. Wernweg, Lewis Wernweg's son, erected a bridge at Camp Nelson, Kentucky, whose design is credited to his father. This latter bridge demonstrates the extraordinary skills of this father-and-son bridge-building team. The bridge was analyzed by professional engineers in 1928 and found, despite its age, to be capable of sustaining modern highway loads. There could be no better testimony to the remarkable skills of a master craftsman who, even prior to the establishment of scientific bridge design, was capable of creating enduring structures.

Of all the bridge builders in the three states considered here, few had a more storied career than Lemuel Chenoweth. Born in 1811 near what is now Beverly, West Virginia, his formal schooling was minimal, but he still managed to teach himself higher mathematics. Eventually, Chenoweth became a furniture and wagon maker and a general carpenter. His expertise in wood joinery naturally led him into the bridge-building business.

The story of the bids he placed on a series of state bridges for the Staunton and Parkersburg Turnpike in 1850 has become legendary. Packing a collapsible bridge model into his saddlebags, he made the trip to the state capital in Richmond. Here a wide range of bidders and bridge styles were proposed to the board of public works. Supposedly his poplar model, assembled with "nary a nail," attracted little attention until Chenoweth placed it between two chairs, stood upon it, and challenged the other bidders to do the same with their models. No one did, and Chenoweth won the contract.

Smith Bridge Company

The Smith Bridge Company was located in Toledo across the Maumee River from the city's so-called lumber district and adjacent to major rail lines, thereby providing ready access to both materials and shipping facilities.
Miriam Wood Collection

While the reliability of this tale may be doubted, no one can question that Chenoweth built many covered bridges in what has become West Virginia between 1851 and his death in 1884. Unfortunately no documentation exists on exactly how many he built. Many were Burr-type arches, and all of them displayed the carefully fitted joinery of this master craftsman.

Miami County, Ohio, native Robert W. Smith was a different kind of builder than Wernweg or Chenoweth. More than any other wooden bridge builder in the three states, Smith was able to exploit a national market and demonstrate that covered bridges could be manufactured as a true industrial product.

Smith was born in West Charleston, Ohio, in 1835. Taught at home by his mother, Smith took time for only a few weeks of actual formal education. He was the son of a cabinet maker and quickly showed his aptitude for structures and construction as an apprentice carpenter, going into business for himself at seventeen. Noteworthy projects included a three-story, continuous stairwell and the development of a barn roof truss that eliminated the need for interior posts.

Smith's interest in bridges stemmed from this early work with roof trusses. In 1866, he created his own unique bridge truss and patented it the following year. By placing both the compression and tension posts as diagonals, he claimed to be able to produce a bridge of "unequalled strength" with fewer materials than other builders. In fact, the Smith bridge truss proved to be highly successful and his business grew rapidly.

Robert Smith

Robert W. Smith from Tippecanoe (Tipp City), Ohio, successfully commercialized wooden bridge construction. *Miriam Wood Collection*

In 1867 Smith formed a bridge company in Tippecanoe City, Ohio (later Tipp City), but, finding a need to be closer to shipping facilities, soon moved the enterprise to Toledo. Here, in partnership with three other men, he created a stock company in 1870 under the name Smith Bridge Company.

The Smith Bridge Company became enormously successful, and its work spread throughout the continental United States, far beyond what a single individual could accomplish. Early on, Smith hired agents to represent him and his patented truss at bridge bid lettings. As an industrial operation, the Smith Bridge Company devised a form of prefabrication. A bridge would be framed and assembled at Toledo, disassembled and shipped to the site where it would be erected with his own crews or with local help supervised by a Smith man. To avoid shipping costs, Smith could also design a bridge and then obtain materials closer to the erection site. He also allowed other builders to use his designs for a royalty fee.

Smith industrialized the highway bridge business to a remarkable extent. Many of his ideas were likely borrowed from the railroads, for helping to orchestrate this expanding business was Daniel Howell, a civil engineer with extensive experience designing rights-of-way and structures for railroad companies, including the Union Pacific. Smith's company also helped represent the transition from wooden trusses to all-metal trusses as he gradually shifted his emphasis toward metal truss bridges. In 1892, he sold the business to the Toledo Bridge Company, and Smith pursued real estate interests until his death in 1898.

Rebirth

A renewed interest in erecting covered wooden truss bridges began in Ashtabula County in northeastern Ohio in the 1980s. John M. Smolen, the county engineer, convinced other county officials of the tourist value of restoring their dozen historic, nineteenth-century covered bridges and maintaining them as vital components of the county highway system. Doing his own design work, training his county forces, and even working with volunteer crews, Smolen gained valuable experience in restoration techniques and adapted modern construction methods for use with wooden trusses. In a county that receives record snowfalls every year, the construction of a new wooden bridge—which is unaffected by de-icing chemicals—-became more and more attractive. Smolen built his first new wooden truss covered bridge in 1983. Three more followed in its wake.

Smolen's idea of adapting this old technology for new construction won over other history and engineering enthusiasts. Along with the rediscovery of wooden trusses among civil engineers, a renewal of construction expertise has emerged. Professional timber framers, who provide traditional building techniques for new homes and other structures, are once again available and have begun using their skills to erect wooden bridges. The construction of new wooden truss bridges is gaining a renewed vitality in the twenty-first century.

Creola Bridge
Due to economic factors, Ohio's highway department built its last covered bridge near Creola in Vinton County in 1919. *Ohio Historical Society*

Sources

Allen, Richard Sanders. *Covered Bridges of the Northeast.* Brattleboro, Vermont: Stephen Greene Press, 1957.

Allen, Richard Sanders. *Covered Bridges of the Middle Atlantic States.* Brattleboro, Vermont: Stephen Greene Press, 1959.

Allen, Richard Sanders. *Covered Bridges of the Middle West.* Brattleboro, Vermont: Stephen Greene Press, 1970.

Allen, Richard Sanders. *Covered Bridges of the South.* Brattleboro, Vermont: Stephen Greene Press, 1970.

Kemp, Emory L. *West Virginia's Historic Bridges.* Charleston: West Virginia Department of Culture and History, 1984.

Nelson, Lee. *The Colossus of 1812: An American Engineering Superlative.* New York, New York: American Society of Civil Engineers, 1990.

"Robert W. Smith." In Clark Waggoner, editor, *History of Toledo and Lucas County, Ohio.* New York: Munsell & Co., 1888.

Sargent, Charles S. *Report on the Forests of North America.* Washington, D.C.: Government Printing Office, 1884.

Wood, Miriam. *The Covered Bridges of Ohio: An Atlas and History.* Columbus, Ohio: author, 1993.

Woodward, K.W. *The Valuation of American Timberlands.* New York, New York: John Wiley & Sons, 1921.

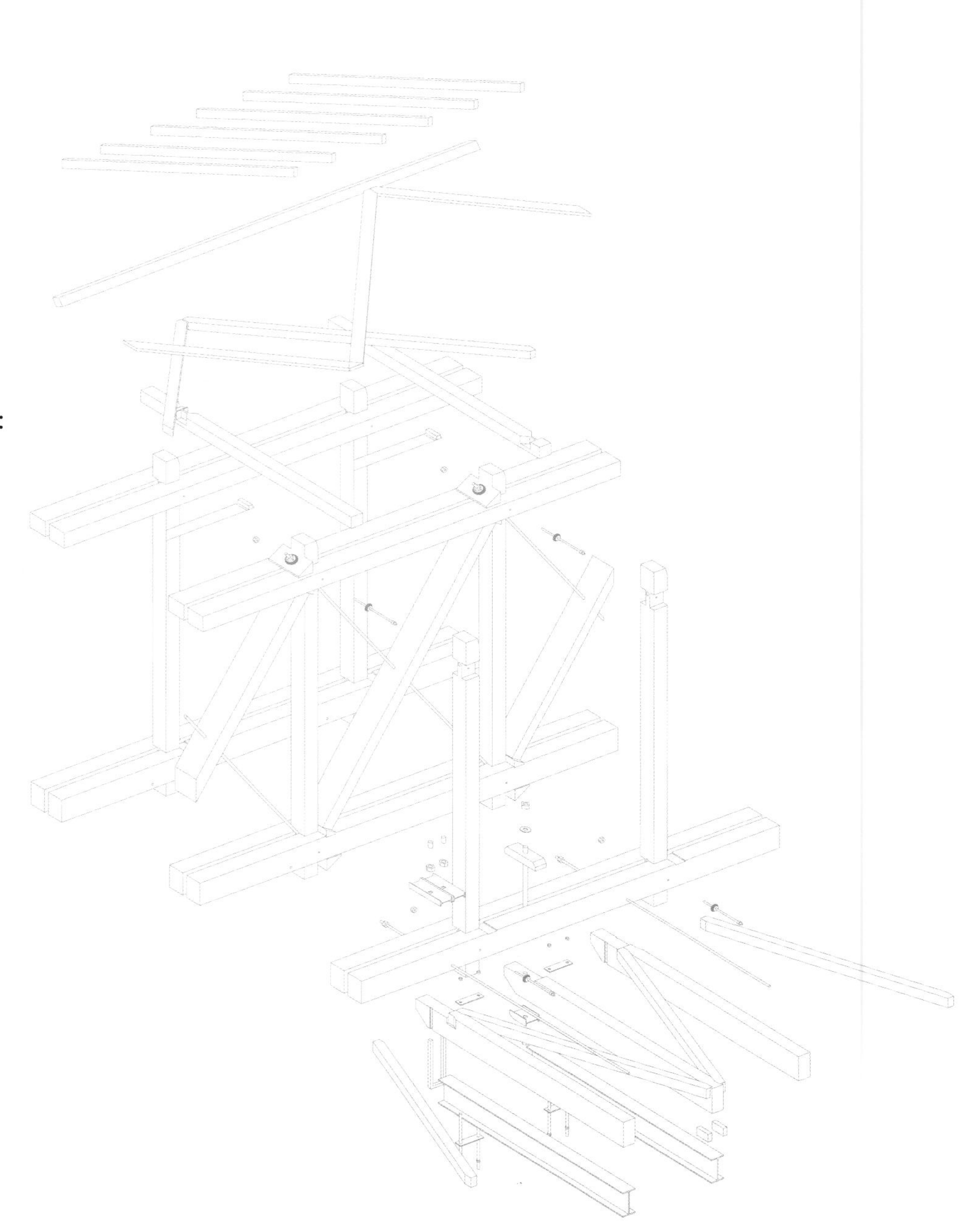

Harshman Covered Bridge
Preble County Ohio ◦ 35-68-03
exploded connections

COVERED BRIDGES

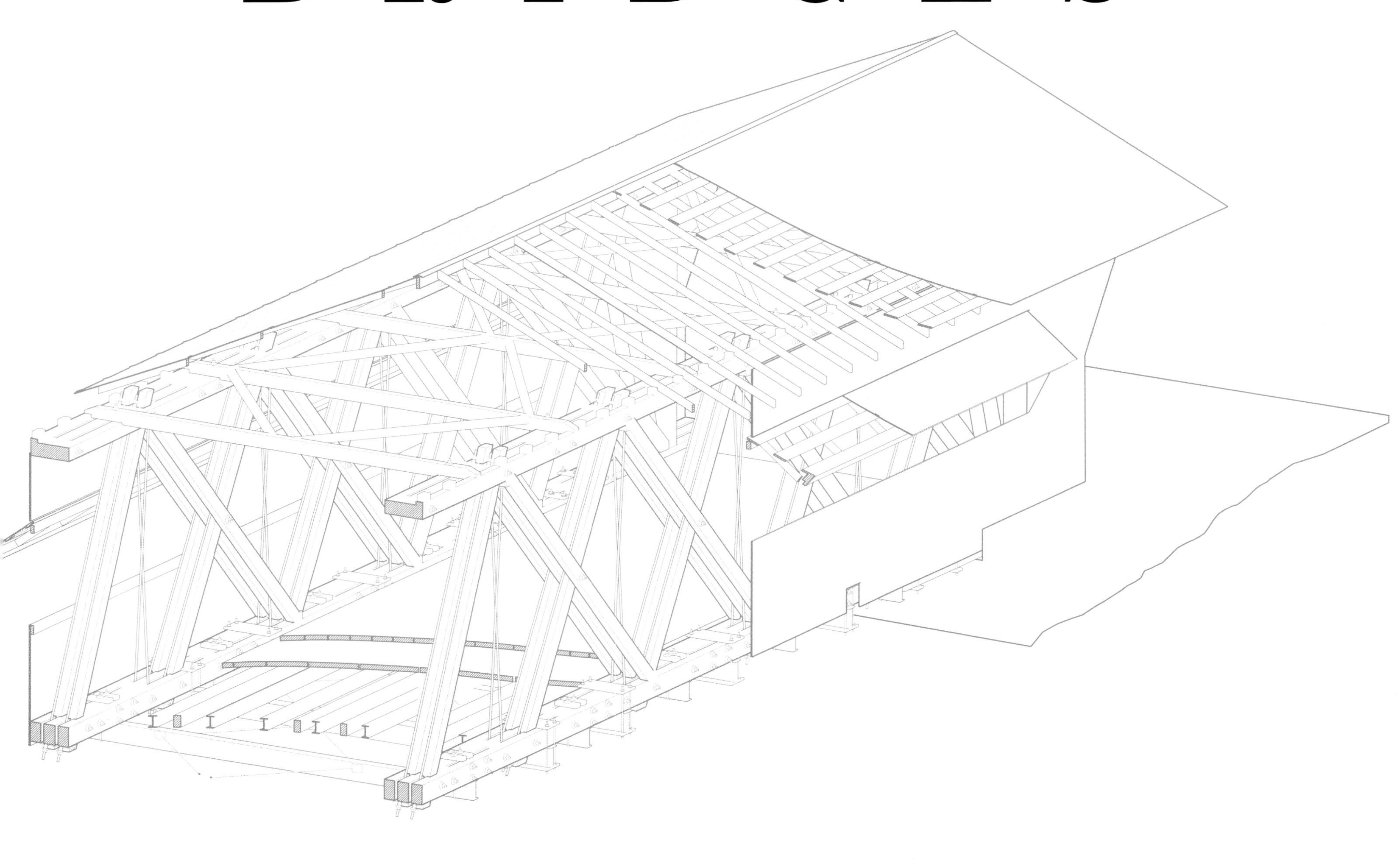

Upper Darby Covered Bridge
Union County Ohio ~ 35-80-01

Dewey Road Covered Bridge • Ashtabula County
Olin, or Dewey Road Bridge is a 115-foot Town lattice truss built in 1873. The Town lattice truss design was especially popular in northeastern Ohio, an area known as the Western Reserve. Connecticut set aside land it owned in the Northwest Territory for residents whose property had been destroyed by the Tories during the Revolutionary War. Many of the early settlers to this region came from New England, and much in the area remains as a reminder of New England, including its picturesque covered bridges and steepled, white churches overlooking village greens. Ashtabula County renovated the Dewey Road Bridge in 1992. •
Bridge number 35-04-03

11'-4"

Creek Road Covered Bridge • Ashtabula County

Creek Road Bridge is a 112-foot Town lattice truss. Few locales have taken advantage of their covered bridges like Ashtabula County. On the second weekend of October, a covered bridge festival is headquartered at the fairgrounds in Jefferson. It features tours of the covered bridges, arts and crafts, and covered bridge items for sale. The Creek Road Bridge, in very scenic Conneaut Township, was completely renovated in 1995. • Bridge number 35-04-05

Middle Road Covered Bridge • Ashtabula County

Middle Road Bridge, southeast of Conneaut, is a 136-foot Howe truss built in 1868. It was closed in 1984 after it was discovered that the structure was sagging from a broken timber. County Engineer John Smolen drew up the plans for the needed repairs, but funds were unavailable. He enlisted the aid of several volunteers to do most of the labor, assisted by employees from Smolen's office. Along with the addition of some new truss members, a new floor, new siding, and a new roof completed the repairs. All who had a part in this 1985 project were proud of what they had accomplished, and the community was lavish in its praise for these volunteers. • Bridge number 35-04-06

Root Road Covered Bridge • Ashtabula County

Root Road Bridge, southwest of Monroe Center, is a 97-foot Town lattice truss built in 1868. Many covered bridges once spanned the Ashtabula River and its branches; four of them still exist today. Ashtabula is an Indian word meaning “fish river.” Major renovation work was done on the Root Road Bridge in 1983, including raising the bridge by two feet, rebuilding one abutment of concrete, and adding a central pier. • Bridge number 35-04-09

Benetka Road Covered Bridge • Ashtabula County

Benetka Road Bridge, northwest of Sheffield, is a 127.5-foot, Town lattice truss with added arches. It was completely rebuilt in 1985 by adding laminated arches to strengthen the old structure. Visitors during the annual covered bridge festival find a welcoming committee that may be a Boy Scout troop, representatives from the county historical society, or some other volunteer group to tell about each bridge. All look forward to greeting their visitors. • Bridge number 35-04-12

Graham Road Covered Bridge • Ashtabula County

Graham Road Bridge sits in a little park just off Kelloggsville Road. It is an 85-foot Town lattice truss built in 1867. Although renovated in the 1960s, by the early 1970s a new bridge was required on Graham Road. In 1972, the county moved the old covered bridge off to a meadow on the south side of the road, and the township trustees established a small park around it. According to some local stories, it was built from the remains of a Rome Township bridge wrecked in the great flood of 1913. Others say this is the original 1867 bridge. The truth is lost in the mists of time. • Bridge number 35-04-13

South Denmark Road Covered Bridge
Ashtabula County

South Denmark Road Bridge is a Town lattice truss built in 1868. The crossroads village of Denmark Center, a short distance from the covered bridge, provided the name for both the road and bridge. Due to repeated damage from overloaded trucks, the county bypassed the old bridge in the mid-1970s but has left it open to light traffic. •

Bridge number 35-04-14

Doyle Road Covered Bridge Ashtabula County

Doyle Road Bridge, northwest of Jefferson, is a 98-foot Town lattice truss built around 1876. Setting on a curve in the road, the bridge affords photographers with a very good late morning side and portal shot.

In 1988, County Engineer John Smolen undertook a complete renovation of this bridge which included new foundations, new laminated arches, a new floor system, a new roof and siding, and a short approach span on the north end. • Bridge number 35-04-16

Mechanicsville Road Covered Bridge • Ashtabula County

Mechanicsville Road Bridge, built in 1867, is a 170-foot Howe truss with arches. Ashtabula County built two Howe truss covered bridges in 1867, this one on Mechanicsville Road and another one over the Conneaut Creek at Conneaut. When the Conneaut Creek bridge was removed in 1925, a local newspaper indicated eleven other county covered bridges would soon be removed. Bypassed in 1989, the Mechanicsville Road Bridge was fully renovated in 2003 and 2004 as part of Ashtabula County's ongoing program of covered bridge preservation. • Bridge number 35-04-18

Harpersfield Covered Bridge • Ashtabula County [overleaf]

Harpersfield Bridge, just south of Harpersfield, is a two-span, 234-foot Howe truss built around 1868. The bridge has a clear span of 228 feet. Old county records do not mention this bridge, but a newspaper article from 1868 indicates that it was nearly completed. Some people felt that an iron bridge should have been built on this spot instead of a wooden covered bridge. The two covered spans measure 234 feet, making it the longest covered bridge in Ohio. The steel span on the north end was built after the 1913 flood cut a new channel in the Grand River. The Harpersfield Bridge carried Ohio Route 534 until the state built a new road to the east in the mid-1950s, and the old road and covered bridge reverted to county ownership. Major renovation that included the replacement of rotted sections of the lower chords, new roofing and siding, and a roofed sidewalk on the west side was done in 1990 and 1991 . National Register of Historic Places • Bridge number 35-04-19

Riverdale Road Covered Bridge • Ashtabula County

Riverdale Road Bridge, northwest of the village of Rock Creek, is a 140-foot Town lattice truss built in 1874. Major renovations in 1980 included massive laminated beams at the base of the trusses that span the length of the bridge. In addition, the portals were renovated and new siding was applied. The county also built ten-foot metal frames at each end of the bridge with signs to warn of the low clearance. Damage from overloaded and oversized vehicles is a great problem with drive-through truss bridges of both wood or metal. • Bridge number 35-04-22

Warner Hollow Covered Bridge • Ashtabula County
Wiswell Road, or Warner Hollow, or Windsor Mills Bridge, just south of Windsor Mills, is a 134.5-foot, Town lattice truss built in 1867. Among Ohio's most scenic covered bridges, this bridge is especially beautiful when viewed from the creek below, perched on its two high piers and abutments. The condition of the bridge steadily deteriorated until it had to be closed in 1971. It underwent extensive renovations in 2002 and 2003, including the replacement of one stone pier with concrete faced with stone. An unusual sunburst design was used on the portal. In May 2004, the bridge was dedicated and reopened to traffic. National Register of Historic Places • Bridge number 35-04-25

State Road Covered Bridge • Ashtabula County

State Road Bridge, east of Kingsville, is a two-span 157-foot Town lattice truss built in 1983. John Smolen, former Ashtabula County engineer, had long dreamed of building new covered bridges in the county. When State Road needed a new bridge, he designed a Town truss bridge based on old bridge plans found in the engineer's office, but he upgraded it to carry modern legal loads. Ninety-seven thousand board feet of Southern pine went into the bridge's construction. Built on the south bank of Conneaut Creek, the bridge was slowly winched into place to rest on modified sandstone abutments and one concrete pier. This was the first genuine covered bridge built in Ohio for public highway use since 1919. • Bridge number 35-04-58

Caine Road Covered Bridge
Ashtabula County

Caine Road Bridge, northeast of Jefferson, is a 96-foot Pratt truss built in 1986. This was the second covered bridge designed by John Smolen. The Pratt truss utilizes both steel and wood components which had not been used in a covered bridge for many years. The Pratt truss was invented in 1844 by two new England builders named Pratt, but fell out of favor for wooden structures and had been used exclusively for metal bridges until the Ashtabula project. • Bridge number 35-04-61

Giddings Road Covered Bridge • Ashtabula County

Giddings Road Bridge, northeast of Jefferson, is a 120-foot Pratt truss built in 1995. The Giddings Road Bridge is another of John Smolen's designs. The trusses were fabricated in Peshtigo, Wisconsin, then numbered and shipped to the Giddings Road site for assembly by B.O.G. Construction Company. The 24-ton trusses were placed on their abutments using four cranes, one of which weighed over 200 tons and sported a 120-foot boom. It took eight hours to set the trusses into place. The main trusses are glue-laminated Southern pine, and the roof and the siding are made of yellow poplar. • Bridge number 35-04-62

Netcher Road Covered Bridge Ashtabula County

Netcher Road Bridge, east of Jefferson, is a 104-foot Haupt truss built in 1999. For this bridge, John Smolen adapted a truss design by Herman Haupt to his own specifications and created a unique and outstanding example of engineering skill. Herman Haupt, a West Point graduate, was a brigadier general with the Union army during the Civil War and was in charge of keeping the Northern railroads in good shape. He also designed a device to blow up the enemy's railroad bridges. Smolen's Haupt truss design is an inverted version of the original with the addition of massive three-hinge, 32-ply laminated arches. The trusses were built of Southern pine by Burke, Parson, Bowlby of Ripley, West Virginia, and shipped to the construction site. The trusses were assembled by Righter Construction Company of Columbus, Ohio. The trusses weigh 24 tons, and four cranes were used to place them into position. Designed to carry heavy loads, the bridge can simultaneously handle two tractor trailers. Red paint and gingerbread trim finish off the exterior of this unique span. Today only two other Haupt truss covered bridges remain in the United States: the Sayres Bridge at Thetford Center in Orange County, Vermont; and the 1894 Bunker Hill Bridge in Catawba County, North Carolina. • Bridge number 35-04-63

Bluebird Farm Covered Bridge • Carroll County

Bluebird Farm Bridge was built by Jim Farley of Sebring, Ohio on the Blue Bird Farm following his restoration of an old barn. After studying the covered bridges in nearby Columbiana County, he drew up plans and erected the bridge on old stone abutments from an earlier bridge. Home-cooked meals can be enjoyed at the farm's restaurant, and the old barn houses a gift and antique shop. • Bridge number 35-10-14

Sells Covered Bridge • Columbiana County

Sells, or Roller Mill Bridge, southwest of Lisbon, is a 50-foot, six-panel, multiple kingpost truss bridge. Robinson and McCracken built the bridge at a total cost of $632, which included the foundations. At one time, a number of covered bridges crossed the West Fork of Little Beaver Creek, but by the early 1950s only three remained. In the early 1980s, a single family used the Sells Bridge, and it was in very poor condition, propped up on wooden cribbing, so the county closed both bridge and road. In 1989, the bridge was dismantled and stored to be later rebuilt. A group of volunteers led by Brian Egli moved the timbers to Scenic Vista Park in 1991, where he led a rebuilding effort. On July 19, 1993, arsonists broke into the park before dawn and, setting the covered bridge on fire, completely destroyed it. Fortunately, Egli had the foresight to keep a complete set of drawings with measurements, and from these plans, he was able to exactly reconstruct it. Funded by insurance and donations, the new Sells Bridge was completed in the fall of 1994. • Bridge number 35-15-01

Jim McClellan Covered Bridge • Columbiana County

Jim McClellan Bridge lies southeast of Hanoverton and is a one-span, 53-foot multiple kingpost truss bridge built in 1879. R.H. McCracken built the bridge to replace an earlier covered bridge at Thompson's Mill. The total cost was only $244, since the foundations from the predecessor bridge were recycled. The McClellan Bridge and road were closed years ago with the intention of establishing a small rural park. Since this never came to pass, the bridge sets in its quiet location largely forgotten and ignored. • Bridge number 35-15-02

CENTENNIAL
BRIDGE
RESTORED 2003

Teegarden Covered Bridge • Columbiana County

Teegarden, or Centennial Covered Bridge lies northwest of Lisbon at Teegarden. Built in 1875, it is a 67-foot multiple kingpost truss bridge. The Columbiana County Commissioners paid Uriah Teegarden for rebuilding the bridge at his mill in 1859 and again in 1867. In 1875 the county contracted with Jeremiah C. Mountz, a well-known Columbiana County bridge builder, farmer, and orchardist, to build a new covered bridge at Teegarden for $441. This bridge is also known as Centennial Bridge since it was painted in February 1876 for the grand sum of thirty dollars. By 1991, the Teegarden Bridge was bypassed and in poor condition. The lower chords on the south end were badly rotted, requiring the installation of cribbing. A bike path provided an excuse for county officials to apply for federal funding to renovate it. In 2001 the bridge was dismantled and trucked off so that new timbers could replace rotten truss members. After months of work, it was trucked back to its original site and reinstalled with a crane. After the finish work of roof and siding, the historic structure began a new phase as part of the bike path. Then, the unthinkable happened—arsonists set fire to the bridge in the early hours of February 23, 2003. Fortunately, a passing motorist turned in an alarm. Thanks to the motorist's starting to fight the fire and the quick response of the local fire department, the damage to the bridge was not severe. The use of fire retardant in the renovation also helped keep the fire from spreading. The high incidence of fire in Columbiana County has encouraged the use of fire retardants during renovations. •

Bridge number 35-15-05

Church Hill Road Covered Bridge • Columbiana County

Church Hill Road Bridge, in Elkton, is a single kingpost truss bridge of only nineteen-feet clear span. This bridge originally spanned Middle Run in Elk Run Township northeast of Lisbon. Confusion in county records means that the best that can be done to date this bridge is to say the decade of the 1870s. In the early 1960s, it was bypassed and a small rural park established nearby. A bronze historic site marker proclaimed it to be America's shortest covered bridge built for a public highway. Columbiana County built many very short covered bridges. In fact, at one time, they had over 300 wooden truss bridges. Vandals began threatening this bridge on its isolated site, and in 1982 the Elkton Historical Society moved it onto the grounds of the Lock 24 Restaurant. It has recently been restored. The lock was a structure on the old Sandy and Beaver Canal. National Register of Historic Places • Bridge number 35-15-08

Thomas J. Malone Covered Bridge • Columbiana County

Tom Malone Bridge, now in Beaver Creek State Park, is a 42-foot multiple kingpost truss bridge. It originally stood in Elk Run Township over Middle Run about one mile west of Elkton. About 1900 the bridge was moved to the nearby Huffman Farm, where it is thought to have served as a barn. When the road was widened about 1912, the covered bridge was again moved. The Elk Run Township trustees moved it to Pine Hollow Road, where it was used as a shed for road equipment. The story might have ended here but for the curiosity of a local historian, the late Tom Malone, who immediately

recognized the shed as a former covered bridge. Envisioning it among other historic buildings in Beaver Creek State Park, he began a crusade to get it moved. In 1971 it was rebuilt over the millrace of the old Gastons Mill. Unfortunately, Mr. Malone did not live to see this project completed. Tom Malone discovered the site of what some feel was the first covered bridge in Ohio which spanned Little Beaver Creek not far from the Ohio River. One abutment of that 1809 bridge still stands and a historic site marker commemorates it. • Bridge number 35-15-96

Helmick Covered Bridge • Coshocton County

Helmick Bridge, east of Blissfield, is a 170-foot, two-span multiple kingpost truss bridge built in 1863. It was built by John Shrake of Licking County, one of Ohio's most prolific covered bridge builders. He worked in a number of eastern and southern Ohio counties. Coshocton County paid Shrake $2,107 to build the bridge at Helmick's mill. This must have included the stonework since no separate masonry contract was recorded. A clue to who did the abutments and pier of this bridge is the name and date carved into one of the abutments: F.A. Victor 1863. This man is listed as a mason in other old county records. The Helmick Bridge consists of two separate multiple kingpost trusses joined at the pier. Frequent flooding of Killbuck Creek necessitated many repairs, done in the 1960s and in 1976. The bridge was finally closed in the 1980s after its condition became too dangerous to carry traffic. A long, steel I-beam was inserted through it to keep the north trusses from collapsing. The Helmick Bridge Restoration Committee slowly raised money to restore this landmark, and in 1995, with federal grant assistance, hired the Brode Construction Company. Eighty percent of the timbers were too rotten for reuse and required replacement. A rededication ceremony was held on September 15, 1996, with a large crowd in attendance. National Register of Historic Places • Bridge number 35-16-02

Charles Harding Memorial Covered Bridge • Cuyahoga County

Charles Harding Memorial Bridge is a 92-foot multiple kingpost bridge built in 1998. In 1998, when Olmstead Falls was unable to afford repairs to a severely damaged bridge on Main Street, the structure was closed. After fifteen years, the local Kiwanis Club offered to sponsor a covered bridge to be set on the old cut-stone abutments, and, in conjunction with the city, hired Don Timmer of Richland Engineering to design it. Under President Dennis Mozser, the club managed to raise over $300,000 in grants and donations that was added to city coffers. The project was put to bid in 1997, and J.J.Y. Construction of Dundee, Ohio, received the contract of $187,000 to build it. A crew of Amish carpenters assembled the bridge timbers and covering on the south approach and then rolled the bridge into place on the abutments. It was named for Captain Charles Harding, the first man from this area to die in World War II, whose sisters had donated generously to the project. Although a full-size bridge, it is for pedestrian and bicycle use only. • Bridge number 35-18-25

Tare Creek Covered Bridge • Geauga County

Tare Creek Bridge is a 50.5-foot Howe truss bridge built in 2004 on Maple Highlands Trail over Tare Creek on an old railroad right-of-way northwest of Middlefield. Tom Sterleker of the Geauga County Parks District decided that a covered bridge on this rails-to-trails path south of Burton Station would be a great idea. John Smolen, former Ashtabula County Engineer, did the structural design. He was quite pleased with the park employees who put it together. The large structural components and flooring were made from Southern pine. The remainder of the timbers were yellow poplar cut by local Amish men. The bridge was assembled on dry land

and then lifted by a crane onto the concrete abutments of an old railroad bridge. The new bridge is ready for any load, including Amish horses and buggies. •

Bridge number 35-28-07

Indian Camp Covered Bridge • Guernsey County

Indian Camp Bridge spans Indian Camp Run about six and one-half miles northwest of Cambridge just off Ohio Route 658. It is a 36-foot multiple kingpost bridge. The Indian Camp Bridge is believed to be very old. The only reference to the bridge being built over this creek was in the 1850s, but the site was not mentioned. The truss timbers here are handhewn—one of the few in the state—and held together by trunnels (wooden pins). Some metal bolts and beams were later added to these old timbers. Severe flooding in June 1998 badly damaged the floor system, necessitating its closure until December. This is the last covered bridge open to traffic in Guernsey County, where more than one-hundred roofed structures once served the highways and railroads. • Bridge number 35-30-04

Armstrong Covered Bridge • Guernsey County

Armstrong, or Clio, Covered Bridge in Cambridge is a 76-foot multiple kingpost bridge built in 1849. Abraham Armstrong was paid $510 to build this bridge over Salt Creek at his grist and saw mills in a hamlet known as Clio in Jefferson Township northeast of Cambridge. Clio, home for a general store, post office and mills, was one of those rural centers so important in the days when a trip to the county seat was an all-day affair. When the state planned a reservoir on Salt Fork in the 1960s, the county intended to move one covered bridge to the city park and give the three others to local farmers. Unfortunately, one of the bridges collapsed under an overloaded truck, and another was burned by vandals. For some reason, the third bridge, the 1891 Gunn Bridge, was left on its original site and stood visible in the reservoir waters for many years. By the mid-1960s, the town of Clio was gone, and only the Armstrong Covered Bridge remained. It was moved into Cambridge in the winter of 1966/1967. • Bridge number 35-30-12

Hindman Memorial Covered Bridge • Jefferson County

Hindman Memorial Bridge is an 89-foot Warren truss bridge built in 1997. The Hindman Memorial Bridge was the first public highway covered bridge in Jefferson County in over sixty years. Modeled after a bridge seen in France, it was designed and built by the county engineer's staff. It memorializes a late county commissioner. The bridge is open-sided and bolted together with steel plates. • Bridge number 35-41-37

Skull Fork Covered Bridge • Harrison County

Skull Fork Bridge lies south of Freeport and is a 45-foot multiple kingpost truss bridge built in 1876. It was known in the 1870s as Griesinger's Bridge and was built by Abraham Slonaker for $327. John Jackson, the mason, was paid $144 for his work. The Skull Fork Bridge, a typical Ohio multiple kingpost truss, was once one of many in the county, but is now the only example. Bypassed in the 1970s, the Four Seasons Garden Club looks after the grounds around it. The county does occasional maintenance on the bridge and is planning a major renovation. • Bridge number 35-34-19

Salt Creek or Johnson's Mill Covered Bridge • Muskingum County

Salt Creek Bridge, northeast of Zanesville, is an 87-foot Warren truss bridge built in 1876. The county commissioners contracted with Thomas Fisher of Dresden for a bridge at Johnson's Mill over Salt Creek for $8 per lineal foot. In later years, it became known as the Salt Creek Bridge. The bridge was sided but not roofed, then a common practice in the county where the roofing would be postponed to save money. Three years later the roof was installed, and the bridge served until 1953 when Muskingum County removed over twenty-five covered bridges. The Salt Creek Bridge was traded to the nearby farmer in return for the land required by a new bridge. He used it for storage until 1960, when, for $300, he sold the bridge and two-thirds of an acre to the newly-formed Southern Ohio Covered Bridge Association (now known as the Ohio Historic Bridge Association). This little group worked hard to restore the bridge, by then in poor condition. The original shingle roof from 1879 was in very bad shape, so money was raised for a new metal roof.

Repairs made to the lower chords with red oak in 1982 did not hold up well. In the mid-1990s, the county commissioners agreed to again assume public ownership so a federal grant application could be filed. The 80% federal funding for the necessary renovations, completed in 1997, were matched with the remainder from the OHBA. The bridge was fireproofed in 2002 and an abutment undermining was eliminated. The OHBA, who is responsible for its maintenance, has a 99-year lease on the bridge. National Register of Historic Places • Bridge number 35-60-31

Everett Road Covered Bridge • Summit County

Everett Road Bridge, southeast of Richfield, is a 100-foot Smith truss bridge originally built in the 1870s. Tentative plans were made by the Summit County Historical Society in the 1960s to move this covered bridge, the last in the county, for future preservation. But in the early 1970s, an overloaded truck collapsed it, forcing the county to completely rebuild it. When the heavy rains of May 1975 turned normally placid Furnace Run into a raging torrent, flood waters and debris hit the old covered bridge and knocked it off its foundations. The broken timbers of the bridge were eventually pulled from the creek and taken to the nearby Hale Farm for storage until it could be rebuilt. Everett Road remained closed. After the area came under the control of the National Park Service in 1980 as part of the Cuyahoga Valley National Park, efforts to reconstruct it began. Officials discovered, however, that the wreckage of the bridge was mostly rotten and unusable. Although park service officials confirmed the Smith truss design, county records did not reveal when and by whom the bridge was built. Almost all new materials were used to rebuild it back on the original site in 1987. It is not open to traffic. National Register of Historic Places • Bridge number 35-77-01

Newton Falls Covered Bridge • Trumbull County

Newton Falls Bridge is a 123-foot Town truss bridge built about 1831. The Newton Falls Covered Bridge was, for many years, the only covered bridge in Ohio with a sidewalk. When a new school opened near to the bridge in 1921, the sidewalk was added so children who lived west of the bridge didn't have to share the roadway with vehicular traffic. This covered bridge is the second oldest in Ohio and the last such bridge in Trumbull County. Little is known of its early history. Major repairs, including steel piers, were made in 1962 and a substantial renovation is being planned for the early twenty-first century. National Register of Historic Places • Bridge number 35-78-01

35-04-12

Benetka Road Covered Bridge • Ashtabula County

Description: 127-foot Town lattice truss plus arch circa 1900, renovated 1985. *Location*: south southwest of Kingsville, in Sheffield Township, over the Ashtabula River. *Directions*: from Interstate I-90, take the State Route 193/84 exit south on State Route 193 for 1.6 miles to Plymouth Ridge Road (also County Road 20). Turn right on Plymouth Ridge Road, heading west 1.3 miles to Benetka Road (also Township Road 350). Turn left on Benetka Road, heading south for .4 miles to the covered bridge. Page 24

35-04-61

Caine Road Covered Bridge • Ashtabula County

Description: 96-foot Pratt truss, built in 1986. *Location*: west northwest of Pierpont, in Pierpont Township, over the West Branch of the Ashtabula River. *Directions*: from Interstate I-90, take the State Route 7 exit south for 12 miles to the intersection of State Route 167 and Caine Road (also Township Road 579). Turn right on Caine Road, heading west 2.4 miles to the covered bridge. Page 35

35-04-05

Creek Road Covered Bridge • Ashtabula County

Description: 112-foot Town lattice truss, renovated in 1995. *Location*: east northeast of Kingsville, in Conneaut Township, over Conneaut Creek. *Directions*: from Interstate I-90, take the State Route 84 exit, heading north for 1 mile to the State Route 84 and State Route 193 split. Take State Route 193 north .2 miles to Creek Road. Turn right on Creek Road (also Township Road 443) and drive northeast 4.5 miles to the covered bridge. Page 20–21

35-04-03

Dewey Road or Olin Covered Bridge • Ashtabula County

Description: 115-foot Town lattice truss, built in 1873, renovated in 1992. *Location*: east southeast of Ashtabula, in Plymouth Township, over the Ashtabula River. *Directions*: from Interstate I-90, take the State Route 11/46 exit and head north for 3 miles. Take the State Route 84 exit, heading east for 3.7 miles to Hadlock Rd. Turn right on Hadlock road and head south for 1.8 miles to Dewey Rd (also Township Road 335). Turn left on Dewey Road towards the east, approximately .2 miles to the covered bridge. Page 19

35-04-16

Doyle Road Covered Bridge • Ashtabula County

Description: 98-foot Town lattice truss plus arch, built in 1876, renovated in 1988. *Location*: northwest of Jefferson, in Jefferson Township, over Mill Creek. *Directions*: from Interstate I-90, take the State Route 11/46 exit, heading south. At the State Route 11 and State Route 46 split, take State Route 46 south for 4 miles to State Route 307. Turn right on State Route 307, heading northeast 1.1 miles to Doyle Road (also Township Road 287). Turn right on Doyle Road, heading north .8 miles to the covered bridge. Page 27

35-04-62

Giddings Road Covered Bridge • Ashtabula County

Description: 120-foot Pratt truss, built in 1995. *Location*: northeast of Jefferson, in Jefferson Township, over Mill Creek. *Directions*: from the intersection of State Route 46 and State Route 307, take State Route 46 north 2.5 miles to Griggs Road. Turn right on Griggs Road, heading east 1.5 miles to Giddings Road. Turn right on Giddings Road, approximately 1.7 miles to the covered bridge. Page 36

35-04-13

Graham Road Covered Bridge • Ashtabula County

Description: 85-foot Town lattice truss, built in 1867, moved in 1972. *Location*: northwest of Pierpont, in Pierpont Township. *Directions*: from Interstate I-90, take the State Route 7 exit to the south for 10 miles to Graham Road (also Township Road 343). Turn right on Graham road, heading west 1.8 miles to the covered bridge located in a small park on the south side of the road. Page 25

35-04-19

Harpersfield Covered Bridge • Ashtabula County

Description: 234-foot, two-span Howe truss, built in 1868. *Location*: south edge of Harpersfield, in Harpersfield Township, over the Grand River. *Directions*: from Interstate I-90, take the State Route 534 exit south to State Route 307. Turn right on State Route 307, approximately .2 miles to Harpersfield Road. Turn left on Harpersfield Road and drive down a hill that leads to the covered bridge. Page 30–32

35-04-18

Mechanicsville Covered Bridge • Ashtabula County

Description: 168-foot Howe truss plus arch, built in 1867. *Location*: southwest of Austinburg, in Austinburg Township, over the Grand River. *Directions*: from Interstate I-90, take the State Route 45 exit south to State Route 307. Turn right on State Route 307, heading west 2.4 miles to Mechanicsville Road (also County Road 9). Turn left on Mechanicsville Road, heading south .8 miles to the covered bridge. Page 28–29

35-04-06

Middle Road Covered Bridge • Ashtabula County

Description: 136-foot Howe truss, built in 1868, renovated in 1984. *Location*: south southeast of Conneaut, in Conneaut Township, over Conneaut Creek. *Directions*: from Interstate I-90, follow State Route 7 south 1.1 miles to South Ridge Road (also County Road 22). Turn left on South Ridge Road, heading east 1.2 miles to Middle Road (also Township Road 425). Turn right on Middle Road, heading south for .2 miles to the covered bridge. Page 22

35-04-63

Netcher Road Covered Bridge • Ashtabula County

Description: 104-foot Haupt truss, built in 1999. *Location*: east of Jefferson, over Mill Creek. *Directions*: from the town of Jefferson and State Route 46, take East Jefferson Street east 1.8 miles to South Denmark Road (also Township Road 291). Turn right on South Denmark Road, heading south to Netcher Road. Turn left on Netcher Road, approximately .2 miles to the covered bridge. Page 37

35-04-22

Riverdale Covered Bridge • Ashtabula County

Description: 140-foot Town lattice truss, built in 1874. *Location*: northwest of Rock Creek, in Morgan Township, over the Grand River. *Directions*: from Interstate I-90, take the State Route 45 exit south for 8 miles to Riverdale Road (also Township Road 69). Turn right on Riverdale Road, heading west .8 miles to the covered bridge. Page 32

35-04-09

Root Road Covered Bridge • Ashtabula County

Description: 97-foot Town lattice truss, built in 1868. *Location*: west southwest of Monroe Center, in Monroe Township, over the West Branch of the Ashtabula River. *Directions*: from Interstate I-90, take the State Route 7 exit south. At the intersection of State Route 7 and State Route 84, continue south on State Route 7 for 2 miles to Root Road (also Township Road 414). Turn right on Root Road, heading west 2.4 miles to the covered bridge. Page 23

35-04-14

South Denmark Road Covered Bridge • Ashtabula County

Description: 94-foot Town lattice truss, built in 1868. *Location*: east southeast of Jefferson, in Denmark Township, over Mill Creek. *Directions*: from the intersection of State Route 167 and State Route 11, take State Route 167 east for 2 miles to the town of Denmark Center and State Route 193. Turn right on State Route 193, heading south 2 miles to South Denmark Road (also County Road 291). Turn right on South Denmark Road, approximately 2 miles to the covered bridge. Page 26

35-04-58

State Road Covered Bridge • Ashtabula County

Description: 157-foot, two-span Town lattice truss, built in 1983. *Location*: north of Kelloggsville, in Monroe Township, over Conneaut Creek. *Directions*: from Interstate I-90, take the State Route 7 exit south 3 miles to State Route 84. Turn right on State Route 84, heading west 2.3 miles to State Road (also County Road 354). Turn right on State Road, heading north 1.6 miles to the covered bridge. Page 34

35-04-25

Wiswell Road, or Warner Hollow, or Windsor Mills, Covered Bridge • Ashtabula County

Description: 134-foot, three-span Town lattice truss, built in 1867. *Location*: west of Orwell, in Windsor Township at Windsor Mills, over Phelps Creek. *Directions*: from the intersection of State Route 45 and State Route 322, head west on State Route 322. At the intersection of State Route 322 and State Route 534, continue west on State Route 322 for 1.6 miles to Wiswell Road (also Township Road 357). Turn left on Wiswell Road, approximately .1 miles to the covered bridge. Page 33

35-10-14

Bluebird Farm Bridge • Carroll County

Description: 40-foot multiple kingpost truss, built in 1996. *Location*: southeast of Carrollton, over Indian Fork. *Directions*: starting at Carrollton Square in Carrollton, take State Route 322 south of the town square two blocks to 3rd Street. Turn left on 3rd Street for approximately .5 miles to Bluebird Farms. The Bluebird Farms driveway is on the left-hand side of the road. The driveway ascends a hill to a parking lot. The bridge is down a steep footpath. Page 38

35-15-08

Church Hill Road Covered Bridge • Columbiana County

Description: 22-foot kingpost truss, built in 1870, moved in 1982. *Location*: west edge of Elkton, in Elk Run Township. *Directions*: from the city of Lisbon, take US Route 30 east to the junction of State Route 11 and State Route 154. Take State Route 154 east 1.4 miles to the covered bridge located on the south side of the road and adjacent to the Lock 24 Restaurant. Page 44

35-15-02

McClellan Covered Bridge • Columbiana County

Description: 53-foot multiple kingpost truss, built in 1879. *Location*: southwest of Lisbon, over the West Fork of the Little Beaver Creek. *Directions*: from the city of Lisbon, take State Route 164 south to State Route 518. Turn right on State Route 518, heading west 1.6 miles to Trinity Church Road. Turn right on Trinity Church Road, heading north 1.4 miles to McClellan Road, a small abandoned road. Park along Trinity Church Road and walk down to the bridge about 200 feet off Trinity Church Road. Please use caution as the roadway to the bridge (McClellan Road) is rough and not well-maintained. Page 40–41

35-15-01

Sells or Roller Mill Covered Bridge • Columbiana County

Description: 50-foot multiple kingpost truss, built in 1878, moved in 1992, burned in 1993, rebuilt in 1994. *Location*: southwest of Lisbon, in Center Township. *Directions*: from the city of Lisbon, take US Route 30 west 1.3 miles to Wayne Bridge Road (also Township Road 764). Turn left on Wayne Bridge Road, heading south 2.3 miles to Vista View Park. Turn right to enter the park and the covered bridge is on the left-hand side of the road. Page 39

35-15-05

Teegarden or Centennial Covered Bridge • Columbiana County

Description: 67-foot multiple kingpost truss, built in 1875. *Location*: northwest of Lisbon, in Salem Township, over Middle Fork of Little Beaver Creek. *Directions*: from the city of Lisbon and US Route 30, take State Route 45 northwest 2.4 miles to Eagleton Road (also Township Road 761). Turn left on Eagleton Road, heading northwest 2.7 miles to the covered bridge on the right-hand side of the road. Page 42–43

35-15-96

Thomas Malone Covered Bridge • Columbiana County

Description: 42-foot multiple kingpost truss, built in 1870, moved in 1971. *Location*: north of East Liverpool, in Middleton Township, over Gastons Mill Stream. *Directions*: from the junction of US Route 30 and State Route 7, take State Route 7 north 2.1 miles to Bell School Road (also Township Road 1131). Turn right on Bell School Road, heading east 1.2 miles to Echo Dell Road. Head north on Echo Dell Road to Beaver Creek State Park. The covered bridge is located just past the park ranger station. Page 45

35-16-02

Helmick Covered Bridge • Coshocton County

Description: 170-foot two-span multiple kingpost truss, built in 1863, rebuilt in 1995. *Location*: east southeast of Blissfield, in Clark Township, over Killbuck Creek. *Directions*: from US Route 36, take State Route 60 north to County Road 25. Turn right on County Road 25. Covered bridge is near intersection of County Road 25 and County Road 343. Page 46

35-18-25

Charles Harding Memorial Covered Bridge • Cuyahoga County

Description: 92-foot multiple kingpost truss, built in 1998. *Location*: in Olmstead Falls, over Plum Creek. *Directions*: in Olmstead Falls, the covered bridge is located just off Main Street. Page 47

35-28-07

Tare Creek Bridge • Geauga County

Description: 50.5-foot, Howe truss built in 2004. *Location*: north of Middlefield, on the Maple Highlands Trail, over Tare Creek. *Directions*: from Interstate I-271, take State Route 422 east to the town of Parkman. From Parkman, take State Route 528 north to State Route 608. Head north on State Route 608 towards Middlefield. Approximately 2 miles past Middlefield, turn left on Burton Windsor Road (also County Road 14), heading west .8 miles. The covered bridge is on an abandoned B&O Railroad right-of-way. You must walk or bicycle to the bridge as cars are prohibited on the Maple Highlands Trail. You can also see the bridge when traveling north on State Route 608: it is on the left-hand side of the road, just past the Middlefield Cheese Factory. Page 48–49

35-30-12

Armstrong or Clio Covered Bridge • Guernsey County

Description: 76-foot multiple kingpost truss, built in 1849, moved in 1966. *Location:* in the north section of Cambridge, in a park over a ravine. *Directions:* in the town of Cambridge, take US Route 22/40 (also Wheeling Avenue) 1.1 miles north to Steubenville Road, turn left on Steubenville Road and travel to 10th Street. Turn right on 10th Street and travel to the city park where the bridge is located. Page 51

35-30-04

Indian Camp Covered Bridge • Guernsey County

Description: 36-foot multiple kingpost truss, built in the mid-nineteenth century. *Location*: north northwest of Cambridge, in Knox Township, over Indian Camp Run. *Directions*: from the town of Cambridge, take State Route 209 north to State Route 658. Take State Route 658 for approximately 5.3 miles to Covered Bridge Road. Turn right on Covered Bridge Road and travel east .1 mile to the bridge. Page 50

35-34-19

Skull Fork Covered Bridge • Harrison County

Description: 45-foot multiple kingpost truss, built in 1876. *Location*: south of Freeport, in Freeport Township, over the Skull Fork of the Stillwater Creek. *Directions*: from the town of Freeport, take State Route 800 south to Skull Fork Road (also County Road 27). Take Skull Fork Road south for 1.8 miles to Covered Bridge Road. Turn left on Covered Bridge Road, heading east for .2 miles. Page 52

35-41-37

Hindman Memorial Bridge • Jefferson County

Description: 89-foot Warren truss, built in 1997. *Location*: northeast of Richmond in Island Township, over Town Fork. *Directions*: in the town of Richmond, take State Route 152/43 north to County Road 56. Turn left on County Road 56 to the covered bridge. Page 52–53

35-60-31

Johnson's Mill or Salt Creek Covered Bridge • Muskingum County

Description: 87-foot Warren, built in 1876, renovated in 1997. *Location*: east northeast of Zanesville, in Perry Township, over Salt Creek. *Directions*: from Zanesville, take US Route 22/40 east approximate 7 miles to Arch Hill Road (also County Road 82). Turn left on Arch Hill Road, heading north 1.9 miles to the covered bridge. Page 54–55

35-77-01

Everett Road Covered Bridge • Summit County

Description: 100-foot Smith truss, built in 1870s, renovated in 1986. *Location*: southeast of Richfield, in Boston Township, over Furnace Run. *Directions*: from Interstate I-77, take Exit 143 onto Wheatley Road (also Township Road 174). Head southeast on Wheatley Road to Revere Road (also Township Road 114). Turn right on Revere Road, heading south for 1.2 miles to Everett Road (also County Road 42). Turn left on Everett Road, heading east for 1.2 miles to the covered bridge. Page 56

35-78-01

Newton Falls Covered Bridge • Trumbull County

Description: 123-foot Town lattice truss, circa 1831. *Location*: in Newton Falls, over the East Branch of the Mahoning River. *Directions*: from the intersection of State Route 5 and State Route 534 (also East Broad Street), take State Route 534 southeast 1.2 miles to River Road. Turn left on River Road, heading north .1 miles to Bridge Street. Take a right on Bridge Street. The covered bridge lies in the center of Newton Falls. Page 57

Town Lattice, 1880

Palos Covered Bridge • Athens County

Palos, or Newton, Bridge in Trimble Township, an 81-foot modified multiple kingpost truss, was built by Daniel Fulton in 1876. The Palos name is probably associated with a stop on the nearby railroad. Numerous repairs have been made to this bridge, including when it was only two years old. Sometime around 1970, the steel pier was added. In 1977, the bridge was sided on the inside to keep vandals from stealing the exterior siding and dumping trash on the lower chords. A complete renovation was finished in 2003 by the Righter Construction Company of Columbus, largely funded by a federal grant. Its deep red paint is a landmark for travelers along Ohio Route 13. National Register of Historic Places • Bridge number 35-05-01

Kidwell Covered Bridge • Athens County

Kidwell Bridge, southwest of Jacksonville, is a 96-foot Howe truss built in 1880 by the Hocking Valley Bridge Works of Lancaster, Ohio, August Borneman's company. The Hocking Valley Bridge Works built many Howe trusses, including this bridge, as well as some of Borneman's own unique combination truss bridges and all-metal trusses. His system of upper and lower cross-bracing consisted of a central iron ring connecting four diagonal tension rods and was positioned between each vertical truss. The deteriorating condition of the Kidwell Bridge led to its closure for many years. The complete renovation by the Righter Construction Company in 2003 came with the aid of a federal grant. When built, the county referred to the location as Kidwell's Mill. National Register of Historic Places • Bridge number 35-05-02

Blackwood Covered Bridge • Athens County

Blackwood Bridge in Lodi Township is a 64.5-foot multiple kingpost built in 1879. It was built by Ebenezer B. Henderson, a prolific bridge builder from Washington County, Ohio. Most of his bridges were built with the popular multiple kingpost truss plan. He charged the county $6.75 per lineal foot to build the Blackwood Bridge and received a total of $492.72. The masonry work cost $1013, over twice as much as the bridge. This was not at all unusual. The bridge was completely renovated in 2003 using 80% federal and 20% county funds. One of the most remote covered bridges in Ohio, its gravel road has barns nearby. Hoof prints of deer can often be seen in the dust coating the floorboards. National Register of Historic Places • Bridge number 35-05-06

BLACKWOOD

BLACKWOOD

Shaeffer or Campbell Covered Bridge • Belmont County

Shaeffer or Campbell Bridge on the Belmont Campus of Ohio University is a 68-foot multiple kingpost truss built in 1875 and was moved to this location in the 1970s. Belmont County lost its last original covered bridge in 1953 when it collapsed under a coal truck. It was another twenty years before Belmont County again had a covered bridge. R.J. Boccabella, Belmont County Engineer, moved this bridge from Fairfield County, south of Amanda. The bridge was dismantled and taken to the county garage at Lloydsville, where it was reconditioned and then rebuilt over a small lake on the Belmont Campus. Visible from the west-bound lanes of I-70, the bridge sets on pilings in the lake and is approached by open spans on each end. Engineer Boccabella designed the approach span railings after those on the summer home of writer Mark Twain. •
Bridge number 35-07-05

Johnson Road or Crabtree Covered Bridge • Jackson County

Johnson Road, or Crabtree, Bridge southwest of Jackson is a 71-foot Smith truss built in 1870. This bridge was once known as the Crabtree Bridge for the family that lived nearby. It was built by R.D. Edwards of nearby Vinton County. Edwards is recorded as building two covered bridges on Johnson Road in 1870 for a total of over $1,300. There were once two other Smith truss covered bridges over Brushy Fork on Johnson Road but both were removed in the 1950s. Jackson County purchased a set of bridge plans from the Smith Bridge Company, and then contracted with local builders to erect a number of these bridges. Smith received a royalty of 50 cents per foot for a 60-foot bridge and 75 cents per foot for a 70-foot bridge. Major renovation work began on the Johnson Road Bridge in 1999 jointly funded by federal and county money. National Register of Historic Places • Bridge number 35-40-06

Byer Covered Bridge
Jackson County

Byer Bridge north of Jackson is an 82-foot Smith truss built in 1872. T.J. Dency built the Byer Bridge and its foundations for $1,269. Major repairs were made to it in 1935 when the state took over this road. Shortly after, the state re-routed Ohio Route 327, and the covered bridge reverted to county ownership. For many years the old bridge on this short section of road received only occasional maintenance. As a result, its condition deteriorated until it was finally closed to traffic (photo lower right). The trusses were badly rotted from a leaky roof and were on the point of collapse when a combination of federal and county funding resulted in its complete renovation in 2004 (photo upper right). National Register of Historic Places •

Bridge number 35-40-08

Buckeye Furnace Covered Bridge • Jackson County

Buckeye Furnace Bridge east of Jackson is a 60-foot Smith truss bridge built in 1871. Dency, McCurdy, and Company built this bridge, including the foundations, for $1,300. Jackson County, part of the Hanging Rock Iron Region, had numerous charcoal iron furnaces. The buildings around Buckeye Furnace, reconstructed by the Ohio Historical Society, complement the old covered bridge. This was not the first bridge on the site. County records mention repairs to a bridge here in 1867. Major repairs were made to this bridge in the 1930s and again in the late 1960s. In 1999 a federal grant paid for eighty percent of a major renovation while the county provided the remaining twenty. National Register of Historic Places • Bridge number 35-40-11

Scottown Covered Bridge • Lawrence County

Scottown Bridge just east of Scottown is an 84-foot multiple kingpost truss bridge variant built in 1877. The bridge was built on the abutments of an earlier bridge by William Thompson for $547. This truss is called a variant of the multiple kingpost since it received so many repairs over the years that it is difficult to determine what is original. Repairs followed the great 1913 flood, and again after the flash flood on Indian Guyan known as the Great Wheat Flood in 1934. Heavy rains washed out whole fields of wheat along Indian Guyan and its tributaries, and this sodden mass of grain hit the old covered bridge, nearly knocking it off its foundations. Much of the bridge siding was torn off and, it is thought, replaced with corrugated metal at this time. Over the years, the Scottown trusses were strengthened by the addition of steel channels, gussets, cables, tension rods, and heavy arch/braces. In 1991 County Engineer David R. Lynd gave this old bridge, Lawrence County's last, a thorough renovation which included a new floor system, new roof, and siding. The new siding is wood with openings along each side. National Register of Historic Places • Bridge number 35-44-05

RENOVATION BY
LAW CO ENGINEER
AND

Foraker Covered Bridge • Monroe County

Foraker Bridge, southeast of Graysville, is a 103-foot multiple kingpost truss bridge built in 1886. The late Clyde Dillon, who was born and raised in Monroe County, credited Isaiah Cline, a well-known stone mason in this area, for the foundations. Dillon's father remembered seeing the bridge built around 1886/1887. In 1938 Stock Bower (see Brown County's New Hope Bridge) added diagonal steel rods to reinforce the trusses and the lower chords and strengthened the floor system with additional beams and stringers. In later years, the county installed steel I-beam piers for more support. Major renovation work was done on this bridge in 2005. The bridge was removed from its foundation while repairs were made to the trusses. National Register of Historic Places • Bridge number 35-56-14

Knowlton Covered Bridge • Monroe County

Knowlton Bridge, north of Rinard Mills, is a 192-foot three-span multiple kingpost truss bridge with arches on the center span. Also known as the Crum, Old Camp, or Long Bridge, this was one of two wooden truss bridges built to span the Little Muskingum in 1866/1867. Fouts and Townsend, bridge builders from nearby Washington County, were contracted for these bridges. It appears that the tied arches on the center span were part of the original structure. At that time, only the center span was covered. The approach spans were open and were replaced in 1884 with covered spans. A major flood in 1896 damaged many county bridges, including the Knowlton, and I.P. and S.N. Cline were paid for repairing it. The Knowlton Bridge was closed to vehicular traffic in the 1980s. Adjacent land owner, Earl Knowlton, sold a ninety-nine-year lease for six acres to the Knowlton Covered Bridge Park Association to create a park. Extensive repairs were made in 1993/1994 including adding a large steel I-beam to the north span and replacing siding. National Register of Historic Places • Bridge number 35-56-18

Barkhurst Mill or Williams Covered Bridge • Morgan County

Barkhurst Mill, northeast of Chesterhill, is an 84-foot multiple kingpost truss bridge with added laminated arches, built in 1872. From the earliest days of Morgan County, this site has been a milling center. The old Barkhurst Mill was built in the 1830s by John Pierpont, but has collapsed after 170 years. In 1872 the county contracted with Licking County builder John Shrake to build the bridge for $8.69 per lineal foot. The three-ply laminated arches are thought to be a later addition, possibly after the 1913 flood. Due to flooding problems on Wolf Creek, iron rods tie this bridge to its abutments. The road is closed and the bridge is not being maintained. The owners of the adjacent farm are working to arouse interest in the preservation of this historic structure. National Register of Historic Places • Bridge number 35-58-15

Rosseau or Fairgrounds Covered Bridge • Morgan County

Rosseau Bridge spans a small run on the county fairgrounds and is a 58-foot multiple kingpost bridge built in 1881. D.D. Scott was paid $6 per lineal foot to build this bridge at the crossroads of Rosseau in southwestern Morgan County. When the county planned to build a new bridge at Rosseau in 1953, County Engineer Ed Ervin moved the bridge to the county fairgrounds with county workers at a cost of only $1,642. This was the first of a series of covered bridge relocations in Ohio. • Bridge number 35-58-32

Helmick Mill or Island Run Covered Bridge • Morgan County

Helmick Mill or Island Run Bridge southwest of Eagleport is a 74-foot multiple kingpost truss bridge built in 1867. Samuel Price built this structure over the rocky ledges of Island Run for $872. It is one of the state's most scenic bridges. A band of Morgan's Raiders rode up the valley of Island Run in July 1863, fleeing from the pursuing Union cavalry. They camped in a field on the old Weaver farm overnight and then crossed the Muskingum River the following day near Rokeby Lock. The Island Run Bridge, Morgan County's last covered bridge open to traffic, is in poor condition and needs a complete renovation. A center pier was placed under the bridge and wooden siding replaced with sheet metal sometime in the 1950s. Despite these changes, it is structurally one of the state's best examples of nineteenth-century layman's engineering. National Register of Historic Places • Bridge number 35-58-35

Adams or San Toy Covered Bridge • Morgan County

Adams Bridge, northwest of Ringgold, is a 58-foot multiple kingpost truss bridge. A man named Adams built this bridge in 1875, a fact not found in old county records. By the late 1980s, this bridge had deteriorated to the point that it had to be closed. Some area residents demanded a new bridge so the road could be reopened, and wanted the old bridge moved to a local park. County Engineer Calvin Parmeter decided to make major repairs to the bridge in 1994, including steel piers and new siding and roofing, but kept it closed to vehicular traffic. National Register of Historic Places • Bridge number 35-58-38

Milton Dye Covered Bridge • Morgan County

Milton Dye Bridge is a 48-foot multiple kingpost truss bridge built in the 1920s. When farmer Milton Dye grew tired of fording a stream on his farm in Brookfield Township, Noble County, he acquired a set of plans for a multiple kingpost truss bridge and began building this covered bridge. As a child, Franz Coyle, son of one of Dye's farm workers, watched with interest as the bridge was built. He estimated the date of construction of the bridge to be during the mid-1920s. The Ohio Power Company bought the Dye Farm for strip mining and in 1965 moved the bridge to Campsite D in their recreation area in nearby Manchester Township, Morgan County. Placed on stone and concrete foundations over Brannons Fork, it served admirably until heavy recreational vehicles weakened it and forced its closure to all vehicular traffic. •
Bridge number 35-58-41

Manchester Covered Bridge • Noble County

The Manchester Bridge south of Olive Green is a 49-foot multiple kingpost bridge. The building date and builder for this bridge are unknown. In the 1960s, a researcher was told by elderly residents that the bridge had been badly damaged in the 1913 flood and was rebuilt two years later. The bridge was thoroughly renovated in 2005. Setting in the midst of a strip mining operation, it is difficult to visit. Although on a township road, the mining company often has the road closed. • Bridge number 35-61-33

Parrish Covered Bridge • Noble County

The Parrish Bridge south of Sharon is an 81-foot multiple kingpost truss bridge built in 1914. The builder of the Parrish Bridge is unknown. It carried county road traffic until bypassed in 1980. The county gave the bridge to the Parrish family, but they found the maintenance too challenging and deeded it back to the county. The bridge was completely rebuilt in 2005. A small rural park has been established around the old bridge. • Bridge number 35-61-34

Park Hill Road or Rich Valley Covered Bridge • Noble County

Park Hill Road Bridge at Caldwell is a 44-foot multiple kingpost truss bridge that once spanned the Middle Fork of Duck Creek northwest of Middleburg. In 1970 the Park Hill Road Bridge and Rich Valley Bridge, which crossed Olive Green Creek at Rich Valley, were removed. Later that decade, parts of both bridges were used to build a little covered bridge in a nice setting on the fairgrounds. It is one of six Ohio covered bridges that have been moved to county fairgrounds. Noble County had twenty-three covered bridges in 1953 remaining from the over one-hundred covered bridges that once stood in its bounds. • Bridge number 35-61-40

Mount Olive Road or Grandstaff Covered Bridge • Vinton County

Mount Olive Road Bridge, north of Allensville and US Route 50, is a 50.5-foot queenpost truss bridge built in 1875. In 1875 George Washington Pilcher of McArthur got the contract to build the masonry for this bridge but ended up also building the bridge because the bridge contractor failed to post his bond. The bridge structure, a simple queenpost truss, cost only $6 per lineal foot. The Pilcher family, who were prominent masons in southeastern Ohio, erected many of the original buildings at Ohio University. Major repairs were made to this bridge in the 1930s by the Champion Bridge Company. The two concrete piers supporting the bridge were added in 1979. This little covered bridge is now bypassed. National Register of Historic Places • Bridge number 35-82-04

Bay or Tinker Covered Bridge
Vinton County

Bay Bridge, north of McArthur, is a 70-foot double multiple kingpost bridge built in 1876. The firm of Graves and Scott originally built this bridge to span Little Raccoon Creek north of Hamden.

The bridge cost $9.50 per lineal foot, an unusually high price due to its double truss timbers. In 1967 when Little Raccoon Creek was dammed to create a lake, the covered bridge was moved intact to the fairgrounds where it spans a small lake. A local contractor did this work for about $2000. • Bridge number 35-82-05

Geer Mill or Humbpack or Ponn Covered Bridge
Vinton County

Ponn Bridge, lying southwest of Wilkesville, is a three-span, double multiple kingpost truss bridge with arches on the center span. This bridge's pronounced "hump," or high camber, makes it unique in Ohio, and it is only one of two in the country. It was built by Martin McGrath and Lyman Wells, contractors from McArthur. It replaced an 1869 covered bridge that was destroyed by arson in May 1874. Although the county offered a large reward, no one was ever charged. The present bridge is a massive structure whose center span combines laminated plank arches between the double truss timbers. The bridge's nineteen-inch camber in both upper and lower chords provides its most common name, Old Humpback. Ponn was a nearby family and Geer's Mill was named for Jacob Geer, the miller in the 1870s and 1880s. The bridge cost $1898. Major repairs were made in 1962 and 2003, but it is now bypassed. National Register of Historic Places • Bridge number 35-82-06

Eakin Mill or Arbaugh Covered Bridge
Vinton County

Eakin Mill Bridge at the little community of Arbaugh is a 122-foot double multiple kingpost bridge with laminated plank arches. Gilman and Ward, contractors from McArthur, built this bridge for $2200 in 1870/1871. The stonework must have been included since there was no separate contract for masonry. When the contract was signed, the site was known as Eakin Mill. The bridge was built with camber although much less than the Humpback Bridge. In the early 1970s, trucks carrying supplies for the construction of the nearby Appalachian Highway damaged the old timber trusses and forced the bridge's closure. For over thirty years, the bridge remained closed, deteriorating steadily. The county struggled to maintain it, propping it up on wooden cribbing and trying to keep the roof in repair. Thanks to a federal grant, the bridge has been completely rebuilt, but only a few of the old timbers were reused. The bridge is again open to traffic. National Register of Historic Places • Bridge number 35-82-07

Cox Covered Bridge
Vinton County

Cox Bridge, north of Creola, is a 40-foot queenpost bridge built in 1884. The county commissioners' journals recorded the low price of $219.20 paid to Diltz and Steel for this bridge. The truss is a variation of the standard queenpost because there is no separate upper chord. During discussions of replacing this little bridge in the late 1980s, area residents indicated their desire to keep it, convincing the county to move it a few yards upstream. County workers jacked up the ends of the bridge and installed metal runners in August 1992. Strips of plywood were laid along the creek banks between the old and new location about twenty feet north, nailed together, and liberally coated with heavy grease. Steel cables were fastened to the metal runners under the bridge and two front end loaders slowly pulled the little bridge to its new site. Area citizens recently worked to give it a facelift, painting the side red and the roof green (see above right). • Bridge number 35-82-10

Shinn Covered Bridge • Washington County

Until 1885, no bridge existed at this crossing, and people were used to fording this branch of Wolf Creek by rowboat. Then a Shinn child nearly drowned after falling from the rowboat. Soon after this incident, area residents petitioned the county for a bridge. Ebenezer B. Henderson, prolific bridge builder from Washington County, was hired to build this bridge for $7.70 per lineal foot. Abuse and neglect caused the bridge to badly deteriorate by the 1990s, and it was closed for several years before the county obtained federal funding for a complete renovation by Amos Schwartz and Company of Indiana. Damage by an overloaded truck has left its future unsure. National Register of Historic Places • Bridge number 35-84-03

Henry Covered Bridge • Washington County

While family members saved the little Shinn girl from drowning, no one could help a little girl who fell from a footbridge over the flood waters of the West Branch of the Little Hocking River and drowned about 1892. Following the tragedy, petitions were sent to the county for a bridge at this crossing. By 1894 the county had arranged for the bridge to be built by E.B. Henderson. It is now bypassed. • Bridge number 35-84-06

ROOT
BRIDGE
33-84-08

Root Covered Bridge • Washington County

Not far from the Henry Bridge and over the same stream is the Root Bridge, built in 1878 by Rolla Merydith, well-known Washington County bridge builder. The Long truss type was built of yellow poplar for $6.50 per lineal foot. The land around the Root Bridge was owned by the Vincent family in the mid-1900s, and through the efforts of Rollin Vincent, land was donated to bypass the bridge and create a park. National Register of Historic Places • Bridge number 35-84-08

Harra Covered Bridge • Washington County

The Harra Bridge was another Long truss built by Rolla Merydith. It cost $7.17 per lineal foot and its timbers are yellow poplar. The foundation stone was quarried on the site, then the Herman Harra Farm. Mike Ryan, an Irish immigrant, had erected a mill dam and grist mill at this site, but until the covered bridge was built in 1878, farmers bringing grain had to ford the creek. The old wooden bridge was bypassed in 1981 and was renovated in recent years. National Register of Historic Places • Bridge number 35-84-11

Bell Covered Bridge • Washington County

In 1888 E.B. Henderson built a bridge at a site known as Bell's Crossing over the Southwest Branch of Wolf Creek near the Shinn Bridge. He received $7.90 per lineal foot for the work. Amos Schwartz Construction of Indiana completely renovated this bridge in 1998. Like some other bridges in southeast Ohio, all four corners of the Bell Bridge are tied to its abutments with iron rods. This sleepy little creek can become a raging torrent during high rainfall. • Bridge number 35-84-12

Mill Branch Covered Bridge • Washington County

The Mill Branch Bridge once spanned the Little Hocking River just east of Ohio Route 339, but its building date is unknown. When the county bypassed the bridge in the 1960s and left it to stand abandoned, the nearby landowner threatened to destroy it. So the county moved the bridge about seven miles north to the Barlow Fairgrounds. Ohio's Bicentennial logo was painted on one side of the bridge. • Bridge number 35-84-17

Schwendeman Covered Bridge • Washington County

Schwendeman Bridge is another of the many bridges built by E.B. Henderson. Interestingly the lumber for the little bridge came from the nearby Marietta Chair Company. The 47-foot multiple kingpost bridge cost only $5.75 per lineal foot and originally spanned Halfway Run on a township road about five miles northwest of Marietta. In 1967 the bridge was moved by the Marietta Jaycess to Jackson Hill Park in Marietta. The bridge made the move intact except for the roof. After twenty years, the old structure was deteriorating and being vandalized. Park officials were glad for the bridge to be moved to Jeff Curran's property in Salem Township south of Macksburg in 1994. • Bridge number 35-84-20

Hills or Hildreth Covered Bridge • Washington County

In 1878, Washington county officials contracted with the Hocking Valley Bridge Works to erect a covered bridge at LaFabers Ford of the Little Muskingum River east of Marietta. August Borneman, owner of the Lancaster, Ohio, company, favored Howe trusses. This is one of three Borneman-built Howe trusses surviving today, which includes the Kidwell Bridge in Athens County and the Johnston Bridge in Fairfield County. The cost of this large Howe truss was $13 per lineal foot. Although E.B. Henderson lost the superstructure contract to Borneman, he won the foundation contract for $3 per perch (a perch is twenty-five cubic yards of stone). The massive foundations of this bridge are part of its scenic charm. Bypassed by a new bridge in 1990, it is well-maintained by the county. Both of the Little Muskingum River covered bridges were built on tall piers to place them above flood waters, necessitating short approach spans on each end. National Register of Historic Places • Bridge number 35-84-24

Hune Covered Bridge • Washington County

About eight and one half miles up the Little Muskingum River from the Hills Bridge sets the Hune Bridge. State Route 26 is known as the "Covered Bridge Highway" even though only three are still standing along this twisty road.Most, if not all, of the covered bridges spanning the Little Muskingum River were built with the main span set high on stone piers and with open-approach spans on each end (see also the Rinard Covered Bridge on next page). Rolla Merydith built this fine covered bridge of yellow poplar in 1878 on his plan number three, a Long truss, for $7.17 per lineal foot, the same as the Harra Bridge. Folks in the 1870s called this crossing Gallaghers Ford despite its closeness to the Hune farm. As a young boy, Dr. H.B. Hune watched the bridge being built and said that the abutment stones and timbers came from his father's farm. Rolla Merydith and his young son boarded with the Hune family as the bridge was built, and the two little boys played together. The bridge was completely renovated in 1998 and is still carrying daily traffic. National Register of Historic Places • Bridge number 35-84-27

Rinard Covered Bridge • Washington County

Rinard Bridge was a little over two miles upstream from the Hune Bridge. The second bridge on this site, it replaced the Henderschott Ford Bridge washed out by a flood in August 1875. Dr. H.B. Hune vividly remembered seeing the covered bridge float by his family farm. The county then contracted with the Smith Bridge Company of Toledo, Ohio, to build a Smith truss replacement at a cost of $13.50 per lineal foot, a total of $2,520. Although the county bypassed the Rinard Bridge, like the Hills and Hune Bridges, it was well-maintained. The Rinard Bridge was washed out on September 18, 2004 in the flooding caused by Hurricane Ivan. A month later, the remains were removed from the river and plans are being made to rebuild this bridge sometime in the next two years. National Register of Historic Places • Bridge number 35-84-28

RINARD
BRIDGE

35-05-06

Blackwood Covered Bridge • Athens County

Description: 64.5-foot multiple kingpost truss, built in 1881. *Location*: east northeast of Pratts Fork, in Lodi Township, over Shade River Branch. *Directions*: from Athens, take US Route 33 south to the town of Pratts Fork. At Pratts Fork, turn left on County Road 45 and drive for 1.7 miles to County Road 44. Turn right on County Road 44, drive for 3.8 miles to County Road 46 (also Blackwood Road). Take a right on County Road 46, approximately .8 miles to the covered bridge. Page 66–67

35-05-02

Kidwell Covered Bridge • Athens County

Description: 96-foot Howe truss, built in 1880. *Location*: south southwest of Jacksonville, in Dover Township, over Sunday Creek. *Directions*: from Athens, take US Route 33 northwest to State Route 13. Take State Route 13 north through the town of Millfield. Approximately 1.5 miles out of Millfield, turn left on Township Road 332 (also Monserat Road), heading west for approximately .5 miles to the covered bridge. Page 66

35-05-01

Palos or Newton Covered Bridge • Athens County

Description: 81-foot multiple kingpost truss, built in 1875. *Location*: north northeast of Glouster, in Trimble Township, over Sunday Creek. *Directions*: from Athens, take US Route 33 northwest to State Route 13. Drive north on State Route 13 to the town of Glouster. Continue north on State Route 13 for 2 miles to Township Road 347. Turn right on Township Road 347, the bridge can be seen on the east side of State Route 13 and Township Road 347. Page 65

35-07-05

Shaeffer or Campbell Covered Bridge • Belmont County

Description: 68-foot multiple kingpost truss, built in 1875, moved in 1973. *Location*: west of St. Clairsville, in Richland Township. *Directions*: from Interstate I-70, take exit 213. Turn left onto US Route 40 and go to the first traffic light. Turn left onto State Route 331, heading north—will cross over I-70. Approximately .2 miles after the overpass is a traffic light. Just past the traffic light, turn left onto the dirt road near a natural science building and greenhouse. The covered bridge is approximately .8 miles down the road. Page 68–69

35-40-11

Buckeye Furnace Covered Bridge • Jackson County

Description: 60-foot Smith truss, built in 1871. *Location*: southeast of Wellston, in Milton Township, over Little Raccoon Creek. *Directions*: from State Route 32 take State Route 124 east. Drive approximately 3.8 miles on State Route 124 to County Road 58 (also Buckeye Furnace Road). Head south on County Road 58 for 2 miles to Township Road 167. Turn right on Township Road 167 and drive .8 miles to the covered bridge. Page 72–73

35-40-08

Byer Covered Bridge • Jackson County

Description: 82-foot Smith truss, built in 1872. *Location*: at Byer, in Washington Township, over Pigeon Creek. *Directions*: take US Route 50 to State Route 327. Take State Route 327 southeast to the village of Byer. In Byer, turn right on 2nd Street and drive a few hundred yard to Township Road 973. Turn left on Township Road 973. Page 71

35-40-06

Johnson Road or Crabtree Covered Bridge • Jackson County

Description: 71-foot Smith truss, built in 1870. *Location*: southwest of Jackson, in Scioto Township, over the Little Scioto River. *Directions*: from State Route 32, take State Route 776 southwest for 5.5 miles to Township Road 291 (also Johnson Road). Turn left on Township Road 291, drive approximately .5 miles to the covered bridge. Page 70

35-44-05

Scottown Covered Bridge • Lawrence County

Description: 79-foot multiple kingpost truss variant, built in 1877, renovated in 1991. *Location*: east of Scottown, in Windsor Township, over Indian Guyan Creek. *Directions*: from the intersection of State Route 775 and State Route 217, take State Route 217 east .8 miles. Turn right on Pleasant Ridge Road (also County Road 67), drive approximately .2 miles to the covered bridge. Page 74–75

35-58-38

Adams or San Toy Covered Bridge • Morgan County

Description: 58-foot multiple kingpost truss, built in 1875. *Location*: south of Portersville, in Union Township, over a branch of Sunday Creek. *Directions*: from State Route 37, take State Route 555 south for 3.2 miles to Township Road 16. Take Township Road 16 southwest for .6 miles to the covered bridge. Page 82

35-56-14

Foraker Covered Bridge • Monroe County

Description: 103-foot multiple kingpost truss, built in 1886, renovated 2005. *Location*: east southeast of Graysville, in Perry Township, over Little Muskingum River. *Directions*: from the town of Woodsfield and the intersection of State Route 78 and State Route 800, take State Route 800 south for 3.5 miles to County Road 40 (also Plainview Road). Turn right on County Road 40, heading south for 5 miles to the covered bridge. Weddle's Country Crafts is located at the bridge site. Page 76

35-56-18

Knowlton Covered Bridge • Monroe County

Description: 192-foot, 3-span multiple kingpost truss plus arch, built in 1867 and 1884 (approaches), renovated in 1995. *Location*: north of Rinard Mills, in Washington Township, over Little Muskingham River. *Directions*: from the town of Woodsfield and the intersection of State Route 78 and State Route 800, take State Route 800 south 2.5 miles to State Route 26. Turn right on State Route 26, heading south—pass through the town of Graysville and pass State Route 537. Approximately 2.5 miles south of State Route 537, turn left on Township Road 384, heading east for .5 miles to the covered bridge. Page 77

35-58-15

Barkhurst Mill or Williams Covered Bridge • Morgan County

Description: 84-foot multiple kingpost truss plus arch, built in 1872. *Location*: northeast of Chesterhill, in Marion Township, over Wolf Creek. *Directions*: from the town of Chesterhill, take State Route 377 north 1.7 miles to County Road 52. Head east 1 mile on County Road 52 to Township Road 21 (also Williams Bridge Road). Bridge is .4 miles ahead on Township Road 21. Page 78–79

35-58-35

Helmick Mill or Island Run Covered Bridge • Morgan County

Description: 74-foot multiple kingpost truss, built in 1867. *Location*: southwest of Eagleport, in Deerfield Township, over Island Run. *Directions*: from the town of Eagleport, take State Route 669 west 2.5 miles to Township Road 201. Head south on Township Road 201 for 1.7 miles and turn left on Township Road 269. Page 80–81

35-58-41

Milton Dye Covered Bridge • Morgan County

Description: 48-foot multiple kingpost truss, circa 1925, moved in 1965. *Location*: northeast of Bristol, over Brannons Fork. *Directions*: from the town of Bristol, head northeast on State Route 78/83. At the State Route 78/83 split, take State Route 83 north for 4.2 miles to Sawmill Road. Head east on Sawmill Road for .5 miles to Campground loop. The bridge is located at Ohio Power Campsite D. Page 83

35-58-32

Rosseau or Fairgrounds Covered Bridge • Morgan County

Description: 58-foot multiple kingpost truss, built in 1881, and moved in 1953. *Location*: southeast edge of McConnelsville. *Directions*: from the town of McConnelsville and the junction of State Route 60 and State Route 376, take State Route 376 south for .5 miles to the covered bridge, located on the fairgrounds. Page 79

35-61-33

Manchester Covered Bridge • Noble County

Description: 49-foot multiple kingpost truss, built in 1915, renovated 2005. *Location*: south of Olive Green, in Sharon Township, over Olive Green Creek. *Directions*: from Interstate I-77, take (exit 25) State Route 78 west 5.6 miles to Township Road 3. Turn left on Township Road 3, heading south 2.1 miles to the covered bridge. Page 84

35-61-34

Parrish Covered Bridge • Noble County

Description: 81-foot multiple kingpost truss, built in 1914, renovated 2005. *Location*: south southwest of Sharon, in Sharon Township, over Olive Green Creek. *Directions*: from Interstate I-77, take (exit 25) State Route 78 west for 2.1 miles to County Road 8. Turn left on County Road 8, heading south for 2.6 miles to the covered bridge. Page 85

35-61-40

Park Hill Road or Rich Valley Covered Bridge • Noble County

Description: 44-foot multiple kingpost truss, moved in 1970. *Location*: southwest of Caldwell. *Directions*: from Interstate I-77, take (exit 25) State Route 78 east for .1 miles, then head north .3 miles to fairground entrance. Page 86

35-82-05

Bay or Tinker Covered Bridge • Vinton County

Description: 70-foot double multiple kingpost truss, built in 1876, moved in 1966. *Location*: the north edge of McArthur. *Directions*: from the town of McArthur, take State Route 93 north for 1.5 miles to the Vinton County Junior Fairgrounds. The bridge is located in the Vinton County Junior Fairgrounds on the west side of State Route 93. Page 88–89

35-82-10

Cox Covered Bridge • Vinton County

Description: 48-foot queenpost truss, built in 1884. *Location*: north of Creola, in Swan Township, over Brushy Fork. *Directions*: from the town of McArthur, take State Route 93 north for 9 miles to County Road 20. Turn left on County Road 20, approximately .2 miles to the covered bridge. The bridge can also be seen from State Route 93 on the west side of the road. Page 93

35-82-07

Eakin Mill or Arbaugh Covered Bridge • Vinton County

Description: 122-foot double multiple kingpost truss plus arch, built in 1870, renovated 2003. *Location*: near Arbaugh, in Vinton Township, over Raccoon Creek. *Directions*: from the town of McArthur, take State Route 93 south to State Route 324. Head southeast on State Route 324 to State Route 160. Turn left on State Route 160, heading east to State Route 32. Take State Route 32 northeast for 3.2 miles to County Road 38A. Take County Road 38A north for .3 miles to the covered bridge. Page 92

35-82-06

Geer Mill, or Humpback, or Ponn Covered Bridge • Vinton County

Description: 165-foot, 3-span double multiple kingpost truss plus arch, built in 1874, renovated 2003. *Location*: southwest of Wilkesville, in Wilkesville Township, over Raccoon Creek. *Directions*: take State Route 160 to the village of Wilkesville. Across from the Wilkesville village square and schoolyard, turn onto County Road 8, heading south 2.5 miles to a wooden Vinton County sign. Turn right on Township Road 7, heading west on the gravel road for .8 miles to the fork in the road. Take a left at the fork to get on Township Road 4. Head south on Township Road 4 down a hill for 1.3 miles to the covered bridge. Page 90–91

35-82-04

Mount Olive Road or Grandstaff Covered Bridge • Vinton County

Description: 50.5-foot queenpost truss, built in 1875. *Location*: northeast of Allensville, in Jackson Township, over Middle Fork of Salt Creek. *Directions*: from the town of McArthur, take US Route 50 west to Allensville. Turn right on County Road 18, heading north for 1.5 miles to Township Road 7. The bridge is located at the intersection of County Road 18 and Township Road 7. Page 87

35-84-12

Bell Covered Bridge • Washington County

Description: 62-foot multiple kingpost truss, built in 1888, renovated in 1998. *Location*: north northwest of Barlow, in Barlow Township, over the Southwest Fork of Wolf Creek. *Directions*: from the town of Barlow and the intersection of State Route 550 and State Route 339, take State Route 339 north for .3 miles to Township Road 39. Turn left on Township Road 39, heading northwest 2.6 miles to the covered bridge. Page 99

35-84-11

Harra Covered Bridge • Washington County

Description: 100-foot Long truss, built in 1878. *Location*: northwest of Watertown, in Watertown Township, over the South Branch of Wolf Creek. *Directions*: from Watertown, take State Route 339 north 2.3 miles to Township Road 172. Take Township Road 172 west for .5 miles to the covered bridge, located on the north side of the road. Page 98

35-84-06

Henry Covered Bridge • Washington County

Description: 45-foot multiple kingpost truss, built in 1894. *Location*: southeast of Bartlett, in Fairfield Township, over the West Branch of the Little Hocking River. *Directions*: from the town of Barlow and the intersection of State Route 339 and State Route 550, take State Route 550 west for 6 miles to Township Road 61. Turn left on Township Road 61, heading south 2 miles to the covered bridge, located on the east side of the road. Page 95

35-84-24

Hills or Hildreth Covered Bridge • Washington County

Description: 122-foot Howe truss, built in 1878. *Location*: east of Marietta, in Newport Township, over the Little Muskingum River. *Directions*: from State Route 7, take State Route 26 north for 5.7 miles to County Road 333. Turn right on County Road 333, the bridge is .3 miles on the left-hand side of the road. Page 102

35-84-27

Hune Covered Bridge • Washington County

Description: 128-foot Long truss, built in 1879, renovated in 1998. *Location*: southwest of Bloomfield, in Lawrence Township, over the Little Muskingum River. *Directions*: from State Route 7, take State Route 26 north for several miles until the town of Dart. The bridge is approximately 3.5 miles north of Dart and can be seen from State Route 26 on the east side of the road (the bridge is about .2 miles to the east). Or, if you are heading southwest on State Route 26, the bridge can be seen approximately 7.4 miles after the junction of State Route 260. Page 103

35-84-17

Mill Branch Covered Bridge • Washington County

Description: 65-foot multiple kingpost truss, moved in 1980. *Location*: at Barlow, in Barlow Township, on the fairgrounds over the brook. *Directions*: from the town of Barlow and the intersection of State Route 339 and State Route 550, take State Route 550 west .1 miles. The covered bridge is located on the north side of the road at the fairgrounds. Page 100

35-84-28

Rinard or Henderschott Ford Covered Bridge • Washington County

Description: 130-foot Smith truss, built in 1876. Washed out in a 2004 flood but is expected to be rebuilt. *Location*: southwest of Bloomfield, in Ludlow Township, over the Little Muskingum River. *Directions*: from the border of Washington County and Monroe County, take State Route 26 south to the town of Bloomfield. Approximately 6 miles out of Bloomfield, take County Road 406 east .1 miles to the covered bridge. The bridge can also be seen from State Route 26 just past County Road 406, on the east side of the road. Page 104–105

35-84-08

Root Covered Bridge • Washington County

Description: 70.5-foot Long truss, built in 1878. *Location*: north of Decaturville, in Decatur Township, over the West Branch of the Little Hocking River. *Directions*: from US Route 50/State Route 32/7, take State Route 555 northwest for 7.3 miles to County Road 6. Turn right on County Road 6, heading north .5 miles to the covered bridge, located on the east side of the road. Page 96–97

35-84-20

Schwendeman or Benedict Covered Bridge • Washington County

Description: 47-foot multiple kingpost truss, built in 1894, moved in 1967, and again in 1994. *Location*: south of Macksburg, in Salem Township. *Directions*: from State Route 60, take State Route 530 northeast 5 miles to County Road 8. Head north on County Road 8 for 1 mile to the covered bridge. The bridge is .7 miles north of State Route 530 and sits below the road and is easily missed. The bridge is located on private property on the east side of the road. Page 101

35-84-03

Shinn Covered Bridge • Washington County

Description: 99-foot multiple kingpost truss plus arch, built in 1886, renovated in 1998. *Location*: southwest of Wolf Creek, in Palmer Township, over the West Branch of Wolf Creek. *Directions*: from Watertown and the intersection of State Route 339 and State Route 676, take State Route 676 west towards Wolf Creek. Approximately .3 miles out of Wolf Creek, turn left on Township Road 91, heading south 2.6 miles to Township Road 447. Turn left on Township Road 447, heading east .2 miles to the covered bridge west of the Wolf Creek (you need not turn south on Township Road 18) The bridge sits low under the roadway and is difficult to see. Page 94

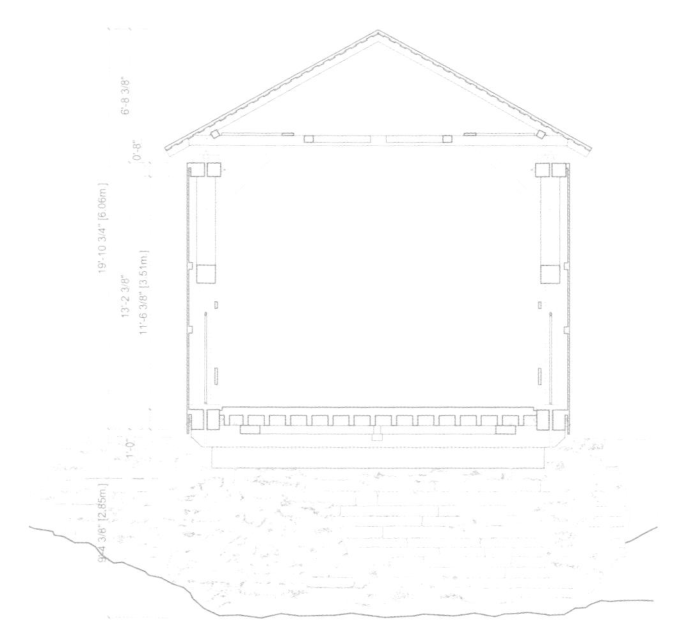

Harshman Covered Bridge, 1861

Harshaville Covered Bridge
Adams County

The Harshaville Covered Bridge, southeast of Seaman, is a 110-foot multiple kingpost truss plus arch, built in 1855. The sleepy village of Harshaville in Adams County had a rude awakening one day in July 1863 when Confederate General John Hunt Morgan and his raiders galloped across the covered bridge and into the village. They robbed the general store and even tied bolts of fabric to their saddles. The fabric unwound and flapped in the breeze as they galloped off down the road. Morgan's Raiders often burned covered bridges to slow their pursuers, but for some reason, they left the Harshaville Bridge alone. The laminated arches and concrete piers were added to this covered bridge in a 1940s renovation. Many members of the Amish community now live in this area. National Register of Historic Places

• Bridge number 35-01-02

Kirker Covered Bridge • Adams County

Kirker Covered Bridge, west of West Union, is a 64-foot multiple kingpost, built in 1890. The Kirker Bridge was named for a prominent Adams County pioneer, Thomas Kirker, whose farm lay in Liberty Township south of the covered bridge. The farm is still in the Kirker family. Thomas Kirker became Ohio's acting governor in 1807 when Governor Edward Tiffin resigned to become a U.S. senator. Thomas Kirker was born in Ireland and emigrated with his family to Adams County. Just north of the old Kirker farm on the west side of Ohio Route 136 is the Kirker Cemetery, where the governor lies buried. Adams County's Bicentennial barn is located on this farm as well. During a 1950s renovation, the Ohio Department of Transportation added steel rods and beams to strengthen the old bridge. The Kirker Bridge has been bypassed for a number of years and is owned and maintained by the county. National Register of Historic Places • Bridge number 35-01-10

Brown Covered Bridge
Brown County

Brown Bridge, northeast of New Hope, is a 144-foot Smith truss built from 1880–1. At their regular meeting on December 10, 1879, the Brown County Commissioners decided to build a bridge over White Oak Creek near the residence of Robert Brown. On January 9, 1880, the abutment contract was awarded to John Kennedy, and the bridge contract went to the Smith Bridge Company of Toledo, Ohio, for $16.50 per lineal foot. Abutment stones came from the Robert Brown farm.

As the foundation work fell behind schedule, the project dragged on into mid-April 1881. The total bill due to the Smith Bridge Company was $2376. John Griffith, a well-known local bridge builder, worked on the superstructure of the bridge. Since he worked on other Smith truss bridges in the county, it is thought he was the local agent or foreman for the company. Visitors to the Brown Bridge will likely be impressed by its width—22.5 foot overall with a 17-foot roadway. Most covered bridge roadways are only 12- to 14-feet wide, and county records provide no explanation for such a wide bridge. It served the area well until bypassed in the 1990s. In 2003 the old bridge was restored to its original condition. •

Bridge number 35-08-04

New Hope Covered Bridge • Brown County (also previous page)
New Hope Bridge, southwest of New Hope, is a 177-foot Howe truss with laminated arches. The first covered bridge on this site was built in 1872 and replaced by the present bridge in 1878. There is no indication why the first bridge failed. Josiah Bryant, well-known Brown County bridge builder, was awarded the 1878 contract at $13.95 per lineal foot. The New Hope Bridge lacks only five inches of being as wide as the Brown Bridge and is among the longer single-span covered bridges in the state. In 1902, the county hired Louis S. Bower Sr. of Fleming County, Kentucky, to renovate this bridge, including the addition of eleven-ply laminated arches. In 1977, the county hired Louis S. "Stock" Bower Jr. to superintend more repairs. After being closed for a number of years, the New Hope Bridge underwent another thorough renovation in 2003/2004. • Bridge number 35-08-05

McCafferty Road Covered Bridge • Brown County

McCafferty Road Bridge, southwest of Vera Cruz, is a 170-foot Howe truss built in 1877 by the Smith Bridge Company. The Smith Bridge Company, founded by Robert W. Smith of Tipp City, Ohio, was best known for building patented Smith trusses but also erected other bridge designs, such as the popular Howe truss. In the McCafferty Road Bridge, iron tension rods throughout the trusses vary in thickness from 1.75 inches to one inch and were designed to accommodate differing stress levels. • Bridge number 35-08-08

North Pole Road Covered Bridge • Brown County

North Pole Road Bridge, northeast of Ripley, is a 166-foot Smith truss built in 1875. This patented truss replaced an earlier bridge on the site that unsubstantiated local stories say was iron. Nonetheless, some folks referred to this covered bridge as the “Iron Bridge.” It was a twin to the Eagle Creek Covered Bridge upstream on Ohio Route 763, also built in 1875 by the same company. A devastating flood struck the Eagle Creek Valley in early March 1997, badly damaging the North Pole Road Bridge and completely destroying its upstream twin. Extensive repairs were made to the North Pole Road Bridge after the flood, and it is in excellent condition. It is another long single-span covered bridge. Old stone walls border the road leading east from the bridge. This quiet location is one of Ohio’s many beauty spots. • Bridge number 35-08-23

George Miller Road Covered Bridge • Brown County

George Miller Road Bridge, southeast of Russellville, is a 160-foot Smith truss built in 1879. John Griffith, agent and foreman for the Smith Bridge Company, supervised construction of this fourteen panel Smith truss, built for $14.75 per lineal foot. The bridge was renovated in the 1990s by the Amish and Mennonite crew of Amos Schwartz Construction of Geneva, Indiana. A visit to this covered bridge is always fun for the family. The creek flows over fossil-bearing limestone, and it is easy to find interesting specimens. • Bridge number 35-08-34

Bebb Park or State Line Covered Bridge • Butler County (see also overleaf)

Governor Bebb Park or State Line Bridge (also once called Fairfield Pike Bridge), spanning a dry gully at the park entrance, was built in 1867/1868. This bridge was once over Indian Creek on Fairfield Pike, west of Oxford. This was long assumed to be its original location. It was actually once part of a two-span bridge crossing a western flood channel of the Great Miami River at Middletown. For $26.00 per lineal foot, the firm of Banden, Butin, and Bowman built this bridge for Butler county. About 1886, the bridge was taken down, divided into two spans and rebuilt at two sites on Indian Creek. It seems to be a late example of the distinctive Lewis Wernwag truss, in which the kingposts are flared on a radius and an arch is added to the trusses. In 1966 the bridge was dismantled and taken to Governor Bebb Park and stored until it was rebuilt in 1970 using funds donated by the Peter Rentschler family of Hamilton. National Register of Historic Places • Bridge number 35-09-02

Black Covered Bridge • Butler County

Black, or Pughs Mill Bridge, north of Oxford, is a mixture of the Long and Childs trusses and was built in 1868. The firm of Banden, Butin, and Bowman built this 223-foot bridge as a single span for $30.25 per lineal foot, an unusually steep price in the 1860s. In June 1869, the county commissioners decided to have the builders come back to erect a central pier and "remodel" the structure with new braces so it would bear on the new pier. The extra work cost $600, and the bridge was completed and accepted in January 1869. The original design was probably a Long truss, but after the remodeling it combined both the Long and Childs truss concepts. Some panels have the wooden counterbraces of the Long truss, and those towards the center have the iron counterbraces of the Childs truss. The bridge served Ohio Route 732 until bypassed about 1950. A major renovation was completed in 1998/1999. The Oxford Museum Association maintains this bridge. National Register of Historic Places • Bridge number 35-09-03

Stonelick or Perintown Covered Bridge • Clermont County

Stonelick, or Perintown Bridge, east of Perintown, is a 140-foot Howe truss built in 1878. Beautiful Stonelick Creek is a tributary of the East Fork of the Little Miami River, a major stream of Clermont County. The Stonelick Bridge was built by M. Collins with a 16.5-foot roadway. Over-loaded vehicles have plagued this bridge and led to a number of repairs. About twenty years ago, a large trash truck broke through the floor and landed in the creek. A rash of vandalism prompted county officials to install lights and infrared cameras. Clermont County values its last covered bridge and is taking measures to protect it. National Register of Historic Places • Bridge number 35-13-02

Martinsville Covered Bridge • Clinton County

Martinsville Bridge, west of Martinsville, is a heavily-reinforced 80-foot multiple kingpost truss bridge. The Martinsville Bridge, the last covered bridge in Clinton County, was built in 1872 by Zimri Wall, founder of the Champion Bridge Company of Wilmington, Ohio. The firm considered this the oldest example of their work. In the 1970s and 1980s, major repairs included the addition of a central concrete pier to support new steel I-beams beneath the bridge. Steel channels and plates were also added to strengthen the structure. Technically, the covered bridge at Lynchburg is partially in Clinton County, but after the bridge closed, Clinton County withdrew all interest in it. National Register of Historic Places • Bridge number 35-14-09

Cemetery Road Covered Bridge • Greene County

Cemetery Road Bridge in Glen Helen Nature Preserve is a 72-foot Howe truss bridge built in 1886. It originally stood over Anderson's Fork northeast of New Burlington in the southern part of Greene County. Local builder Henry E. Hebble built it for $14 per lineal foot. The original bridge totaled 130 feet. When construction began on Caesar's Creek Reservoir in the late 1970s, all structures on or near Anderson's Fork had to be removed from the area that would be flooded in a 100-year flood. Ralph Ramey, director of Glen Helen in 1979, decided to relocate the covered bridge to his nature preserve. Ramey and his Boy Scout troop moved only a 72-foot center section on a low-boy truck. Since then, maintenance has been a regular struggle due to vandalism. The most recent renovation was done in early 2000. • Bridge number 35-29-01

West Engle Mill Road Covered Bridge • Greene County

West Engle Mill Road Bridge lies southeast of Spring Valley and is a 148-foot Smith truss bridge built in 1877. The history of this covered bridge is mysterious. The commissioners' journals hold only a few tidbits on it. In 1887 Lucas & Thomas were given the contract to dismantle and move a bridge from Spring Valley Road to West Engle Mill Road over Andersons Fork. The original building date of the bridge was probably in the 1870s. Bypassed by a new structure in the mid 1980s, the old bridge stands abandoned and in poor condition. • Bridge number 35-29-03

Stevenson Road Covered Bridge
Greene County

Stevenson Road Bridge lies northeast of Xenia and is a 99-foot Smith truss bridge. The Smith Bridge Company built this bridge for $11 per lineal foot. The commissioners stipulated that it be a double truss. The masonry work cost $7 per perch. Situated on a main county road and on a curve at the foot of a hill, drivers have occasionally lost control of their vehicles and crashed into the bridge. Despite the addition of steel beams, the bridge has continued to deteriorate and had to be closed. A new bridge built upstream allowed the old covered structure to be preserved. •

Bridge number 35-29-15

Charlton Mill Road Covered Bridge • Greene County

Charlton Mill Road Bridge lies southwest of Cedarville and is a 128-foot Howe truss bridge that was built in 1883. Henry E. Hebble built the bridge at Charlton Mill, but the old county commissioners' journals failed to record the cost. We can estimate the price at about $14 per lineal foot. The creek it spans was named for Nathaniel Massie, an important early surveyor in this section of Ohio, the Virginia Military District. The Charlton Mill Bridge became the last covered bridge carrying traffic in Greene County. • Bridge number 35-29-16

Ballard Road Covered Bridge • Greene County

Ballard Road Bridge sits six miles east of Xenia near the entrance to the historic Dean Farm. It was built in 1883 by J.C. Brown and Henry E. Hebble did the masonry. The county records do not indicate prices. It is Ohio's only green covered bridge. Ballard Road dead-ends just south of the bridge since US Route 35 is now re-routed through the Dean Farm. The old covered bridge's lovely setting is only slightly diminished by the highway's close proximity. National Register of Historic Places • Bridge number 35-29-18

HELP PRESERVE
THIS

Jediah Hill Covered Bridge • Hamilton County

Jediah Hill Bridge lies about one and a half miles north of Mt. Healthy and is a 44-foot queenpost truss bridge built in 1850. Jediah Hill built this little covered bridge at his mill. His young grandson was the first to cross the new bridge, driving his dog cart. It is the county's last covered bridge. A concrete pier was placed under the old bridge prior to 1950. The first of two major renovations occurred in 1956 after ice storm damage. During this renovation, the original 6 x 10-inch oak timbers were treated with wood preservative and the roof was replaced. By the 1970s, the old bridge led to a private housing development where the only access for heavy emergency vehicles was a locked gate that meant delays during emergencies. The covered bridge had to either be rebuilt for modern traffic loads or be moved to a location downstream. Those arguing to keep the bridge on its original site after widening and raising its overhead clearance won the day. The old trusses are still there, but the bridge is supported by steel I-beams and the concrete pier was removed. In October 1981 the year the bridge was rebuilt, Jediah Hill's old mill burned to the ground. The bridge reopened to traffic in 1982. National Register of Historic Places • Bridge number 35-31-01

Lynchburg Covered Bridge • Highland County

Lynchburg Covered Bridge at Lynchburg is a 120-foot Long truss bridge built in 1870. It was the work of well-known builder and designer, John C. Gregg, who built a number of Long truss covered bridges in Highland County in the 1860s and 1870s. Costing $3,138 to complete, the bridge was bypassed in 1969 and then closed to all traffic in 1974 after severe damage by a windstorm. At this time, Clinton County withdrew all support for the bridge, leaving Lynchburg struggling to maintain it through funds raised at an annual covered bridge festival. Damaged in an arson attempt a few years ago, the local community worked hard to raise funds for a major renovation. Now restored, this is Highland County's last covered bridge. National Register of Historic Places • Bridge number 35-36-06

Eldean Covered Bridge • Miami County

Eldean Bridge, north of Troy, is a two-span 224-foot Long truss bridge built in 1860. In March 1860 the Miami County Commissioners announced their intention to build a Long truss bridge at Allen's Mill. The bridge cost $11.75 per lineal foot and $2.95 per perch for the pier masonry and $2.73 per perch for the abutments. Total cost of the superstructure was $2,632 and $1,337 for the stonework. Both bridge and foundations were built by James and William Hamilton. The name Allen's Mill was soon superceded by Eldean, a nearby community on the Miami and Erie Canal. The Eldean Bridge, second longest covered bridge in Ohio and the last such bridge in Miami County, was bypassed in 1963 and closed to traffic. When vandalism threatened the old bridge, the county decided to reopen it to light traffic as a deterrent. The Eldean Bridge is the nation's best example of a Long patent truss. Renovation work is underway in 2006. National Register of Historic Places • Bridge number 35-55-01

Fletcher Covered Bridge • Miami County

Fletcher Bridge is a 45-foot Smith truss bridge built in 1998. Deputy Auglaize County Engineer Dan Bennett designed this little covered bridge for Fletcher using the truss design patented by Miami County native Robert W. Smith. About forty community volunteers and the designer provided the labor to build it from white oak timbers and roofed it with cedar shingles. Many visitors joined village residents for the July 4, 1998, dedication ceremony. • Bridge number 35-55-103

Germantown Covered Bridge • Montgomery County

Germantown Bridge, in Germantown, is a 100-foot suspension truss bridge built in 1865. It is a product of Dayton bridge designer and builder David H. Morrison. County records indicate the commissioners contracted for "an iron suspension bridge with a roof" to carry Dayton Pike over Little Twin Creek in 1865. This unusual bridge combines both wood and iron truss members and features an inverted arch. It was never sided. In 1906, the bridge collapsed under a threshing machine. It was repaired and kept in service until 1911, when it was moved into

Germantown to span the same creek on Center Street. About 1960, when plans were announced to replace it, the Southern Ohio Covered Bridge Association (now known as the Ohio Historic Bridge Association) helped persuade officials to repair the bridge instead. In early winter 1981, a car smashed into one of the end posts, and, in a few minutes, the bridge collapsed. The locals quickly rallied to save their precious bridge, and by a massive effort involving donations of finances, labor, and machinery, once again rebuilt the bridge. It now serves only pedestrians and bicycles. National Register of Historic Places • Bridge number 35-57-01

Feedwire Covered Bridge • Montgomery County

Feedwire, or Carillon Park Bridge, spanning the bed of the Miami and Erie Canal, is a four-panel, 56-foot Warren truss bridge built in 1870. R.W. Smith, founder of the Smith Bridge Company, built this bridge to span Little Sugar Creek on Feedwire Road northwest of Bellbrook in Greene County. At one time, thirteen Warren truss covered bridges stood in Greene County. The wooden Warren truss was something of an oddity and is thought by some to be a variation of the Smith truss. In 1948 the bridge was moved to Carillon Historical Park where the arches and projecting portals were added. • Bridge number 35-57-03

Jasper Road or Mud Lick Covered Bridge • Montgomery County

Jasper Road, or Mud Lick Bridge, southwest of Germantown on a private estate, is a 71-foot Warren truss bridge. Like the Feedwire Road Bridge in Carillon Historical Park, the Jasper Road Bridge is also a transplant from Greene County. It was built in 1870 by John W. McLane over Caesar's Creek, several miles southwest of Jamestown, for $6.95 per linear foot. Dayton industrialist Huston Brown had this bridge moved to his estate in 1964 and rebuilt over Mud Lick Creek. The arch-brace was added sometime after 1930. • Bridge number 35-57-36

Photograph courtesy of the Ohio Historic Bridge Association

Valentine or Bill Green Covered Bridge • Pickaway County

Valentine, or Old Bill Green Bridge, southeast of Orient, is 36-foot multiple kingpost truss. The late William Green obtained a Fairfield County covered bridge to add to his collection of early American buildings and artifacts with the aid of the Ohio Historic Bridge Association. The bridge was rebuilt to span the arm of a lake in Green's meadow. It was originally built in Fairfield County in 1872 over Muddy Prairie Run on Hamburg Road by William Black for $550. In 1908 the county paid J.W. Buchanan $198 to move the little bridge about one-half mile, place it over the same creek on Delmont Road, and install new joists and roof. The bridge has gone by various names, Kerns or Craiglow Bridge on Hamburg Road, and the Valentine Bridge on Delmont Road. In 1971 the bridge was moved to Grant Thomas's farm where it stood over a pond until Green bought it in 1978. The Bill Green Bridge was blown down in a windstorm in March 2004. The new owner of the remains of the Bill Green Covered Bridge has plans to rebuild and incorporate the bridge in the approach to his new house. • Bridge number 35-65-15

Harshman Covered Bridge • Preble County

Harshman Bridge, north of Fairhaven, is a 104-foot Childs truss bridge built in 1894. A devastating "cyclone" struck western Ohio in 1887, whose heavy rains and wind greatly damaged roads and bridges as well as private property. Robert Eaton Lowery, the Preble County engineer, was a Delaware County native who knew of Everett S. Sherman's work and told him of bridge building jobs in Preble County following the great storm. Sherman took his Childs truss bridge model and met with Preble county officials, where he placed his model between two chairs, climbed up and stood on it. Because Sherman was not a small man, the commissioners were impressed with the strength of the Childs truss, and hired the bridge builder. From 1887 to 1895, Sherman built fifteen Childs truss covered bridges in Preble County and a number of small pony bridges of his own design. The Harshman Bridge was built near the end of his career in Preble County. The original contracts called for all these bridges to be finished with two coats of white paint, and they remain so today. National Register of Historic Places • Bridge number 35-68-03

Dixon Branch Covered Bridge • Preble County

Dixon Branch Bridge in Lewisburg is a 60-foot Childs truss bridge built in 1887. The bridge's name comes from its original location in Dixon Township over Dixon Branch of Four Mile Creek. Major repairs in 1961 included work on the lower chords, a new roof, and fresh paint. After a windstorm blew off the roof in 1963, the county decided to replace the bridge and offered it to the Civitan Club of Lewisburg who, under the direction of Seth S. Schlotterbeck, moved it to the park. Schlotterbeck was deputy county engineer for many years, and it was largely due to his efforts that so many of the county's covered bridges were preserved. He studied them carefully and developed plans for their maintenance while also gathering many anecdotal stories. Most of his recollections and pictures are today preserved by the Ohio Historic Bridge Association. Preble County's covered bridges are a fitting memorial to the late Seth Schlotterbeck as well as Everett Sherman. • Bridge number 35-68-04

Roberts Covered Bridge • Preble County (see also overleaf)

Roberts Bridge at Eaton is a two-lane 79-foot Burr truss bridge built in 1829. This is Ohio's oldest covered bridge and last two-lane covered bridge. Construction began in 1829 when Orlistus Roberts, nearby landowner on Seven Mile Creek and a skilled cabinet and clock maker, was hired by the turnpike company. Work was well underway when, in August 1830, Roberts died suddenly and left his seventeen-year-old apprentice, Lyman Campbell, to finish the bridge. He also married Roberts's widow, Mary. Today, the graves of all three Preble County pioneers can be seen at the old Roberts farm less than a mile north of the original site of the Roberts Bridge on the former Camden to Eaton Pike Road. After the road was relocated in the 1930s, the Roberts Bridge was left serving a short section of isolated road, leading to fears about the safety of the old landmark. On the night of August 5, 1986, an arsonist doused the timbers of the bridge with an accelerant and set it on fire. A sheriff's deputy saw the blaze from miles away and phoned in an alarm. The fire department managed to extinguish the fire, but the bridge was seriously damaged. Dr. Emory Kemp of West Virginia University, an expert on wood trusses, recommended gently removing the charring on the wood with sand blasting and covering them with plastic to keep them dry. The bridge was, of course, closed. A private committee moved the skeleton of the old bridge into Eaton over Seven Mile Creek where it was repaired, resided, and reroofed. It was rededicated in September 1991. National Register of Historic Places • Bridge number 35-68-05

Roberts

Brubaker Covered Bridge • Preble County

Brubaker Bridge, northwest of Gratis, is an 85-foot Childs truss bridge built in 1887. The only Childs truss bridges anywhere in the United States are in Delaware and Preble counties in Ohio and were built by Everett S. Sherman. The lumber in these bridges was pine from lumber dealers in Cadillac, Michigan, and the stone abutments were of local limestone. Deputy County Engineer Seth Schlotterbeck told an amusing story about the Brubaker Bridge. The siding on some covered bridges made it impossible to see oncoming traffic after automobiles became

common, especially, as at the Brubaker, where the approaches were at right angles to the crossing. A petition was sent to the county commissioners asking their permission to create long windows in the siding. When the commissioners refused, the local folks did it anyway. The commissioners were indignant, but nothing was ever done, and the windows were eventually made even bigger. Ironically, it also led to greater weathering that led to a recent major renovation. National Register of Historic Places • Bridge number 35-68-06

Christman Covered Bridge • Preble County

Christman Bridge, northwest of Eaton, is a 92-foot Childs truss built in 1895. The Christman Bridge is the first bridge on the site and was named for the adjacent landowners. The limestone foundations were quarried downstream from the bridge site. In 1961 a metal roof replaced the original red cedar shingle roof and the bridge was repainted. During the repainting, Deputy Engineer Seth Schlotterbeck salvaged poplar from another bridge to repair deteriorated gingerbread trim on the portals. It was, he claimed, his favorite of all Preble County's Sherman-built covered bridges. National Register of Historic Places • Bridge number 35-68-12

Geeting Covered Bridge • Preble County

Geeting Bridge, west of Lewisburg, is a 100-foot Childs truss bridge built in 1894. Like the Christman Bridge, this is the first and only bridge on the site. The price of $18.50 per lineal foot gave the builder, Everett Sherman, a total of $2,691. The bridge was named for adjacent land-owner Dave Geeting. Like the rest of the county's covered bridges, the Geeting Bridge sets on abutments of local blue limestone. Deputy Engineer Seth Schlotterbeck made new trim for the portals of this bridge in 1961. Like the other Sherman-built bridges in the county, the floor of the bridge is suspended from the lower chords by iron stirrups. In the 1940s, all the floor beams were doubled using new and salvaged oak beams. National Register of Historic Places • Bridge number 35-68-13

Warnke Covered Bridge • Preble County

Warnke Bridge, northeast of Lewisburg, is a 52-foot Childs truss built in 1895. This was the last covered bridge built by Everett S. Sherman. According to Seth Schlotterbeck, Sherman made his last bid to build a covered bridge in Preble County a year later, but when the county decided instead to build an iron bridge, Sherman moved to Richmond, Indiana, where he died in 1897 at the age of sixty-six. He was buried at Berkshire Cemetery in his native Delaware County. John Warnke, for whose family the bridge was named, told Schlotterbeck that the county built this covered bridge because they "mistrusted" an earlier iron bridge. Warnke was the inspector for the abutment excavations and received $2.00 for his work. National Register of Historic Places • Bridge number 35-68-14

Buckskin Covered Bridge • Ross County

Buckskin Bridge just west of South Salem is a 99-foot Smith truss bridge built in 1873. In March 1873, the county commissioners received a petition for a bridge at Caldwell's Crossing of Buckskin Creek. The county awarded a contract to the Smith Bridge Company to build a Smith truss for $14.50 per lineal foot. Smith had proposed to erect a Howe truss for $18.75 per lineal foot, so the county opted for the cheaper bridge. The Buckskin name comes from an old legend of a huge hollow sycamore tree nearby, where the Indians would hang buckskins to dry. On one such occasion, a group of white hunters attacked and stole their buckskins, giving the township and creek their name. An idea to move the bridge from its busy county highway was thoroughly vetoed by area residents. Plans for a complete renovation were announced in 2004. National Register of Historic Places • Bridge number 35-71-02

Otway Bridge • Scioto County

Otway Bridge, built in 1874, northwest of Portsmouth is a 129-foot Smith truss bridge with added arches. The Otway Covered Bridge is among the most interesting timber truss bridges in Ohio. It was built by the Smith Bridge Company of Toledo, Ohio, for $14.30 per lineal foot and was supervised by Nicholas Schakert, one of the county commissioners. As the firm sometimes arranged, the timbers came from the nearby Thompson and Freeman saw mill instead of being shipped from Toledo. W.H. Wheeler built the abutments for $2.89 per perch and used massive stones, unusually large for bridge foundations, from a nearby quarry. Laborers, hired to work on the bridge, were paid $1.10 per day. One of the young workers created much excitement when he walked across the upper chords on stilts. The arches and iron tension rods were added in an 1896 renovation, although the reason for such extensive renovations in a twenty-two-year-old bridge was unclear. The arches rest on the lower chords. An eighty-one-foot steel truss, built in 1923, is the east end approach to the covered bridge. Originally this was a low, or pony, Smith truss and was likely sided. The old covered bridge was vital to the Otway community. The first bridge on the site, the road it carried became part of the state highway system in the 1930s and has since been designated an Ohio Scenic Highway. When the state revealed its plans for a replacement bridge on a new alignment in the 1960s, a small preservation group was established which has struggled against great odds to keep their old bridge in repair. National Register of Historic Places • Bridge number 35-73-15

35-01-02

Harshaville Covered Bridge • Adams County

Description: 110-foot multiple kingpost truss plus arch, built in 1855. *Location*: southeast of Seaman, at Harshaville, in Oliver Township, over Cherry Fork. *Directions*: from State Route 32, take State Route 247 south 1.5 miles to Grace's Run Road (also County Road 1). Turn left on Grace's Run Road, heading east 1.5 miles to the covered bridge. Page 113

35-01-10

Kirker Covered Bridge • Adams County

Description: 64-foot multiple kingpost truss, built in 1890. *Location*: west of West Union, in Liberty Township, over the East Fork of Eagle Creek. *Directions*: take State Route 247 to West Union. In West Union, take State Route 41 southwest 4 miles to State Route 136. Turn right on State Route 136, heading north 1.5 miles to the covered bridge. Page 114

35-08-04

Brown Covered Bridge • Brown County

Description: 144-foot Smith truss, built in 1878, renovated 2004. *Location*: northeast of New Hope, on the border of Pike and Scott Townships over White Oak Creek. *Directions*: from US Route 68 and the main intersection in the town of New Hope, take New Hope-White Oak Station Road (also County Road 5) northeast 2.5 miles to the bridge, located on the west side of the road. Page 115–116

35-08-34

George Miller Road Covered Bridge • Brown County

Description: 160-foot Smith truss, built in 1878. *Location*: southeast of Russellville, in Byrd Township, over the West Fork of Eagle Creek. *Directions*: from the intersection of State Route 125 and US Route 62 (just south of Russellville), take US Route 62 south 1.2 miles to George Miller Road (also County Road 15). Turn left on George Miller Road, heading east 2.4 miles to the covered bridge. Page 120

35-08-08

McCafferty Road Covered Bridge • Brown County

Description: 170-foot Howe truss, built in 1870. *Location*: southwest of Fayetteville, in Perry Township, over the East Fork of the Little Miami River. *Directions*: traveling east on US Route 50, drive .5 miles past the Clermont/Brown County line to McCafferty Road (also County Road 105). Turn right, or south, on McCafferty Road, heading .2 miles to the covered bridge. You can also see the bridge from US Route 50. Page 118

35-08-05

New Hope Covered Bridge • Brown County

Description: 170-foot Howe truss plus arch, built in 1878, renovated 2004. *Location*: southwest of New Hope, in Scott Township, over White Oak Creek. *Directions*: traveling south on US Route 68, drive approximately 1 mile past the town of New Hope to Bethel-New Hope Road (also County Road 5). Head west on Bethel-New Hope Road, approximately .1 mile to the covered bridge, located on the right, or north, side of the road. Page 117

35-08-23

North Pole Road Covered Bridge • Brown County

Description: 166-foot Smith truss, built in 1875. *Location*: northeast of Ripley, in Huntington and Union Townships, over Eagle Creek. *Directions*: from US Route 52, take US Route 62/68 northeast 1.4 miles to North Pole Road (also County Road 13). Turn right on North Pole Road, heading east 3 miles to the covered bridge. Page 119

35-09-03

Black or Pughs Mill Covered Bridge • Butler County

Description: 223-foot, 2-span Long, built in 1868, renovated 1998/99. *Location*: on the north edge of Oxford, in Oxford Township, over Four Mile Creek. *Directions*: from the town of Oxford and the intersection of US Route 27 and State Route 732, take State Route 732 north .8 miles to Corso Road. Turn left on Corso Road, heading north .3 miles to the covered bridge. Page 124–125

35-09-02

Fairfield Pike or Governor Bebb Park Covered Bridge • Butler County

Description: 125-foot Wernwag truss, built in 1867–1868, moved 1886 and 1966. *Location*: south of Scipio, in Bebb Park, over Dry Fork Creek. *Directions*: from the city of Hamilton, take State Route 129 (also Hamilton-Scipio Road) west for approximately 12 miles to California Road. Turn left on California Road, heading south to State Route 126 (also Cincinnati-Brookville Road). Turn right on State Route 126, heading northwest for .25 miles. Look for the Bebb Park entrance on the left, and turn left onto Bebb Park Lane to the covered bridge. Page 121–123

35-13-02

Stonelick or Perintown Covered Bridge • Clermont County

Description: 140-foot Howe truss, built in 1878. *Location*: east of Perintown, in Stonelick Township, over Stonelick Creek. *Directions*: from the town of Stonelick, take US Route 50 approximately 1 mile west to Stonelick Road (or County Road 116). Turn right on Stonelick Road, heading north 1.3 miles to the covered bridge. Page 126

35-14-09

Martinsville Covered Bridge • Clinton County

Description: 80-foot multiple kingpost truss, built in 1871. *Location*: northwest of Martinsville, in Clark Township, over Todds Fork of the Little Miami River. *Directions*: in the town of Martinsville, from the junction of State Route 134 and State Route 28, take State Route 28 west 1.8 miles to Martinsville Road (also County Road 14). Turn right on Martinsville Road, heading north .6 miles to the covered bridge. Page 127

35-29-18

Ballard Road Covered Bridge • Greene County

Description: 80-foot Howe truss, built in 1883. *Location*: west of Jamestown, in Jasper Township, over Massie Creek. *Directions*: from Jamestown, take US Route 35 west for 4.8 miles to Ballard Road (also Township Road 6). Turn left on Ballard Road, heading south .5 miles to the covered bridge. Page 132–133

35-29-01

Cemetery Road or Glen Helen Covered Bridge • Greene County

Description: 72-foot Howe truss, built in 1886, moved and shortened in 1975. *Location*: southeast of Yellow Springs, in Miami Township, over Yellow Springs Creek. *Directions*: in Yellow Springs, at the junction of State Route 343 and US Route 68, take US Route 68 south .3 miles to Corry Street. Head south on Corry Street for .9 miles to Grinnel Road (also County Road 27). Head east on Grinnel Road for 3 miles. The bridge is in the Glen Helen Nature Preserve. Page 128

35-29-16

Charlton Mill Road Covered Bridge • Greene County

Description: 128-foot Howe truss, built in 1883. *Location*: southwest of Cedarville, in Xenia Township, over Massie Creek. *Directions*: from the town of Cedarville, take US Route 42 southwest approximately 2.2 miles to Charlton Mill Road (also Township Road 29). Turn right on Charlton Mill Road, heading west .9 miles to the covered bridge. Page 131

35-29-15

Stevenson Road Covered Bridge • Greene County

Description: 95-foot Smith truss, built in 1877. *Location*: northeast of Xenia, in Xenia Township, over Massie Creek. *Directions*: from the city of Xenia, take US Route 68 north approximately 3 miles to Brush Row Road. Turn right on Brush Row Road, heading east 1.8 miles to Stevenson Road (also County Road 76). Turn left on Stevenson Road, heading north .5 miles to the covered bridge. Page 130

35-29-03

West Engle Mill Road Covered Bridge • Greene County

Description: 148-foot Smith truss, built circa 1877. *Location*: southeast of Spring Valley, in Caesar Creek Township, over Anderson Fork of Caesar Creek. *Directions*: from the city of Xenia, take US Route 68 south approximately 8 miles to Spring Valley-Paintersville Road (also County Road 75). Turn right on Spring Valley-Paintersville Road, heading west 3.5 miles to Engle Mill Road. Turn left on Engle Mill Road, heading south .5 miles to the covered bridge (bypassed). Page 129

35-31-01

Jediah Hill Covered Bridge • Hamilton County

Description: 54-foot queenpost truss, built in 1850, renovated in 1981. *Location*: north of Mount Healthy, in Springfield Township, over West Fork of Mill Creek on Covered Ridge Road *Directions*: take the I-275 outerbelt to US 127. Travel south on US 127 approximately 2.5 miles to Miles Road. Turn left on Miles Road, travel .2 miles and turn right to cross the bridge. Page 134

35-36-06

Lynchburg Covered Bridge • Highland County

Description: 120-foot Long truss, built in 1870. *Location*: the west edge of Lynchburg, in Clark Township, over the East Fork of the Little Miami River on Covered Bridge Lane *Directions*: from Hillsboro, take State Route 50 west approximately 9 miles to State Route 134. Turn right and travel north on State Route 134 to the town of Lynchburg. Turn left on High Street and the bridge is just ahead (bypassed). Page 135

35-55-01

Eldean Covered Bridge • Miami County

Description: 224-foot, 2-span Long truss, built in 1860, renovated in 2005. *Location*: north of Troy, in Concord Township, over the Great Miami River on old Eldean Road (County Road 33) *Directions*: from I-75, take exit 78, County Road 25A; turn right on County Road 25A and travel south; at the second traffic light, turn left on Eldean Road and travel east .1 mile to the bridge (bypassed). Page 136–137

35-55-103

Fletcher Covered Bridge • Miami County

Description: 45-foot Smith truss, built in 1998. *Location*: at Fletcher, in Brown Township, over Gustin Ditch. *Directions*: from Piqua, take US Route 36 east approximately 6 miles into the town of Fletcher (where it becomes Main Street). Turn left (north) on North Street to Downing Street and then turn right on Downing Street to the covered bridge. Page 138

35-57-03

Carillon Park or Feedwire Road Covered Bridge • Montgomery County

Description: 56-foot Warren truss plus arch, built in 1870, moved and renovated in 1948. *Location*: south end of Dayton, in Carillon Park, over the Miami and Erie Canal. *Directions*: get off Interstate I-75 in Dayton on the Miami Boulevard Exit. Head east along the river to Stewart. Go across the river to Patterson Boulevard, and take a right into Carillon Park. The park is at 2001 South Patterson Boulevard. Page 140

35-57-01

Germantown Covered Bridge • Montgomery County

Description: 100-foot suspension truss, built in 1865. *Location*: in Germantown, over the Little Twin Creek. *Directions*: in Germantown, at the junction of State Route 4 and State Route 725, take State Route 725 west .5 miles to Plum Street. Head north on Plum Street for .1 mile to Center Street. Head east on Center Street to the covered bridge. Page 138–139

35-57-36

Jasper Road or Mud Lick Covered Bridge • Montgomery County

Description: 71-foot Warren truss plus arch, built in 1869, moved in 1964. *Location*: southwest edge of Germantown, in German Township. *Directions*: from Germantown, take State Route 725 west 2.5 miles to Signal Road. Turn left on Signal Road, heading south .7 miles to Oxford Road. Turn right on Oxford Road. The bridge is located on private property at 11345 Oxford Road but is easily seen from the road. Page 141

35-65-15

Valentine or Old Bill Green Covered Bridge • Pickaway County

Description: 36-foot multiple kingpost truss, built in 1872, moved in 1908, 1971, and 1978. *Location*: southeast of Orient. *Directions to former site*: from US Route 62/ State Route 3, head east on State Route 762 to Thrailkill Road (also Township Road 152). Turn right on Thrailkill Road, heading west. The covered bridge was located on Green Farm, private property. Page 142

35-68-06

Brubaker Covered Bridge • Preble County

Description: 85-foot Childs truss, built in 1887, renovated in 2005. *Location*: northwest of Gratis, in Gratis Township, over Sams Run. *Directions*: from the town of Gratis and the intersection of State Route 503 and State Route 122, take State Route 122 northwest .4 miles to Brubaker Road (also Township Road 328). Turn left on Brubaker Road, heading west for .6 miles to the covered bridge. Page 147

35-68-12

Christman Covered Bridge • Preble County

Description: 92-foot Childs truss, built in 1895. *Location*: northwest of Eaton, in Washington Township, over Seven Mile Creek. *Directions*: at the intersection of US Route 35 and State Route 127, take State Route 127 north 1.5 miles to Washington-Jackson Road (also County Road 50). Turn left on Washington-Jackson Road, heading west .7 miles to Eaton-Gettysburg Road (also County Road 11). Head northwest on Eaton-Gettysburg Road for .4 miles to Eaton-New Hope Road (also Township Road 142). Turn left on Eaton-New Hope Road, heading west to the covered bridge. Page 148

35-68-04

Dixon Branch Covered Bridge • Preble County

Description: 60-foot Childs truss, built in 1887, moved in 1964. *Location*: the east edge of Lewisburg, in Civitan Park. *Directions*: from the intersection of US Route 127 and US Route 40, take US Route 40 east to State Route 503. Turn right on State Route 503, heading south .6 miles to East Dayton Street (also County Road 15). Turn left on East Dayton Street, approximately .3 miles to Civitan Park. Page 144

35-68-13

Geeting Covered Bridge • Preble County

Description: 100-foot Childs truss, built in 1894. *Location*: west of Lewisburg, in Monroe Township, over Price Creek. *Directions*: from the city of Lewisburg and the junction of State Route 503 and US Route 40, take US Route 40 west 3 miles to Yohe Road. Turn left on Yohe Road, driving south .5 miles to Price Road. Turn right on Price Road, heading west .2 miles to the covered bridge. Page 149

35-68-03

Harshman Covered Bridge • Preble County

Description: 104-foot Childs truss, built in 1894. *Location*: north of Fairhaven, in Dixon Township, over Four Mile Creek. *Directions*: from the city of Eaton, take US Route 127 south to the intersection of US Route 35 and State Route 122. Turn right on State Route 122, heading west 7.2 miles to Concord-Fairhaven Road (also Township Road 218). Turn left on Concord-Fairhaven Road, driving south 3.2 miles to the covered bridge. Page 143

35-68-05

Roberts Covered Bridge • Preble County

Description: 79-foot, double roadway Burr truss, built in 1829, moved and repaired in 1991. *Location*: in Eaton, over Seven Mile Creek. *Directions*: from the city of Eaton, take US Route 127 (also South Barron Street) south to St. Clair Street. Turn right on St. Clair Street, heading west .1 mile to South Beech Street. Turn right on South Beech Street, the covered bridge is located on the left-hand side of the road in Crystal Lake Park. Page 145–146

35-68-14

Warnke Covered Bridge • Preble County

Description: 52-foot Childs truss, built in 1895. *Location*: northeast of Lewisburg, in Harrison Township, over Swamp Creek. *Directions*: from the city of Lewisburg and the junction of State Route 503 and US Route 40, take US Route 40 east .4 miles to Verona Road (also County Road 36). Turn left on Verona Road, heading northeast 1.5 miles to Swamp Creek Road (also Township Road 403). Turn right on Swamp Creek Road, heading east .2 miles to the covered bridge. Page 150

35-71-02

Buckskin or South Salem Covered Bridge • Ross County

Description: 99-foot Smith truss, built in 1873. *Location*: the west edge of South Salem, in Buckskin Township, over Buckskin Creek. *Directions*: east of the town of Greenfield, at the intersection of State Route 28 and State Route 41, take State Route 41 south 2.2 miles to Lower Twin Road (also County Road 54). Turn left on Lower Twin Road, heading east 2.2 miles to the covered bridge. Page 151

35-73-15

Otway Covered Bridge • Scioto County

Description: 129-foot Smith truss plus arch, built in 1874. *Location*: the west edge of Otway, in Brush Creek Township, over Scioto Brush Creek. *Directions*: from US Route 23, take State Route 348 west to the town of Otway. In Otway, at the intersection of State Route 73 and State Route 348, continue southwest on State Route 348 for another .2 miles to the covered bridge, located on the north side of the road. Page 152–153

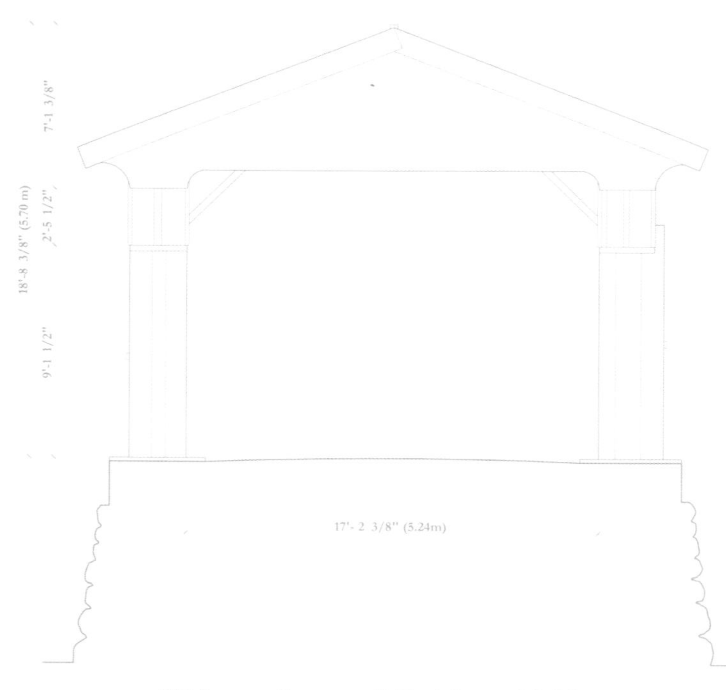

Eldean Covered Bridge, 1860

Memorial Covered Bridge • Auglaize County

Memorial, or St. Marys, Covered Bridge in St. Mary's is a 108.5-foot Howe truss built in 1992. Its construction was a community effort. Deputy County Engineer Dan Bennett designed the bridge and donated the plans to a Memorial Bridge Committee in January 1992. Ground was broken for the concrete abutments on June 2nd. The trusses were built in the adjoining parking lot. On August 10th, cranes lifted the trusses into place on the abutments. Then the finishing work of roof, siding, and flooring began. The Memorial Bridge was officially dedicated on October 11, 1992. Perhaps the most important part of the story of the building is that volunteers gave five thousand hours to this project. The community raised eighty-five thousand dollars in cash donations and sixty thousand dollars in donated materials. People in North Carolina donated oak shingles from several trees felled in Hurricane Hugo. Farmers in Auglaize County had developed a friendship with their counterparts in North Carolina, donating hay to each other in times of drought. When the North Carolina farmers heard about the bridge project, they immediately thought of making shingles from the felled oak trees. While the Memorial Bridge is an authentic, full-sized Howe truss, it is used for pedestrian and bikes only. It has become a tradition at the nearby high school for young couples to stroll through the bridge in their fancy gowns and tuxes on prom night. A crowd gathers to watch and cameras flash as families record this big event in the lives of their children. • Bridge number 35-06-54

McColly Covered Bridge • Logan County

McColly Bridge, southeast of Bloom Center, is a 142-foot Howe truss bridge built in 1876. The Anderson Green Company of Sidney, Ohio, specialists in sturdy Howe trusses, built many covered bridges in this part of the state. They were paid $13.35 per lineal foot for the McColly Bridge. T. B. Stillwell, well-known masonry contractor, laid up the original stone foundations. Sometime in the late 1970s or early 1980s, the timber floor beams were replaced by steel beams. In the mid-1990s, it was closed because of structural concerns. A federal grant allowed the county to completely renovate the bridge in 2000. The Righter Construction Company of Columbus built the new foundations from concrete poured in lined forms that imitate stone. The superstructure work was done by Amos Schwartz of Geneva, Indiana, an expert in timber truss renovation, who recreated the original timber floor. The siding had been painted white for many years even though the old siding showed traces of red paint and older people in the area remembered when the bridge was painted red. So the county decided on red paint but painted the interior, including the floor, white. A new standing seam metal roof was installed over the old wooden shingles. National Register of Historic Places • Bridge number 35-46-01

Bickham Covered Bridge • Logan County

Bickham Bridge east of Russells Point is a 94-foot Howe truss bridge built in 1877, by the Smith Bridge Company of Toledo, Ohio, for $10.85 per lineal foot. Like the McColly Bridge, the Bickham Bridge had long been painted white. Following a thorough renovation in 2002, an examination of the old siding showed that it was originally red so the color was restored. Like the McColly Bridge, its interior was painted white and the stone work capped with concrete formed like old stone. The metal roof was retained after first being removed to repair the old sheathing. • Bridge number 35-46-03

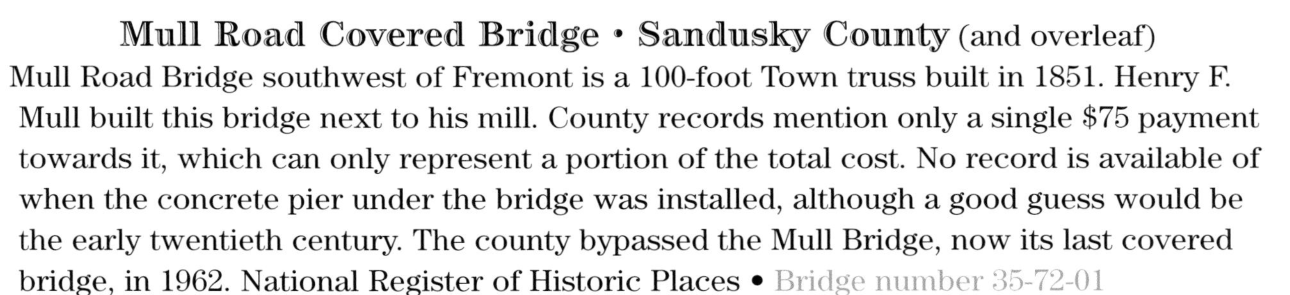

Mull Road Covered Bridge • Sandusky County (and overleaf)

Mull Road Bridge southwest of Fremont is a 100-foot Town truss built in 1851. Henry F. Mull built this bridge next to his mill. County records mention only a single $75 payment towards it, which can only represent a portion of the total cost. No record is available of when the concrete pier under the bridge was installed, although a good guess would be the early twentieth century. The county bypassed the Mull Bridge, now its last covered bridge, in 1962. National Register of Historic Places • Bridge number 35-72-01

Upper Darby or Pottersburg Covered Bridge • Union County (also overleaf)

Upper Darby Bridge northeast of North Lewisburg is a 94-foot Partridge truss bridge built in 1868. Also known as the Beltz Mill Bridge, this is one of at least sixteen covered Partridge truss bridges built for Union County by Reuben L. Partridge. (For more on Partridge and his bridge-building career, see Franklin County's Bergstresser Bridge.) The roofed windows on this bridge were added during a 1930s renovation. The steel cables and rods were also not part of the Partridge design and were installed by the county at an unknown date. County records mention a bridge here as early as 1854. In 2006, County Engineer Steve Stolte announced that the county would build two new covered bridges. One will replace this bridge which has been moved about a mile away to serve a multipurpose trail and where it will continue to be in use by the public after renovation. The other new bridge will be over Big Darby Creek on Buck Run Road replacing an aging steel truss structure. The two new covered bridges will utilize Pratt trusses designed by John Smolen. • Bridge number 35-80-01

10'-0"

Spain Creek Covered Bridge • Union County

Spain Creek Bridge, northeast of North Lewisburg, is a 79.5-foot Partridge truss bridge built in the 1870s. In the late 1980s, Union County Engineer Steve Stolte completely renovated this old bridge by installing glu-lam beams at floor level and attaching them to the base of the trusses. A new floor system, new floor beams, new roof and siding, and a deep red paint job completed this project. Like the other Union County covered bridges, roofed side windows were added. •

Bridge number 35-80-02

Culbertson or Treacle Creek Covered Bridge • Union County

Culbertson, or Treacle Creek, or Winget Road Bridge south of Milford Center is a 111-foot Partridge truss bridge built in the 1870s. The general consensus is that this bridge was moved to Winget Road many years ago, but from an unknown location, probably nearby. Winget Road dead-ends into a farmyard, and heavy farm equipment crossed the bridge for many years. In 1961 the county installed metal piers to strengthen it and in 1977 created a ford for heavier vehicles. The bridge is kept in good condition by the county. • Bridge number 35-80-03

Little Darby or Bigelow Covered Bridge • Union County

Little Darby or Bigelow Bridge (sometimes known as Axe Handle Road Bridge), south of Milford Center, is a 123-foot Partridge truss bridge built in 1873. This bridge is familiar to many travelers since it is so close to a state highway. In 1990, County Engineer Steve Stolte supervised the bridge's complete rehabilitation. It included new concrete foundations and laminated arches with steel rods from which the new floor system was hung, completely bypassing the old truss system. A nearby hog farm often ripens the air around the old bridge. Reuben Partridge was quite active as bridge builder in central Ohio, erecting structures in Delaware, Fayette, Franklin and Fairfield Counties. His largest was a three-span covered Partridge truss bridge over the Scioto River in nearby Delaware County. In 1900, at the age of seventy-seven, Partridge was fatally injured after falling from a Union County bridge being demolished. • Bridge number 35-80-04

Lockport Number 2 Covered Bridge • Williams County

When construction began on a new covered bridge to span the Tiffin River in 1998, Williams County had not had a covered bridge for over fifty years. A covered bridge once stood at this Lockport site, and folks suggested building another to replace an aging steel truss bridge. The timbers for this massive Howe truss were cut at Riverbend Timber Framing and shipped to the bridge site. Construction was handled by the S.E. Johnson Company. There are long windows on each side of the bridge and a roofed sidewalk on the south side. • Bridge number 35-86-06

Fairgrounds Covered Bridge Williams County

A covered bridge had long been a dream of fairground officials, and although designed by John Smolen with Pratt trusses, the project had a serious setback during construction in December 2003. Construction equipment was prematurely parked on the bridge before the steel diagonal rods had been installed. Without warning, the bridge fell into the river. Forced to start anew, the contractor had the bridge up and ready for traffic nine months later on the opening day of the 2004 fair in September. The structural timbers are all Glu-Lam Southern pine while the siding is red pine from northern Wisconsin. • Bridge number 35-86-26

Parker Covered Bridge • Wyandot County

The first covered bridge at the Parker farm on the Sandusky River was built by J.C. Davis in 1873. Only two years later, the county announced plans for a second bridge at the site. The fate of the first bridge is unknown. The second Parker Bridge was completed in 1876 by the firm of Bope and Weymouth for $2,732. After the great 1913 flood, the county salvaged timbers from the wrecked Indian Mill covered bridge and repaired the Parker Bridge. Major repairs were made in 1966 and 1980. In May 1991, a family at the north end of the bridge reported it was on fire, but by the time the fire department arrived, the south end of the bridge had collapsed. A committee almost immediately began raising funds to repair it, and through the efforts of the county engineer and many volunteers, the bridge was completely renovated. The names of contributors are found in the brick roadway approaches. National Register of Historic Places • Bridge number 35-88-03

Swartz Covered Bridge • Wyandot County

Moses Weymouth was paid $1,380 for building the Swartz Bridge, the first and only bridge on the site. Daniel Swartz did the stonework for $4.85 per perch. Major repairs in 1966 included a new shingle roof of red cedar imported from British Columbia. The county also resided the bridge after vandals had torn off most of the boards. A complete 1974 renovation included a new floor system. By the early 1990s, a new roof was necessary and the graffiti on the inside of the bridge was painted over. No sooner than the workmen left, the vandals returned, and even before the dedication ceremony could be held, the county was forced to paint over the new interior graffiti. National Register of Historic Places • Bridge number 35-88-05

35-06-54

Memorial or St. Marys Covered Bridge • Auglaize County

Description: 108.5-foot Howe truss, built in 1992. *Location*: in St. Marys, over St. Marys River. *Directions*: from Interstate I-75, take US Route 33 west 11 miles to the State Route 66 exit. Head south on State Route 66 towards St. Mary's. State Route 66 turns west onto Spring St. Go one full block to Chestnut Street. Turn left onto Chestnut Street, going south, to Memorial Park. Located on the right-hand side of the road. Page 161

35-46-03

Bickham Covered Bridge • Logan County

Description: 94-foot Howe truss, built in 1877. *Location*: east of Russells Point, in Richland Township, over the South Fork of the Great Miami River. *Directions*: from Bellefontaine, take US Route 33 north to State Route 366. Turn right on State Route 366, heading east 2.6 miles to County Road 38. Turn left on County Road 38, heading north .3 miles to the covered bridge. Page 163

35-46-01

McColly Covered Bridge • Logan County

Description: 142-foot Howe truss, built in 1876. *Location*: southwest of Lewistown, on the Washington Township and Bloomfield Township line, over the Great Miami River. *Directions*: from Bellefontaine, take State Route 47 west to State Route 235. Turn right on State Route 235, heading north 4 miles to County Road 13. Turn left on County Road 13, heading west .9 miles to the covered bridge. Page 162

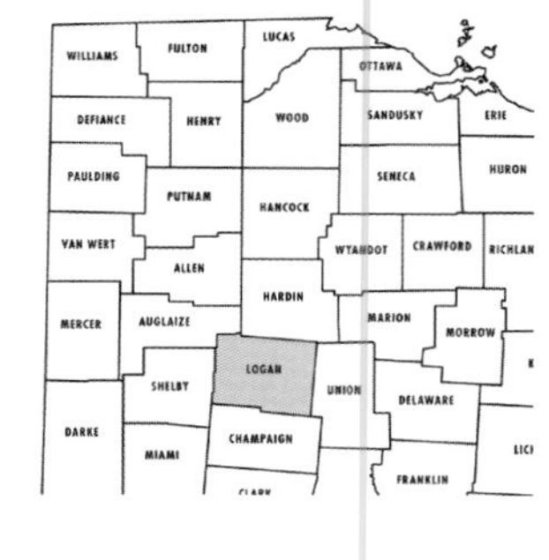

35-72-01

Mull Road Covered Bridge • Sandusky County

Description: 100-foot Town lattice truss, built in 1851. *Location*: southwest of Fremont, over the East Branch of Wolf Creek. *Directions*: from the junction of State Route 12 and State Route 53, head south on State Route 53 2.2 miles to Township Road 9 (also Mull Road). Turn right on Township Road 9 and travel for a mile to the covered bridge. Page 164–166

35-80-04

Bigelow or Little Darby or Axe Handle Road Covered Bridge • Union County

Description: 123-foot Partridge truss, built in 1873, renovated in 1990. *Location*: west of Chuckery, in Union Township, over Little Darby Creek. *Directions*: from Marysville, take US Route 36/State Route 4 south. Stay on State Route 4 south when the highway splits. Follow State Route 4 to the town of Irwin and State Route 161. Turn left on State Route 161, heading east 4 miles to Axe Handle Road (also County Road 87). Turn right on Axe Handle Road, heading north .1 mile to the covered bridge. Page 172

35-80-03

Winget Road, or Treacle Creek, or Culbertson Covered Bridge • Union County

Description: 111-foot Partridge truss, built in 1868. *Location:* northeast of Irwin, in Union Township, over Treacle Creek. *Directions:* from Marysville, take US Route 36 south past Milford Center. Approximately 4 miles after Milford Center, turn left on Homer Road (also County Road 86). Follow Homer Road for 1.2 miles to Winget Road (also Township Road 82). Turn left on Winget Road, heading east .3 miles to the covered bridge. Page 171

35-80-02

Spain Creek Covered Bridge • Union County

Description: 79.5-foot Partridge truss, circa 1870, renovated in 1988/89. *Location:* northeast of North Lewisburg, in Allen Township, over Spain Creek. *Directions:* from Marysville, take State Route 245 west 7 miles to Inskeep-Cratty Road (also County Road 163). Turn right on Inskeep-Cratty Road, heading north .1 mile to the covered bridge. Page 170

35-80-01

Upper Darby or Pottersburg Covered Bridge • Union County

Description: 94-foot Partridge truss, built in 1868. *Location:* northeast of North Lewisburg, in Allen Township, formerly over Big Darby Creek. *Directions:* from the Spain Creek Covered Bridge, continue northwest on Inskeep-Cratty Road about 1 mile where you will see the bridge. The bridge site is 2 miles northwest on Insekeep-Cratty Road to North Lewisburg Road (also County Road 164). Turn right on North Lewisburg Road, follow .1 mile to the bridge location. Page 167–169

35-86-26

Fairgrounds Covered Bridge • Williams County

Description: 120-foot Pratt truss built in 2004. *Location:* in Montpelier, over the St. Joseph River. *Directions:* from the town of Bryan, take State Route 15 north to State Route 107. Turn left on State Route 107, heading west to Montpelier. Take State Route 107 to the fairgrounds which is located on the north side of the road. The covered bridge is located near the rear of the fairgrounds. Page 174

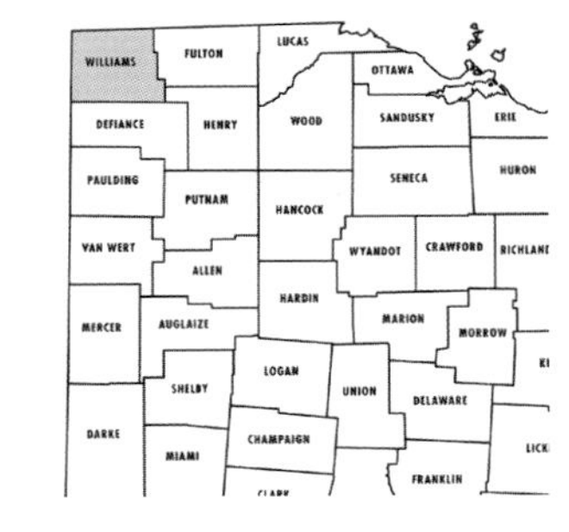

35-86-06

Lockport Covered Bridge Number 2 • Williams County

Description: 166-foot, 3-span Howe truss, built in 1999. *Location:* the south edge of Lockport, in Brady Township, over the Tiffin River. *Directions:* from the junction of State Route 2 and State Route 191 in Stryker, take State Route 2 northeast about 1.2 miles to County Road 21N. Turn left on County Road 21N, cross the Tiffin River, and at the junction of County Road G40 stay to the right on County Road 21N and travel approximately 1.25 miles to the south edge of Lockport. The covered bridge is across the street from the Lockport Mennonite Church. Page 173

35-88-03

Parker Covered Bridge • Wyandot County

Description: 172-foot Howe truss, built in 1873, renovated in 1992. *Location:* northeast of Upper Sandusky, in Crane Township, over the Sandusky River. *Directions:* from the city of Upper Sandusky, take US Route 23 to State Route 67. Head north on State Route 67 for 3.5 miles to Township Road 39. Turn left on Township Road 39, heading west 1.2 miles to Township Road 40. Turn left on Township Road 40, approximately .2 miles to the covered bridge. Page 175

35-88-03

Swartz Covered Bridge • Wyandot County

Description: 108.5-foot Howe truss, built in 1878, renovated in 1992/93. *Location:* northeast of Little Sandusky, in Antrim Township, over the Sandusky River. *Directions:* from the city of Upper Sandusky, take US Route 23 south to State Route 294. Turn left on State Route 294, heading east 2.2 miles to County Road 130. Turn left on County Road 130, heading north 2 miles to the covered bridge. Page 176–177

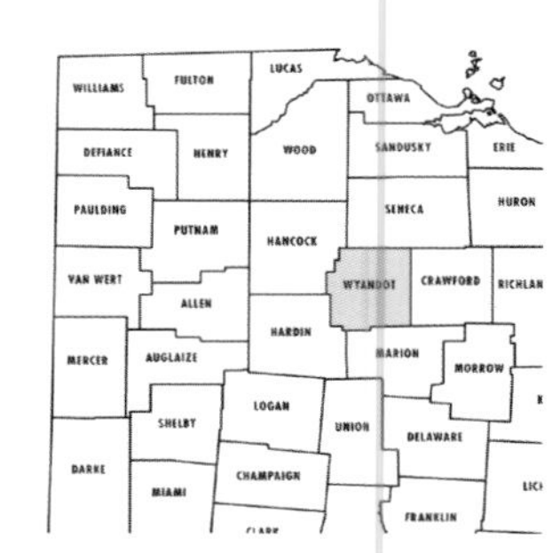

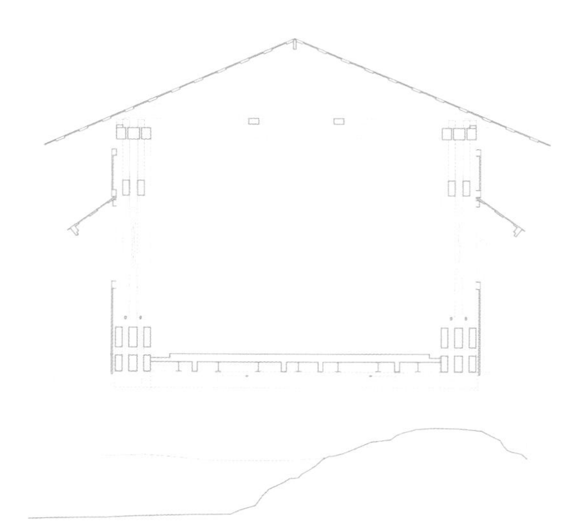

Pottersburg or Upper Darby Covered Bridge • 1872

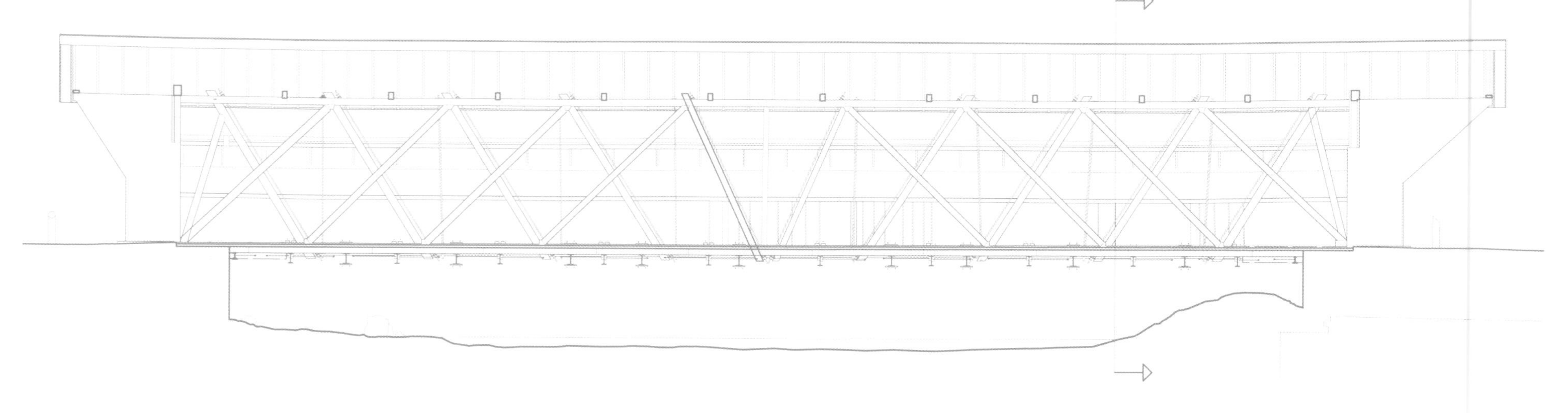

Chambers Road Covered Bridge • Delaware County

Chambers Road Bridge lies northeast of Olive Green and is an 86-foot Childs truss bridge built in 1883. The Childs truss was patented in 1846 by Horace Childs, a bridge builder and agent for the Long truss, in Henniker, New Hampshire. This truss design uses iron tension rods in place of the wood counterbraces of a Long truss. As far as is known, no Childs trusses were built in New England and it appears that the Chambers Road Covered Bridge is the first of this truss style ever built. Everett S. Sherman, of Delaware County, Ohio, son of bridge builder David T. Sherman, was the first to use the Childs truss design. The younger Sherman's name began to appear in Delaware County records by the late 1860s, proposing to build bridges on the Howe, Burr, or Sherman plan. He also worked in other central Ohio counties such as Madison and Marion, and in 1887, he moved to Preble County in western Ohio where he built fifteen Childs truss covered bridges. The Chambers Road Bridge is Delaware County's last covered bridge. Renovated in 1982–1983, the abutments were rebuilt with concrete and a concrete pier was added. Steel I-beams that now support the old structure likely saved it from collapse in April 2004 when a speeding motorist lost control and crashed into the south truss. National Register of Historic Places • Bridge number 35-21-04

Hizey Covered Bridge • Fairfield County

Hizey Bridge is on a private lane in Pickerington. The bridge is an 83-foot variation of the multiple kingpost truss. Built in 1891 by the well-known Fairfield County bridge builder James W. Buchanan, the Hizey Bridge spanned Poplar Creek on Poplar Creek Road. The name of the builder and date were stenciled on the north portal of the bridge until a county paint job in the 1960s obliterated it. The county rehired Buchanan in 1914 to repair this bridge, and it is likely that the arches were added to the trusses at this time. This was doubtless due to damage from the great 1913 flood. Because of its condition, the county closed the Hizey Bridge in 1979. In 1986 it was given to Jim Visintine, who, working by himself, disassembled and moved it to his property on Tollgate Road for rebuilding over Sycamore Creek on the lane leading to his home. No arches were used in the rebuilding of the bridge. With the arches removed, the center panel of the bridge was actually a queenpost truss. Similar to a multiple kingpost, this design features a secondary chord between the central posts and was found in other bridges built by Mr. Buchanan. Jim Visintine's recent death makes the Hizey Bridge a fitting memorial to a man who loved covered bridges enough to dismantle, move, and rebuild one by himself. • Bridge number 35-23-07

John Bright Covered Bridge • Fairfield County (also previous page)

John Bright Bridge, on the Ohio University Campus north of Lancaster, is a 75-foot suspension truss bridge with arches. Built in 1881, this bridge is one of the most unique covered bridges in the country. It is a combination wood and metal suspension truss built by August Borneman for $933. The Fairfield County Commissioners' Journals record the contract for it as a "combination bridge, roofed and sided." At some later date, perhaps after the 1913 flood, wooden arches were added. It was in an area of Liberty Township known as the Bright Settlement, named for early settlers along Poplar Creek. August Borneman emigrated from Prussia about 1864 and began the Ohio Iron and Bridge Company in partnership with William Black. These men appear in the records of other Ohio counties listed simply as Black and Borneman. William Black patented an all-metal inverted arch suspension truss bridge in 1875 which may have inspired the John Bright Bridge design. Black and Borneman parted ways in the late 1870s, and Black moved his business to Urbana, Ohio. In 1878 Borneman founded the Hocking Valley Bridge Works in Lancaster. From 1878 to 1889, Gus Borneman won most of the Fairfield county bridge-building contracts and many in other Ohio counties. His career was doing well when, in 1889, he died suddenly in the prime of his life. In 1988 the John Bright Bridge was moved to the campus at Lancaster. National Register of Historic Places • Bridge number 35-23-10

George Hutchins Covered Bridge • Fairfield County (also overleaf)
George Hutchins Bridge, south of Lancaster, is a 62.5-foot multiple kingpost bridge, built in 1904. This bridge is a typical Fairfield County multiple kingpost truss built by J.W. Buchanan to replace an earlier bridge on Clear Creek southeast of Amanda. In the late 1980s, the old bridge was dismantled and put into storage where it remained for more than ten years. The Hutchins Bridge was finally rebuilt in a scenic location in Alley Park. • Bridge number 35-23-13

Hanaway Covered Bridge • Fairfield County

Hanaway, or Clearport Covered Bridge, southeast of Amanda, is an 86-foot multiple kingpost truss bridge built in 1901. This bridge is another product of J.W. Buchanan, builder of numerous bridges in Fairfield County in the early twentieth century. Fairfield County records referred to these as "House Bridges" in the 1890s. The last covered bridge was built in the county in 1919. All told, Fairfield County had over 270 wood truss bridges on their highways, canals and railroads and still had forty-three standing in 1953 when the first list of Ohio covered bridges was published. Early 1930s photos show this bridge with high-boarded siding on both sides. Since the bridge sat on a curve in the road, sometime later roofed windows were cut into both sides to improve visibility for traffic. Bypassed about 1990, the Hanaway Bridge deteriorated rapidly until the bridge was nearly lost. Fairfield County obtained a federal grant for restoration and hired Shaw and Holter of Lancaster to do the work. The bridge was raised and placed on a temporary support platform, or falsework. Stone from old bridge abutments was used for repairs, and many rotten truss timbers were replaced. The Hanaway Bridge is now one of five bridges administered by the Fairfield County Historic Parks District. •
Bridge number 35-23-15

Johnston Covered Bridge
Fairfield County

Johnston Bridge lies 5.5 miles southeast of Amanda, and is a 98-foot Howe truss bridge built in 1887. The Johnston Bridge is one of the few remaining covered bridges built by August Borneman and the Hocking Valley Bridge Works. He was paid $14.50 per lineal foot. Located on a sharp curve, increased traffic loads

made it necessary to bypass this bridge and build a new crossing in 1990. Early 1930s pictures of the bridge show roofed windows, but it was likely boarded up completely at one time. Federal funds helped to renovate this bridge, now part of the Fairfield County Historic Parks District. National Register of Historic Places

• Bridge number 35-23-16

Zeller-Smith Covered Bridge • Fairfield County

Zeller-Smith, or Sycamore Park Covered Bridge at Pickerington is a 79-foot multiple kingpost truss bridge built in 1905–1906. This J. W. Buchanan-built covered bridge originally spanned Sycamore Creek on Busey Road two miles south of Pickerington. This simple multiple kingpost truss cost only eight dollars per lineal foot. The county closed the old bridge in 1984 and two years later moved it intact to Sycamore Park. Seven of the fifteen covered bridges remaining in Fairfield County were built by J. W. Buchanan who built at least twenty-five covered bridges for the county, twelve after 1900. • Bridge number 35-23-19

Shade Covered Bridge • Fairfield County

Shade Bridge lies south of Sugar Grove and is a 127.5-foot multiple kingpost truss bridge dating to 1871. It was built by John Shrake of Licking County, one of the few "outside" builders to work in Fairfield County in the nineteenth century, for $13.75 per lineal food. The arches on the trusses are thought to be a later addition. Like other Fairfield County covered bridges, the Shade Bridge deteriorated steadily until 1978 when an overloaded truck forced its closure. As William Pierson and his family were dismantling the old bridge, it suddenly collapsed. Most of the pieces were salvaged and taken to their farm for rebuilding. The Piersons used the old bridge as a museum. • Bridge number 35-23-20

McCleery Covered Bridge • Fairfield County

McCleery Bridge was originally a 97-foot multiple kingpost truss built in 1864 to span Walnut Creek. McCleery Bridge was the first major bridge contract awarded to Jacob R. "Blue Jeans" Brandt. The bridge cost $12.50 per lineal foot, giving Brandt a total of $1362. He was meticulous, demanding the best workmanship from the carpenters in his crew. His nickname "Blue Jeans" came from his blue denim clothing and his habit of keeping a clean suit of clothes in case a change was necessary. Brandt's wife bought denim by the bolt to make the suits. James W. Buchanan learned bridge building from Jacob Brandt. In addition to building bridges, Brandt built houses, barns, and churches in other Ohio counties. The McCleery Bridge's condition forced the county to close it in the early 1980s.

In 1983, James Walter moved a 54-foot section of the bridge to his property off Pleasantville Road where it set on concrete block foundations for twenty years. In 2003 plans were made to incorporate it in a bike path near the John Bright Bridge. An evaluation of the old covered bridge for insurance purposes found that its timbers are American chestnut, a rarity in Ohio where most covered bridges were built of white oak or yellow poplar. • Bridge number 35-23-25

Shryer Covered Bridge • Fairfield County

Shryer Bridge is a 69-foot multiple kingpost bridge built in 1891. From the commissioners' journals we know only that J.W. Buchanan received a partial payment of $60 in January 1891 for this bridge. It replaced the St. Michaels Church Bridge that was built in 1880 on this site by August Borneman. While the small church still stands near the bridge site, the fate of the Borneman bridge is unknown. In 1987 as the county readied to build a new bridge for PawPaw Creek, the Bill Shryer family moved the 1891 bridge to their front yard west of Baltimore, easily visible to the passing motorists. Annual Easter sunrise services are held at the bridge. • Bridge number 35-23-27

Charles Holliday Covered Bridge • Fairfield County

Charles Holliday Bridge lies in Millersport and is a 98-foot multiple kingpost truss bridge built in 1898. This bridge, which cost only $355, was built by J. W. Buchanan from the remains of an 1891 bridge he had built on this site. At least four covered bridges were built at this crossing to serve Lake Road. August Borneman erected two and Buchanan built the others. The first three stood only briefly before needing replacement. In 1983 the county closed the Holliday Bridge (also known as the Andrews or Trovinger Bridge) and gave it to the Millersport Lions Club for the Corn Festival grounds. • Bridge number 35-23-30

R. F. Baker Covered Bridge • Fairfield County

Baker Bridge is a 69-foot multiple kingpost truss built in 1871. James Arnold built this bridge, also known as the Winegardner Bridge, for a family that lived nearby, for $9.45 per lineal foot. It spanned Little Rush Creek northeast of Rushville on Thornville Road. Arnold and his son also laid up the abutments for $5.49 per perch (a perch is twenty-five cubic yards of stone). A unique feature of the Baker Bridge were exterior wooden braces giving the appearance of flying buttresses. With the construction of Rush Creek Reservoir in 1981, it was moved to Fairfield-Union High School to span a pond behind the athletic field. National Register of Historic Places • Bridge number 35-23-33

Jon Raab Covered Bridge • Fairfield County

Raab Bridge is a 44-foot Queenpost truss bridge built in 1891. Although the county commissioners' journals referred to this bridge as a Buckingham truss, it is actually a simple queenpost truss. By Buckingham truss, the county meant a multiple kingpost, named after Catharinus Buckingham of Zanesville Y Bridge fame. The Raab Bridge originally spanned Raccoon Run on Ireland Road southwest of Rushville. Despite repairs made in the 1960s, it had to be replaced in 1974, and was moved across the fields to the Raab farm for use as a shed. The Raabs are descendants from Jonathan W. Raab, a farmer and mason who worked on a number of Fairfield County bridges. • Bridge number 35-23-37

Hartman Number 2 Covered Bridge
Fairfield County

The Lockville Park, or Hartman, Covered Bridge is a 48-foot queenpost bridge built in 1888. This bridge was built by William Funk for $7.50 per lineal foot to span Pleasant Run on Wheeling Road northeast of Lancaster. In 1888 the bridge was known as the Hartman Bridge. Incapable of carrying the increasingly heavy traffic of the area, the county moved the bridge and rebuilt it over the canal in Lockville Park in 1967. Lockville is a small community that grew up around the Ohio and Erie Canal as evidenced by the massive sandstone locks nearby. •

Bridge number 35-23-38

Mink Hollow Covered Bridge • Fairfield County

Mink Hollow Bridge lies southwest of Lancaster in scenic Oil Mill Hollow, and is a 51-foot multiple kingpost bridge built about 1887. The late Charles Goslin, Fairfield County historian, claimed this bridge was incorrectly named since it is actually located in Oil Mill Hollow. Mink Hollow is a few miles away. The Oil Mill Hollow name came from the nearby mill (known as Borchers Mill) that converted flax seed into linseed oil. Whatever the truth, Mink Hollow is the only name now associated with this little bridge. Its only reference in the county records was a roofing project in 1887. The bridge's low boarded siding and roofed windows were likely replacements for the original full boards to accommodate faster automobile traffic. The truss design is unique to Ohio. Instead of the usual central kingpost or open center panel in a multiple kingpost, the Mink Hollow Bridge has a central X brace. Now bypassed and maintained by the Fairfield County Historic Parks District, Mink Hollow's expensive lights have been vandalized and left the parks director without funding to replace them. National Register of Historic Places • Bridge number 35-23-43

Rock Mill Covered Bridge • Fairfield County (also overleaf)

Rock Mill Bridge lies northwest of Lancaster and is a 37-foot queenpost truss bridge built in 1901. This is the best-known and loved covered bridge in Fairfield County. Spanning the Hocking River where it flows through a dramatic gorge, it was the last covered bridge in the county open for traffic until recently. Taken down and hauled away for renovation, it is back in place and carries only foot and bicycle traffic. The bridge is in a very lovely setting, next to the 1824 Rock Mill that operated until the early twentieth century. The covered bridge is the second on this site and was erected by veteran bridge builder "Blue Jeans" Brandt for $575. It was the last bridge built by Brandt, although he continued to repair bridges for a few more years before he died in 1911. He used his long farm lane to lay out bridge trusses before taking them to the erection site. National Register of Historic Places • Bridge number 35-23-48

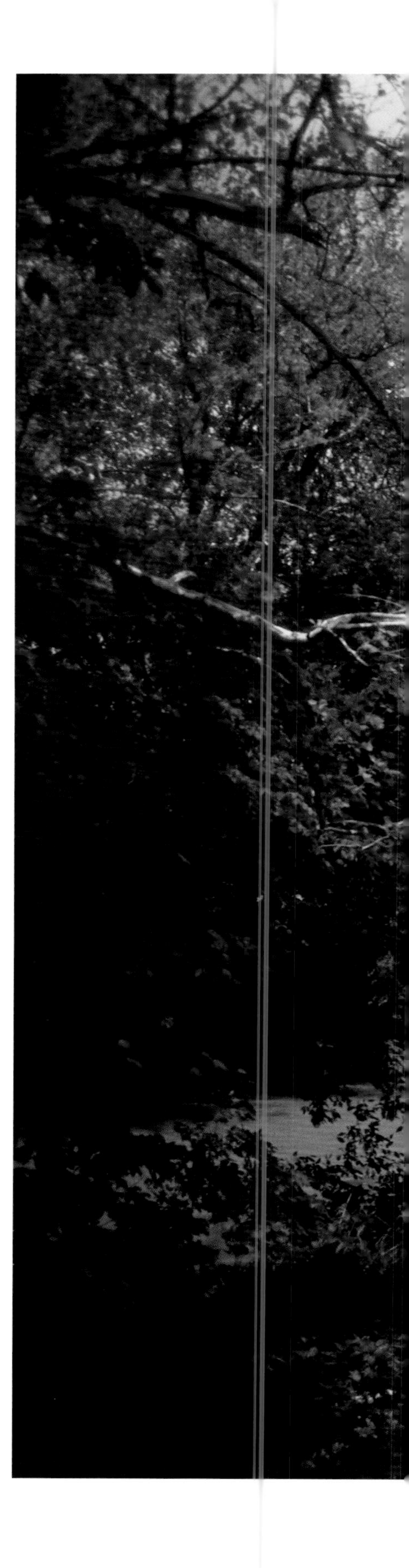

Roley School Covered Bridge • Fairfield County

Roley School Bridge in Lancaster is a 49-foot multiple kingpost bridge built in 1899. This little bridge was built by J. W. Buchanan to span the Ohio and Erie Canal just south of Baltimore. The fourth covered bridge on the site, it cost $7.80 per lineal foot. The canals never overcame the competition from the railroads in Ohio in the mid 1850s, although they continued to operate into the early twentieth century but were no longer profitable. The flood of March 1913 finished the canal era in Ohio. In 1914 Buchanan was hired to move the bridge to Roley Road where it spanned PawPaw Creek for the next fifty-eight years. Like so many covered bridges, it set on a curve and the county cut a window on one side to improve visibility. By 1972 the time had come for a new bridge on Roley Road and it was moved to the fairgrounds. • Bridge number 35-23-49

Bergstresster Covered Bridge • Franklin County (also overleaf)

Bergstresser Bridge lies at the south edge of Canal Winchester and is a 134.5-foot Partridge truss bridge built in 1887. Also known as the Dietz Bridge, it was built by the Columbus Bridge Company under the supervision of Reuben L. Partridge. Partridge was born in 1823 in Essex County, New York, and moved to Union County, Ohio with his widowed mother as a thirteen-year-old. After attending a one-room school for a short time, he learned the carpenter and wagon maker's trade. He developed a roof truss for barns while working in the Union County area as a carpenter. In 1872 he received a wood bridge truss patent that was very similar to Robert Smith's. By the 1880s Partridge was the vice-president in charge of construction for the Columbus Bridge Company. During his long career, he built bridges in Delaware, Fairfield, Fayette, and Franklin Counties. For Franklin County, the Bergstresser Bridge was a late covered bridge. The commissioners had been replacing the old timber truss bridges with all-metal trusses for many years. The Columbus Bridge Company proposed building either wood or iron and the county chose the cheaper alternative because the Kramer's Ford was a relatively unimportant site. The Bergstresser Bridge road became a state highway in the 1930s and remained a state route until bypassed in the mid-1950s. Ownership reverted to the county, who maintained it until 1991 when Canal Winchester became the owner. Prior to the transfer, the county had the bridge completely renovated. The bridge is now closed to all but pedestrian and bicycle use. National Register of Historic Places • Bridge number 35-25-03

Brannon Fork, or Blackburn, or Wesner, Covered Bridge, south of Canal Winchester, is a 60-foot multiple kingpost bridge. This small bridge was built in 1885 to span Brannons Fork in southeastern Muskingum County. The county

Brannon Fork or Wesner Covered Bridge • Franklin County

closed the old bridge in 1961 due to strip-mining. Coal trucks forded the creek beside the bridge. The Old Wheels Club of Zanesville bought the bridge from the county, marked the timbers with chalk, dismantled it, and stored it in a barn with the intention of rebuilding it on their own property. In 1967 attorney Art Wesner obtained the bridge timbers and rebuilt them on his property near Grove City over Big Run. Many people helped in the rebuilding, but their efforts were severely hindered because the chalk markings had all rubbed off. The foundations came from Fayette County's last covered bridge which had burned two years earlier. In 1999 the bridge was donated to the Franklin County metropolitan Parks who again dismantled it and moved it to Slate Run Farm close to the main park road. • Bridge number 35-25-65

Fairgrounds Covered Bridge • Franklin County

Fairgrounds Bridge is a 31-foot Town lattice bridge built in 1993 on the county fairgrounds in Hilliard. This small pedestrian bridge was built from plans drawn up by former Ashtabula County Engineer John Smolen for the Canal Greenway Bridge in Licking County in 1991. The Town lattice truss was common among early Franklin County bridges, making the design especially appropriate. It was located on the fairgrounds near several historic buildings. • Bridge number 35-25-147

Boy Scout Camp Covered Bridge Licking County

Boy Scout, or Rainrock, Bridge northwest of Rocky Fork is a 49-foot multiple kingpost truss bridge of unknown date. This small bridge was built to span a branch of Rocky Fork five miles southwest of Fallsburg and was also known as the Rainrock Bridge after a nearby community. The builder is unkown. When the county decided to build a new bridge at this site, the old bridge was moved to the nearby Boy Scout Camp for placement over a ravine. In June 1976 the bridge was completely rebuilt and rededicated by the Boy Scouts and their leaders. • Bridge number 35-45-04

Girl Scout Camp or Shoults Covered Bridge • Licking County

Girl Scout Camp Bridge northwest of Fallsburg is a 74-foot multiple kingpost truss built in 1874. Samuel Miller built this bridge for only $4.69 per lineal foot. In the 1890s a man named G.W. Shoults, who may have lived nearby, repaired this bridge for $48 and some folks refer to it as the Shoults Bridge. Mercer was also a common name along the Wakatomika Valley in the 1800s, and more than one covered bridge bore this name. The numbering system helps keep from getting these bridges confused. The Girl Scout Camp Bridge is no longer used for through traffic as the road is not maintained south of the bridge. In 2003 a neighbor offered to do repairs and painting if the county would help to pay for it, to which they happily agreed. For a brief time, the bridge sported new siding, painted a deep red. Vandals soon had much of that torn off so they can jump in the creek for a swim. Nighttime parties leave all manner of trash behind, making maintenance difficult. • Bridge number 35-45-05

Gregg Mill Covered Bridge • Licking County

Gregg Mill, or Pine Bluff Bridge northwest of Fallsburg is a 124-foot multiple kingpost truss bridge built in 1881. County records indicate that work was underway on the Gregg Mill abutments in 1881 but nothing was recorded about the builder or price of the superstructure. Frampton Road crosses Wakatomika Creek five times and there were covered bridges at each crossing. Gregg Mill Bridge is now the lone survivor. The center pier of this bridge was a later addition. In 1993 the county completely rebuilt the bridge. •

Bridge number 35-45-06

McLain or Lobdell Covered Bridge • Licking County

McLain, or Lobdell Bridge, on the east edge of Alexandria, is a 52.5-foot multiple kingpost truss bridge. It was built sometime between 1866 and 1875, a period when the county records are missing. Another mystery is the poem that once graced the portal of this bridge:

All things save this
Have changed within our day,
Beside this quiet road
Nestled in these joyous hills,
You point your modest structure
Toward the sky,
Unsought and all unthanked
You give us still,
Some fragrance of your peace
As we go by.

The name Frank Phillips and the date, 1871, follow. Could he have been the builder? His name does not appear anywhere else in old county bridge building records. In the late 1940s, the siding was removed to facilitate repairs to the lower chords and for some reason, never replaced. The bridge stood unhoused for over twenty years. Bypassed in 1970, it stood abandoned until 1977 when it was moved, renovated, and resided. • Bridge number 35-45-17

Davis Farm Covered Bridge • Licking County

Davis Farm Bridge, on a private farm road, is a 50-foot multiple kingpost truss bridge built in 1947. Cecil Davis built this little bridge of old barn timbers in 1947 to provide access to his farm. The Davis Bridge was only the second authentic timber truss built in Ohio since 1919, but since the bridge was privately owned and used, there was little or no publicity about it. •
Bridge number 35-45-25

Canal Greenway Covered Bridge • Licking County

Canal Greenway Covered Bridge, on an abandoned railroad right-of-way, is an 80-foot Town truss bridge built in 1991. It was designed by former Ashtabula County Engineer John Smolen for pedestrian and bicycle use only and is only eight feet in width and heigth. Built by the Ohio Civilian Conservation Corps from kiln-dried Southern yellow pine, it cost ten thousand dollars. The Owens-Corning Fiberglass Company donated the roof shingles, and the bridge sets on the concrete abutments of an old railroad bridge. The railroad paralleled the Ohio and Erie Canal, which provided the name for this bike path and bridge. The bridge is visible from the east-bound lanes of I-70 east of Ohio Route 37. • Bridge number 35-45-160

Parks or South Covered Bridge • Perry County

Parks Bridge, north of Somerset, is a 66-foot multiple kingpost dating to 1883. It was built by William Dean, a well-known local builder who completed twenty-five timber truss bridges in Perry County between 1874 and 1886. Costing $7.85 per lineal foot, it has a noticeable camber or curve to the upper and lower chords. It was painted red with white portals for many years, and the portals were decorated with red gingerbread trim. In an excess of Bicentennial-inspired patriotic zeal, Perry County's covered bridges were all painted with red, white, and blue horizontal stripes and stars designs and dates on the white portals. Unfortunately the Parks Bridge lost its unique gingerbread trim and the colors on all the bridges bled and ran, making them look quite tawdry. All three highway bridges were recently repaired and repainted red with both white and blue trim. National Register of Historic Places • Bridge number 35-64-02

Hopewell Church Covered Bridge • Perry County

Hopewell Church Bridge is a 55-foot multiple kingpost truss bridge built in 1874. Hiram Dennison erected this bridge for $4.85 per lineal foot. Isaac Cotterman, a well-known stone mason in Perry County, did the foundation for $3.00 per perch. Vandals tried to burn it in July 2000, but thanks to alert neighbors, the bridge was saved. Still, it was closed for several years before being repaired. The young men responsible for this arson were caught and imprisoned. This has always been a great bridge to photograph with both a bridge and church in one shot. Newly-renovated and freshly painted, this bridge makes a lovely rural scene. With luck, you can see an Amish horse-and-buggy crossing the bridge. National Register of Historic Places • Bridge number 35-64-03

Jacks Hollow Covered Bridge • Perry County

Jacks Hollow Bridge, northeast of Mount Perry, is a 66-foot multiple kingpost bridge built in 1879. Perry County builder William Dean built this bridge for $7.25 per lineal foot. When first completed, a distillery stood close by, but all traces of it have vanished today. Unfortunately, the area is rather remote, making the bridge a frequent target for vandals. An arson attempt in the early 1990s resulted in damage serious enough to close it for repairs. Like both the Parks and Hopewell Church bridges, the Jacks Hollow Bridge was recently renovated. National Register of Historic Places • Bridge number 35-64-05

Bowman Mill or Redington Covered Bridge • Perry County

Bowman Mill Bridge on the New Lexington fairgrounds is an 82-foot multiple kingpost bridge built in 1859. Gottlieb Bunz, a Hocking County bridge builder and mason, built the bridge superstructure for $6.50 per lineal foot and the stone abutments for $2.50 per perch. The stone center pier does not appear to be part of the original structure. Built at Bernard Bowman's Mill west of Somerset, the only mention of the bridge in county records after construction was for a minor repair in 1879 and a new roof in 1884. When the Rush Creek Reservoirs threatened to flood it in 1987, the county moved the bridge to the fairgrounds. National Register of Historic Places • Bridge number 35-64-06

Ruffner or Moore Covered Bridge • Perry County (also previous)

Ruffner Bridge is an 81-foot Smith truss bridge built in 1875. William Black built this bridge to span Little Rush Creek on Gun Barrel Road in northeastern Fairfield County. Since it is a Smith patent truss, Black is thought to have been an agent for the Smith Bridge Company. The bridge cost over $15 per lineal foot, much more than the average Fairfield County multiple kingpost of the 1870s. Carroll Moore's long-time desire to move a covered bridge to his farm matched Fairfield County's intention to remove the bridge in 1986. Moore remodeled the bridge with roofed windows running the length of the bridge. Visitors are welcome to see the old bridge in its new setting. • Bridge number 35-64-84

35-21-04

Chambers Road Covered Bridge • Delaware County

Description: 86-foot Childs truss, built in 1883. *Location:* northeast of Olive Green, in Porter Township, over Big Walnut Creek. *Directions:* from Interstate I-71 heading north from Columbus, take State Route 61 south to State Route 656 about 1.7 miles to Chambers Road (also Township Road 63) and turn left, heading east one mile to the covered bridge. Page 181

35-23-30

Charles Holliday Covered Bridge • Fairfield County

Description: 98-foot multiple kingpost truss, built in 1897, moved in 1982. *Location:* southeast edge of Millersport, in Walnut Township. *Directions:* from Columbus, take Interstate I-70 east to State Route 37. Head south on State Route 37 for 3.5 miles to State Route 204. Head east on State Route 204 to the town of Millersport. In Millersport, head south on Lancaster Street .2 miles to Chatauqua Boulevard. Turn left on Chatauqua Boulevard, approximately .5 miles to Gate 4. The bridge is located on the Corn Festival Grounds. Page 193

35-23-15

Hanaway or Clearport Covered Bridge • Fairfield County

Description: 86-foot multiple kingpost truss, built in 1901. *Location:* south of Clearport, in Madison Township, over Clear Creek. *Directions:* from Lancaster, take US Route 22 southwest to State Route 159. Head south on State Route 159 for a few miles to the east end of the town of Amanda and old State Route 22. Approximately .3 miles south of the old State Route 22 intersection, turn left on Amanda-Clearport Road (also County Road 69). Head east on Amanda-Clearport Road 3.4 miles to County Road 24. Turn right on County Road 24, heading south .4 miles to the covered bridge, located on the east side of the road. Page 187

35-23-38

Lockville Park or Hartman Number 2 Covered Bridge • Fairfield County

Description: 48-foot queenpost truss, built in 1888, moved in 1967. *Location:* at Lockville, in Violet Township, over Ohio and Erie Canal. *Directions:* from Lancaster, take US Route 33 northwest to the town of Carroll. At the traffic light in Carroll, turn left on Winchester Pike (also County Road 23), heading west 1.5 miles to Pickerington Road (also County Road 20). Turn right on Pickerington Road, heading north 1.4 miles to a small park where the covered bridge located. Page 197

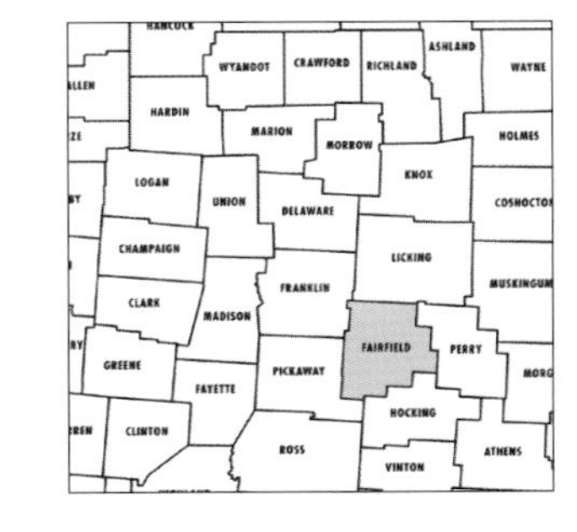

35-23-07

Hizey Covered Bridge • Fairfield County

Description: 83-foot multiple queenpost truss plus arch, built in 1891, renovated in 1989. *Location:* northeast of Pickerington, in Violet Township, over Sycamore Creek. *Directions:* from the intersection of State Route 256 and State Route 204, take State Route 204 east 4.3 miles to Toll Gate Road. Turn right on Toll Gate Road, heading south a mile to the covered bridge. The bridge is on a private drive at 12549 Toll Gate Road, but can be seen from the road. Page 182

35-23-13

George Hutchins Covered Bridge • Fairfield County

Description: 62-foot multiple kingpost truss, built in 1904 to span Clear Creek two miles southeast of Amanda. Moved to Alley Park in 1988, rebuilt in 2000. *Location:* south of Lancaster, in Alley Park, over a branch of Lake Loretta near the Charles Goslin Nature Center. *Directions:* from Lancaster, take US Route 33 south a few miles to Stump Hollow Road. Turn right on Stump Hollow Road, heading west a few yards to the stop sign. Turn left on Old Logan Road, follow for .5 miles to Alley Park. Page 185–187

35-23-10

John Bright Covered Bridge • Fairfield County

Description: 75-foot suspension truss plus arch, built in 1881. *Location:* northeast of Lancaster, in Pleasant Township, over Fetters Run. *Directions:* from Lancaster and the intersection of US Route 22 and State Route 37, take State Route 37 north 2 miles to the Ohio University Lancaster Branch Campus, on the east side of the road. Turn east into the south parking lot and drive to the back of the campus parking lot. The covered bridge is located 200 yards behind the campus buildings and can be seen from the parking lot. Page 183–184

35-23-16

Johnston Covered Bridge • Fairfield County

Description: 98-foot Howe truss, built in 1887. *Location:* southeast of Clearport, in Madison Township, over Clear Creek. *Directions:* from Lancaster, take US Route 22 southwest to State Route 159. Head south on State Route 159 for a few miles to the east end of the town of Amanda and old US Route 22. Approximately .3 miles south of the old US Route 22 intersection, turn left onto Amanda-Clearport Road (also County Road 69), heading east 5 miles to the covered bridge, located on the right, or south, side of the road in a small park. Page 188

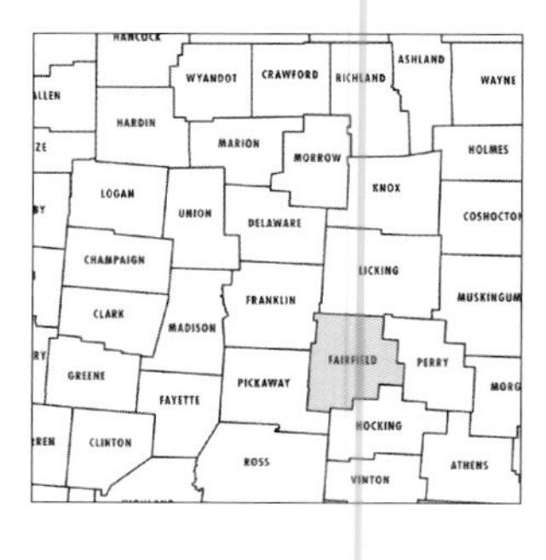

35-23-37

Jon Raab Covered Bridge • Fairfield County

Description: 44-foot queenpost truss, built in 1891, moved in 1974. *Location:* east of Lancaster, in Pleasant Township. *Directions:* from Lancaster, take US Route 22 northeast 1.8 miles past the intersection of State Route 37 to Ireland Road (also Township Road 344). Turn right on Ireland Road, heading east a mile, the bridge is on the south side of the road at 5695 Ireland Road on the Raab Farm, private property. Page 196

35-23-25

McCleery Covered Bridge • Fairfield County

Description: 54-foot multiple kingpost truss, built in 1864, moved in 1983. *Location:* south of Baltimore, in Greenfield Township. *Directions:* from Pickerington, head east on State Route 256 to the town of Baltimore. Continue past Baltimore to State Route 158. Turn right on State Route 158, heading south 2.4 miles to Pleasantville Road (also County Road 17). Turn right on Pleasantville Road, heading west .2 miles. The bridge is on the south side of the road on private property. Please note, this bridge is scheduled to be relocated as follows: from the junction of US Route 22 and State Route 37 in Lancaster, take State Route 37 (Granville Pike) north .7 miles to Fair Avenue and turn right. Travel .6 miles on Fair Avenue to Arbor Valley Drive and turn left. Travel about .2 miles to the bridge. Page 191

35-23-43

Mink Hollow Covered Bridge • Fairfield County

Description: 51-foot multiple kingpost truss, built in 1887. *Location:* northeast of Clearport, in Hocking Township, over Arney Run. *Directions:* from Lancaster, take US Route 22 southwest to State Route 159. Head south on State Route 159 about 4.5 miles (through the town of Amanda) to Amanda-Clearport Road (also County Road 69). Turn left on Amanda-Clearport Road, heading east 4 miles to Hopewell Church Road. Turn left on Hopewell Church Road, heading north 1.3 miles to Crooks Road (also County Road 24). Turn right on Crooks Road, approximately 2.2 miles to the covered bridge. Page 198

35-23-33

R.F. Baker Covered Bridge • Fairfield County

Description: 69-foot multiple kingpost truss, built in 1871, moved in 1981. *Location:* west of Rushville, in Richland Township. *Directions:* from Rushville and the intersection of State Route 664 and US Route 22, take US Route 22 southwest 2.2 miles to Fairfield Union High School. Turn left into the High School parking lot. The covered bridge is behind the high school, across the athletic field. Page 194–195

35-23-48

Rock Mill Covered Bridge • Fairfield County

Description: 37-foot queenpost truss, built in 1901. *Location:* northwest of Lancaster, in Bloom Township, over Hocking River. *Directions:* from Lancaster, take US Route 33 north approximately 4 miles to the traffic light at Lithopolis Road (formerly the site of the town of Hooker). Turn left at Lithopolis Road (also County Road 39), heading west 2.7 miles to Rock Mill Road (also County Road 41). Turn left on Rock Mill Road, approximately .1 mile to the covered bridge. Page 199–201

35-23-49

Roley School Covered Bridge • Fairfield County

Description: 49-foot multiple kingpost truss, built in 1899, moved in 1972. *Location:* in Lancaster on the fairgrounds. *Directions:* from Lancaster and the intersection of US Route 22 and State Route 37, take State Route 37 north .7 miles to East Fair Avenue. Turn left on East Fair Avenue and drive one block to the county fairgrounds. The covered bridge is located just inside the main gate on the fairgrounds. Page 202

35-23-20

Shade Covered Bridge • Fairfield County

Description: 127.5-foot Burr truss, built in 1871, moved and partially rebuilt in 1983. *Location:* southeast of Sugar Grove, in Berne Township. *Directions:* from Lancaster, take US Route 33 south to Sugar Grove Road. Turn left and head east on Sugar Grove Road .4 miles to Buckeye Road (also Township Road 400). Head south on Buckeye Road for 1.6 miles to Sullivan Road (also Township Road 298). Head east on Sullivan Road, approximately .5 miles to the bridge, located on the right on Pierson Farm, private property. Page 190

35-23-27

Shryer Covered Bridge • Fairfield County

Description: 69-foot multiple kingpost truss, built in 1891, moved in 1987. *Location:* west of Baltimore, in Liberty Township. *Directions:* from Pickerington, take State Route 256 east 4 miles to Bader Road (also Township Road 251). Turn right on Bader Road, heading south a mile to Basil-Western Road (also County Road 13). Turn right on Basil-Western Road, heading west 1.5 miles to the covered bridge, on the north side of the road. The bridge is located on Bill Shryer's Farm, and is on private property. Page 192

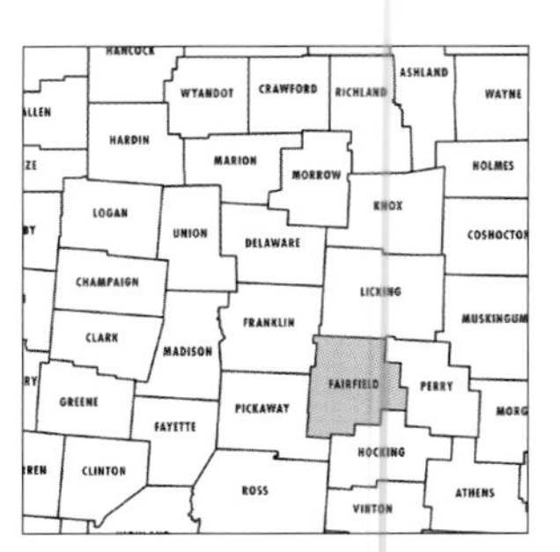

35-23-19

Zeller-Smith or Sycamore Park Covered Bridge • Fairfield County

Description: 79-foot multiple kingpost truss, built in 1905, moved in 1986. *Location:* southeast edge of Pickerington, in Violet Township, over Sycamore Creek. *Directions:* from Columbus, take Interstate I-70 east to (exit 112A) State Route 256. Head south on State Route 256 for 3.8 miles to a traffic light and turn left—still on State Route 256. Continue to the next traffic light, turn right onto Lockville Road (County Road 20), heading south past the Pickerington City Hall building. Once past the Pickerington City Hall, cross a small bridge, and immediately turn left onto Covered Bridge Lane and into Sycamore Park (the bridge is off Lockville Road). The parking lot is 200 yards in and the covered bridge is just beyond the lot. Page 189

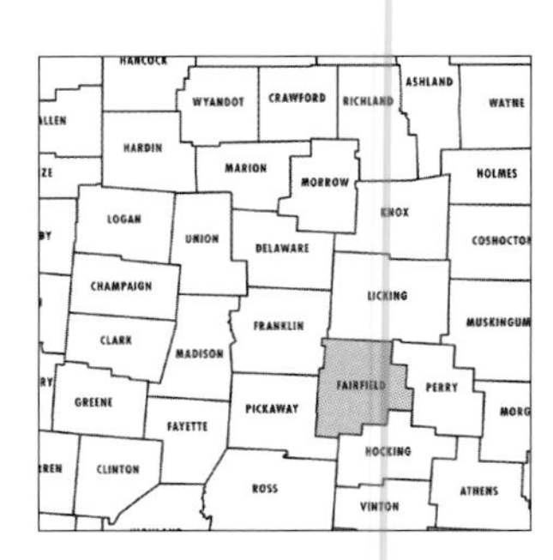

35-25-03

Bergstresser Covered Bridge • Franklin County

Description: 134.5-foot Partridge truss, built in 1887. *Location:* on the south edge of Canal Winchester, over Little Walnut Creek. *Directions:* from US Route 33, take State Route 674 south .8 miles to Groveport Road. Turn left on Groveport Road, heading east to the town of Canal Winchester. In Canal Winchester, turn right on Washington Street, approximately 1.5 miles to the covered bridge, located on the right-hand side of the road. Page 202–204

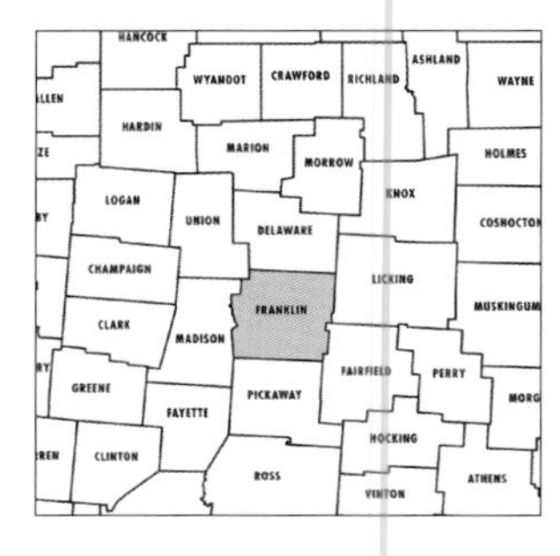

35-25-65

Blackburn or Brannon Fork or Wesner Covered Bridge • Franklin County

Description: 60-foot multiple kingpost truss, built in 1885, moved in 1967 and again in 1999 for rebuilding in Slate Run Park. *Location:* south of Canal Winchester *Directions:* from US Route 33, take State Route 674 approximately 3.2 miles past the Pickaway County line to Duvall Road. Stay on State Route 674 to the main entrance of Slate Run Park. (There is another entrance to the park by turning right on Duvall Road and heading west 1.6 miles to Slate Run Park). The bridge is actually located in Pickaway County. Page 204–205

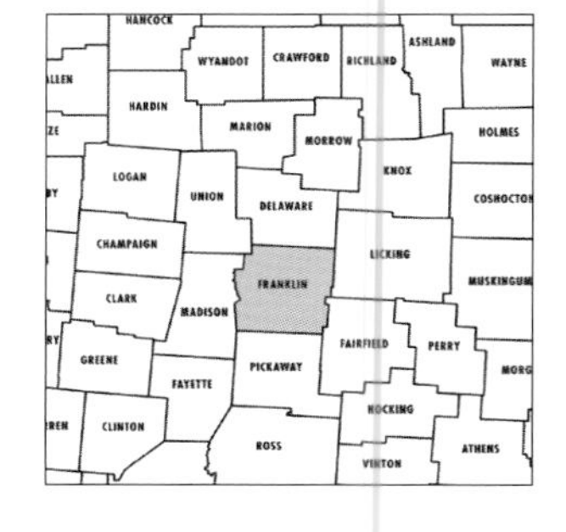

35-25-147

Fairgrounds Covered Bridge • Franklin County

Description: 31-foot Town lattice truss, built in 1993. *Location:* in Hilliard, on the fairgrounds. *Directions:* From I-270 (the outerbelt), take exit 13 which is marked Fishinger Road and Cemetery Road. Take Cemetery Road westbound and follow the Franklin County Fairground's signs (the fairgrounds are in Hilliard, on North Main Street about .8 miles north). Page 206–207

35-45-04

Boy Scout Camp or Rainrock Covered Bridge • Licking County

Description: 49-foot multiple kingpost truss, moved in 1974. *Location:* north of Rocky Fork, in Eden Township. *Directions:* from State Route 79, head north on Rainrock Road (also Township Road 244) .2 miles to Rocky Fork Road (also Township Road 210). Turn left on Rocky Fork Road, approximately a mile to the Boy Scout Camp where the covered bridge is located beyond the pond and up the hill. Page 208

35-45-160

Canal Greenway Covered Bridge • Licking County

Description: 80-foot Town lattice truss, built in 1991. *Location:* southwest of Hebron, on abandoned rail right-of-way. *Directions:* From Columbus, take I-70 East to State Route 79. Head north on State Route 79 to the town of Hebron. Make a left turn on Canal Road and travel approximately 2.5 miles southwest to the covered bridge which is located on the west side of the road, across from the Hebron State Fish Hatchery. Page 214–215

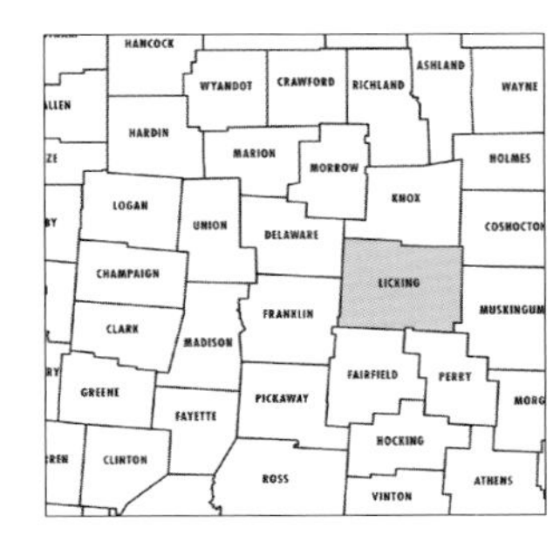

35-45-25

Davis Farm Covered Bridge • Licking County

Description: 50-foot multiple kingpost truss, built in 1947. *Location:* south of Hickman, over Rocky Fork of Licking River. *Directions:* from State Route 79, head southeast on Hickman Road 1.5 miles to the Davis Farm. The bridge is located on the Davis Farm, private property. Page 213

35-45-06

Gregg Mill Covered Bridge • Licking County

Description: 124-foot multiple kingpost truss, built in 1881, renovated in 1992. *Location:* north of Fallsburg, in Fallsbury Township, over Wakatomika Creek. *Directions:* from State Route 79, head northwest on State Route 586 for 1.4 miles to Frampton Road (also County Road 201). Head east on Frampton Road 1.4 miles to the covered bridge. Page 210–211

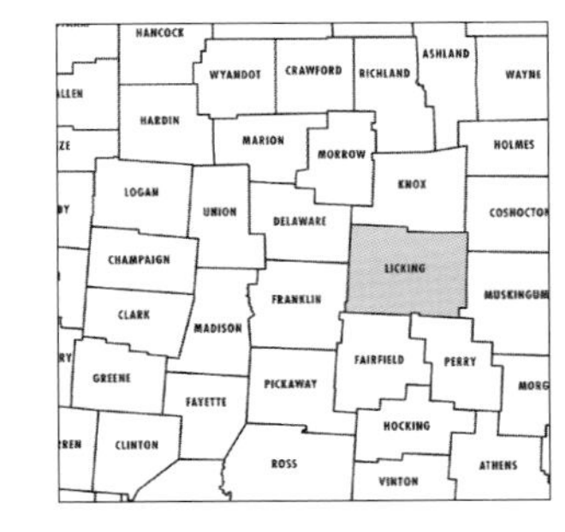

35-45-17

McLain or Lobdell Covered Bridge • Licking County

Description: 52.5-foot multiple kingpost truss, built in 1871, moved in 1977. *Location:* at the south edge of Alexandria. *Directions:* from the town of Alexandria, head south on State Route 37 approximately .5 miles to Firemans Park where the bridge is located. Page 212

35-45-05

Shoults or Mercer or Girl Scout Camp Covered Bridge • Licking County

Description: 74-foot multiple kingpost truss, built in 1879. *Location:* northwest of Fallsburg, in Fallsbury Township, over Wakatomika Creek. *Directions:* from State Route 79, head northwest on State Route 586 for 2.5 miles to Girl Scout Road (also Township Road 225). Turn right on Girl Scout Road, heading east 1.4 miles to the covered bridge. Page 209

35-64-06

Bowman Mill or Redington Covered Bridge • Perry County

Description: 82-foot multiple kingpost truss, built in 1859, moved in 1987. *Location:* the west edge of New Lexington. *Directions:* on the northwest outskirts of New Lexington, at the intersection of State Route 13 and State Route 37, head west on State Route 37 for .3 miles to the fairgrounds. The bridge is located at the entrance to the fairgrounds. Page 220

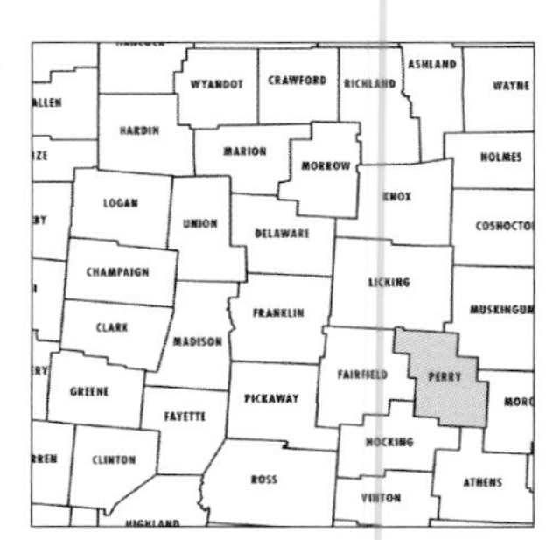

35-64-03

Hopewell Church Covered Bridge • Perry County

Description: 55-foot multiple kingpost truss, built in 1874. *Location:* north of Somerset, in Hopewell Township, over Painter Creek. *Directions:* from the town of Somerset, head east on US Route 22 to State Route 668. Turn left on State Route 668, heading northeast 2.6 miles to Gower Road (also County Road 33). Turn left onto Gower Road, heading north 2 miles to Cooperriders Road (also County Road 51). Turn right on Cooperriders Road, heading east .3 miles to the covered bridge. Page 217

35-64-05

Jacks Hollow Covered Bridge • Perry County

Description: 60-foot multiple kingpost truss, built in 1879. *Location:* northeast of Mount Perry, in Madison Township, over Kents Run. *Directions:* from the town of Mount Perry, take Gratiot Road (also County Road 34) north 1.9 miles to Kroft Road (also County Road 67). Turn right on Kroft Road, heading east 1.9 miles to Township Road 108. Turn left on Township Road 108, heading north .8 miles to the covered bridge. Page 218–219

35-64-02

Parks or South Covered Bridge • Perry County

Description: 66-foot multiple kingpost truss, built in 1883. *Location:* north of Somerset, in Hopewell Township, over Painter Creek. *Directions:* from the town of Somerset, head east on US Route 22 to State Route 668. Turn left on State Route 668, heading northeast 2.6 miles to Gower Road (also County Road 33). Turn left on Gower Road, heading north .9 miles to the covered bridge. Page 216

35-64-84

Ruffner or Moore Farm Covered Bridge • Perry County

Description: 81-foot Smith truss, built in 1875, moved from Fairfield County in 1986. *Location:* southeast of Thornville, in Thorn Township, over a pond. *Directions:* from Interstate I-70, head south on State Route 13 (exit 132) for 7 miles. The covered bridge is located on the east side of the highway on a private farm. Page 221–222

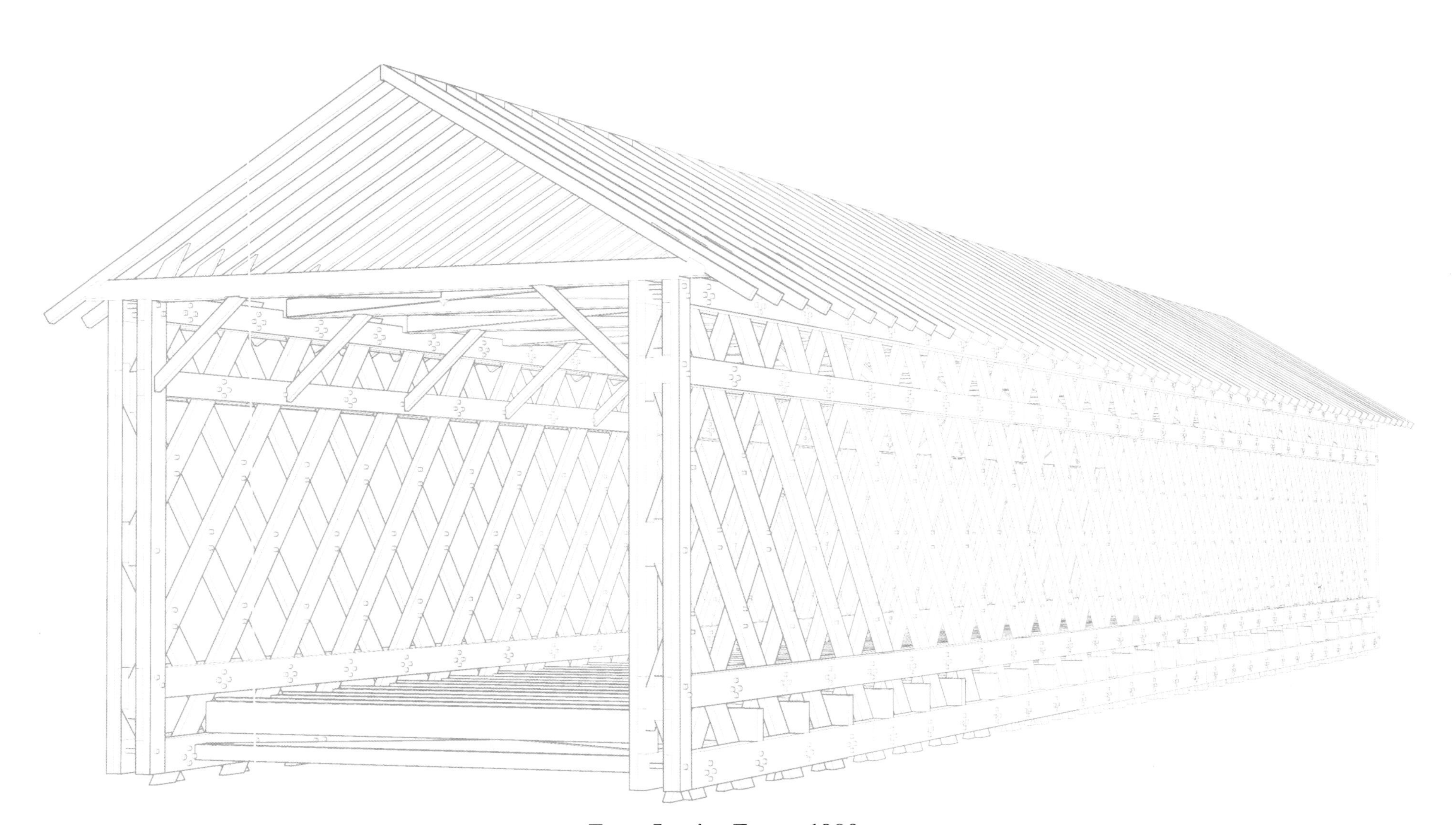

Town Lattice Truss, 1880

Colville Covered Bridge • Bourbon County

The first covered bridge on Colville Pike was built in 1877, repaired by Louis Bower in 1913, and again in 1937 and 1976 by his son, Louis S. Bower. By late 1990s, the condition of the Colville Pike Bridge was so bad that local authorities closed it. In 2002 the old bridge was removed and, in a two million dollar project, replaced by a completely new structure crafted as much like the original as possible. It is a handsome bridge, with a marked camber in the upper and lower chords. The original limestone abutments were reinforced with concrete years ago and are still in place. National Register of Historic Places • Bridge number 17-09-03

Walcott or White Covered Bridge • Bracken County

The Walcott Bridge, also called White in recognition of its long-standing paint color, was bypassed about 1954. G.N. Murray, founder of the county historical society, and his family stepped in to preserve and maintain the old structure. Vernon White indicated that the truss timbers are poplar and the lower chords are oak. The original structure set on dry-laid abutments. The current bridge has an unusual mix of two popular truss designs, multiple kingpost and queenpost. Some of the timbers used in the bridge were thought to have been taken from a bridge built on this site in 1824. In 2001, the bridge was completely rebuilt of new timbers and lengthened slightly a few yards east of its original location on new concrete foundations faced to look like stone. The sterile, park-like setting around the bridge has displeased some who wonder why the old bridge could not be renovated on its original site. All that remains of the original bridge are some thin slabs of the old truss timbers that have been veneered onto the face of five of the new truss diagonals. National Register of Historic Places • Bridge number 17-12-01

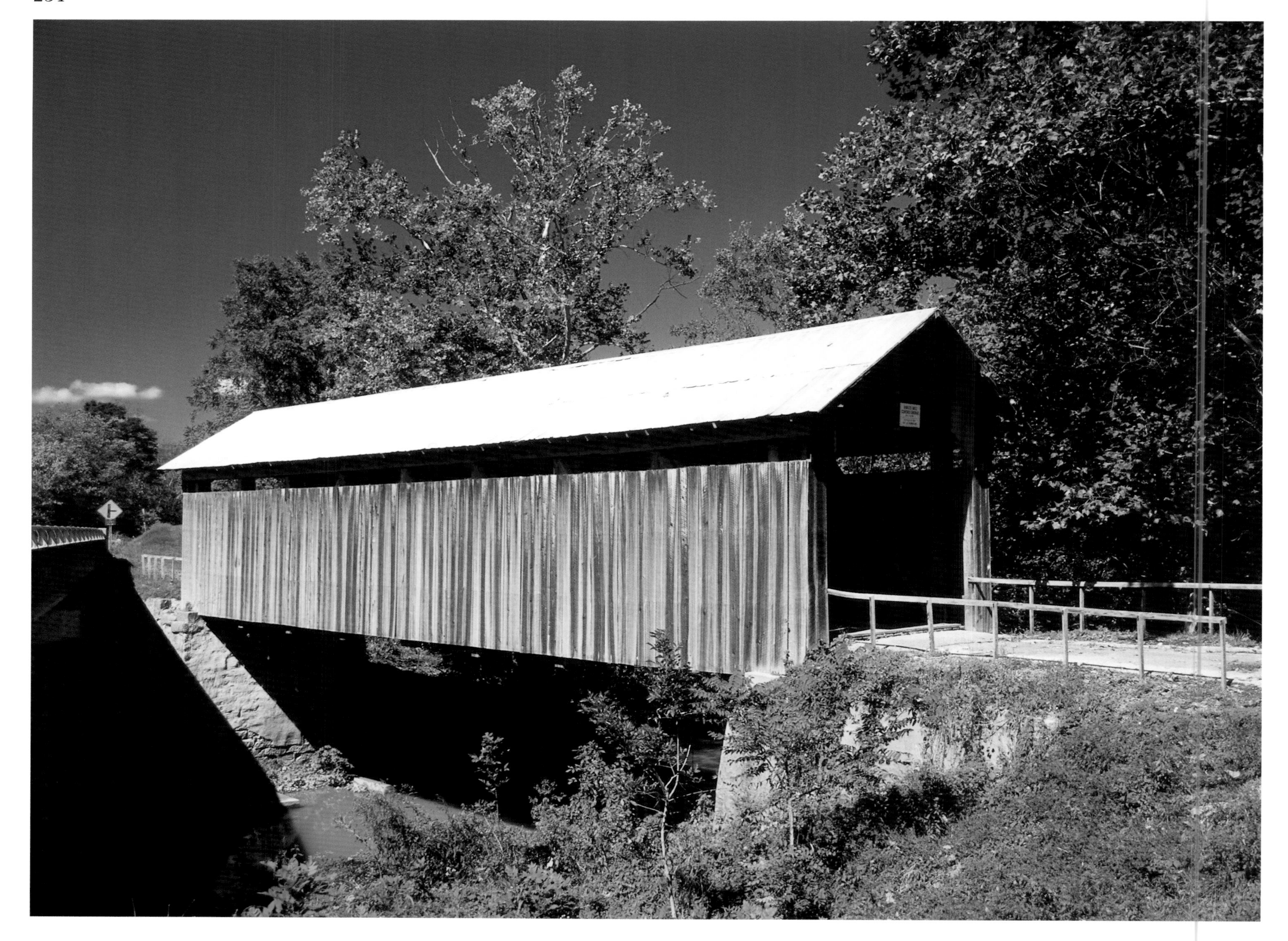

Ringo's Mill Covered Bridge • Fleming County

Ringo's Mill Bridge takes its name from the old mill that operated here in the 1880s. Bypassed and abandoned in 1968, its builder is unknown but it was probably the same man who built the Hillsboro Bridge. The trusses of yellow pine are fastened with large bolts and the lower chords are oak and pine. No trunnels were used in this or the Hillsboro Bridge. In 1982 Kentucky formed the Buffalo Trace Covered Wooden Bridge Authority, which included Louis S. "Stock" Bower of the Bower bridge building family. The Authority funded renovation of the Ringo's Mill Bridge under the supervision of Stock Bower. When his health declined, L. A. Thompson of Flemingsburg was contracted to finish the job. Under his direction, decayed sections of the lower chords and trusses were replaced with white oak. Vertical planks were substituted for the old horizontal siding, and the roof was painted. National Register of Historic Places • Bridge number 17-35-04

Hillsboro or Grange City Covered Bridge • Fleming County

Fleming County had eighteen wooden bridges standing in the 1950s. The Hillsboro, or Grange City Bridge has been described as a twin of the Ringo's Mill Bridge, and Vernon White thought they were probably built by the same man. The bridge sets on sandstone abutments that are in poor condition. The original shingle roof and horizontal siding were replaced with galvanized sheet metal in the 1930s. The metal siding was replaced in the 1980s with vertical wooden planks. In 1968 the old bridge was bypassed. Four flood high-water marks—including one fourteen inches above the floor—have been cut into the truss timbers. Foundation damage is apparent from the most recent flood in 1997. National Register of Historic Places • Bridge number 17-35-05

Goddard Covered Bridge
Fleming County

Although the date of the Goddard Bridge is unknown, its truss design (the only example in Kentucky) suggests it is very old. The trusses are fastened together with wooden pins called tree nails or, more commonly, trunnels. Town lattice trusses were common in the early nineteenth century, and the bridge may have been built by the Morehead to Flemingsburg Turnpike Company. O.G. Ragan's *History of Lewis County* (1912) credits

a Thomas Hinton of Fleming County with building a Town lattice truss on a Lewis County road. This could have been the same man who built the Goddard bridge. The bridge originally stood on Route 32 but was moved years ago to its present location. Too short for the new site, one end was placed on a concrete pier and an uncovered extension was added to reach the opposite abutment. Louis S. "Stock" Bower supervised the restoration of this bridge in 1968. The founder of this well-known family of bridge builders, Jacob N. Bower, learned his craft from Lewis Wernwag (see introduction). The Bowers built bridges in Maryland, Pennsylvania, West Virginia, Kentucky, and southern Ohio. They eventually settled permanently in Fleming County, Kentucky, where they continued their trade. Of the three Fleming County covered bridges, the Goddard Bridge is the only one that still carries traffic. National Register of Historic Places • Bridge number 17-35-06

Switzer Covered Bridge • Franklin County

Built by George Hockensmith, the Switzer Bridge is the last covered bridge in Franklin County. Louis Bower repaired it in 1906 and carved his initials and the date inside the bridge. In 1954, it was bypassed. Thirty years later, L. A. Thompson added new siding and painted the roof. He also replaced decayed sections of the lower chords and truss members with new white oak timbers. The surrounding community was shocked in March 1997 when a devastating flood tore the bridge from its foundations and dumped it into the creek. The bridge was completely rebuilt the following year by Intech Contracting using as much of the old wood as possible but over half is new. The unusual sawtooth design on the portals was repeated in the rebuilt bridge, and it was designated by the General Assembly as Kentucky's official covered bridge. A small park surrounds the bridge. National Register of Historic Places • Bridge number 17-37-01

Bennett Mill Covered Bridge • Greenup County (also overlead)

Using massive sandstone from an abandoned iron furnace for foundations, a bridge was erected to serve the B.F. and Pramley Bennett Mill in the 1870s. Because of this, many sources incorrectly give an 1850s date for the Bennett Mill Bridge. Isaac H. Wheeler of Sciotoville Ohio (just across the Ohio River) was granted a patent in 1870 for the unusual truss design. Research has identified five Wheeler truss bridges in Scioto County, Ohio, and one in Lawrence County, Ohio, but all have been demolished making the Bennett Mill Bridge a rare treasure. In the fall of 2003, the bridge was dismantled and faithfully rebuilt to look much like it always did but only fifteen percent of its timbers are from the old bridge. The work was done by Intech Contracting and included a slight elevation to reduce future flooding problems. • Bridge number 17-45-01

WEIGHT
LIMIT
3
TONS
13'0"

Oldtown Covered Bridge • Greenup County

The Oldtown Bridge was built in two unequal spans. The 145-foot main span with double trusses is over the river, and the short span with single truss members is only 41-feet long. There is no record of the builder of the Oldtown Bridge. The bridge sets on sandstone abutments and has received major renovations. A sign declares its capacity to be 360 people. National Register of Historic Places • Bridge number 17-45-02

Cabin Creek Covered Bridge • Lewis County

Various sources list the date of construction for the Cabin Creek Bridge as 1867, 1870, 1873, or 1875. Louis Bower's repairs to this bridge in 1914 added laminated arches and steel rods to the multiple kingposts. The bridge was bypassed in 1983 by a new bridge and a realigned road. The abutments of the old bridge are flat limestone rock laid without mortar. Two concrete pillars just in front of each abutment help carry the load. A steel I-beam arrangement on the southeast corner helps buttress against an outward lean that threatens the bridge. This bridge is scheduled for renovation in 2006. • Bridge number 17-68-03

Dover Covered Bridge • Mason County

The Dover Bridge, probably Kentucky's oldest, was built as a toll bridge and is still open to traffic. Stock Bower, whose company repaired the bridge in 1928, claimed that it was the third bridge on this site after the first burned and the second washed away in a flood. The double set of trusses, with one inside the other, is unusual. Steel I-beams were added in 1966 and a new roof was installed in 1968 after a tornado tore off the old one. The bridge was bypassed in the fall of 2004. National Register of Historic Places • Bridge number 17-81-01

Valley Pike or Bouldin Covered Bridge • Mason County

This small, privately-owned bridge, the Valley Pike, or Bouldin Bridge, is still used by the Bouldin family. At only twenty-four feet in length, it is the shortest covered bridge in Kentucky and one of the shortest in the United States. Bower repaired this bridge in 1972 and was told then that it was 108 years old. The truss timbers are poplar and the foundations are limestone laid with mortar. The bottom two feet of the end posts were replaced by Bower. He also put three steel I-beams under the floor to carry the roadway traffic. • Bridge number 17-81-02

Johnson Creek Covered Bridge • Robertson County

Famed bridge builder Jacob Bower built the Johnson Creek Bridge as a single-span Smith truss. The off-center stone pier was added at an unknown date. Stock Bower, grandson of Jacob, said that the four-ply laminated arches and iron rods extending below the lower chord of the bridge were added by his father, Louis, in 1906. A different set of steel rods reach to the lower chords from the upper chords. The abutments, like the pier, are built of flat limestone with mortar but have been faced with concrete. Surprisingly, the truss timbers at the center of the bridge are less than three by five inches. Bypassed by a new bridge in 1965, an arsonist damaged this bridge three years later. Repairs were not made until the early 1970s. A new roof was put on the bridge in 1986, and further renovations are scheduled for 2006. • Bridge number 17-101-01

Beech Fork Covered Bridge • Washington County

According to Vernon White and the Kentucky Transportation Cabinet, the Beech Fork Bridge was built by L. H. and William F. Barnes. Also known as Mooresville Bridge, the bridge was bypassed by a new bridge in 1975. In 1982 the deteriorating pier on the upstream side was rebuilt, a new roof replaced the old rusty one, and new siding was added. The trusses of this bridge are single and the two arches are bolted to the trusses, one on either side. Both trunnels and iron bolts hold the trusses together. A true two-span bridge, the center end-posts of each truss rest on the pier about five feet apart. The arches rest on the lower chords and may be part of the original structure. On the west end, the arches rest in metal "shoes" which protect the joint from weather. The area around the bridge is well-mown, security lights are at each end, and the area is monitored by cameras, all indications of the obvious pride local folks take in their last covered bridge. National Register of Historic Places • Bridge number 17-115-01

17-09-03

Colville Pike Bridge • Bourbon County

Description: 120-foot multiple kingpost truss reconstructed in 2002. *Location*: on Colville Pike over Hinkston Creek northwest of Millersburg. *Directions*: from US Route 68 on south edge of Millersburg turn right on Kentucky Route 1893 and go 4.2 miles to Colville Road and turn right. Bridge is 1.1 miles ahead. Page 231

17-12-01

Walcott or White Bridge • Bracken County

Description: originally a 73-foot combination kingpost and queenpost truss, built in the 1880s and reconstructed about 2002. *Location*: four miles north northwest of Brooksville over Locust Creek. *Directions*: from the junction of Kentucky Route 9 and Kentucky Route 19 west of Maysville, take Kentucky Route 9 four miles to Kentucky Route 1159 and turn right on 1159 about .1 miles and right again to covered bridge which is in a small park. The bridge is easily visible from the west bound lane of Kentucky Route 9. Page 232–233

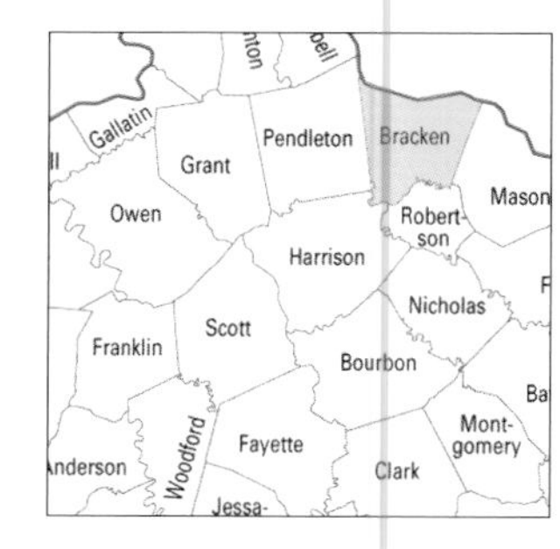

17-35-06

Goddard Bridge • Fleming County

Description: 63-foot Town lattice truss of unknown date. *Location*: southeast of Flemingsburg at Goddard over Sand Lick Creek on Maddox Road. *Directions*: take Kentucky Route 32 Southeast from Flemingsburg about 6 miles to Goddard. The bridge is just off Route 32 to the left. Page 236–237

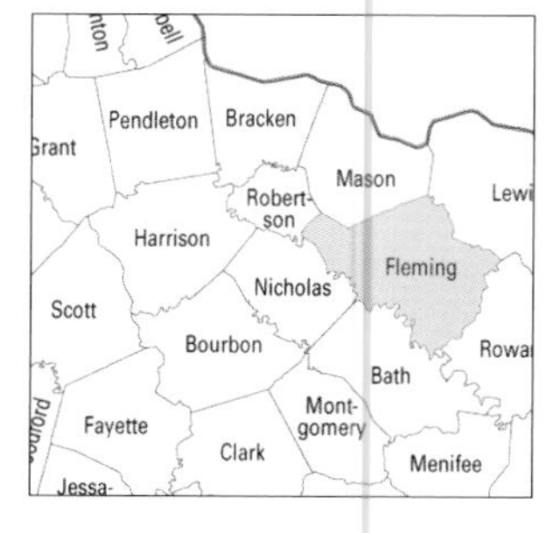

17-35-05

Hillsboro or Grange City Bridge • Fleming County

Description: 86-foot double multiple kingpost truss, built about 1867. *Location*: south of Hillsboro over Fox Creek on a bypassed section of Kentucky Route 111. *Directions*: from the junction of Kentucky Route 158 and Kentucky Route 111 at Hillsboro, take Kentucky Route 111 south three miles to covered bridge on the west side of the highway. Page 235

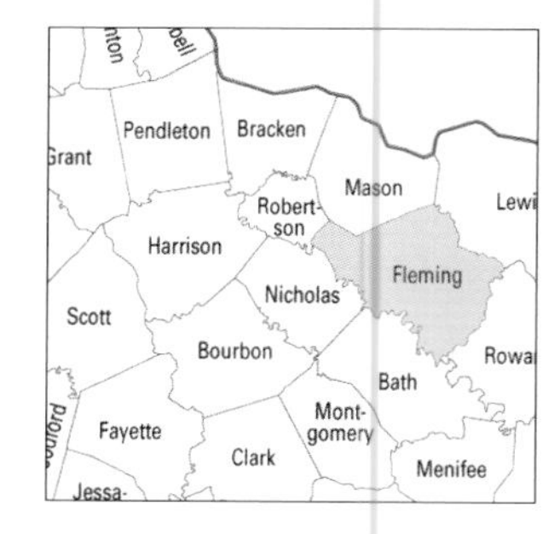

17-35-04

Ringo's Mill Bridge • Fleming County

Description: 88-foot double multiple kingpost truss built in 1867. *Location*: between Hillsboro and Sharkey on bypassed section of Kentucky Route 158 over Fox Creek. *Directions*: from the junction of Kentucky Route 32 and Kentucky Route 111, about 4 miles southeast of Flemingsburg, take Kentucky Route 111 south to Hillsboro and turn left onto Kentucky Route 158 and drive 3.7 miles south to Ringos Mill on east side of highway. Page 234

17-37-01

Switzer Bridge • Franklin County

Description: 120-foot Howe truss, built about 1855. *Location*: east of Frankfort over North Elkhorn Creek at Switzer. *Directions*: from Georgetown, north of Lexington, take U.S. Route 460 west about 10 miles to Kentucky Route 1262 and turn right and drive 3.5 miles to the bridge. Page 238

17-45-01

Bennett Mill Bridge • Greenup County

Description: 155-foot Wheeler truss, built about 1875. *Location*: south of South Shore over Tygarts Creek on Tygarts Creek Road. *Directions*: at South Shore, take Kentucky Route 7 south 8.2 miles to Tygarts Creek Road and turn left to bridge. Bridge is just off Kentucky Route 7. Page 239–240

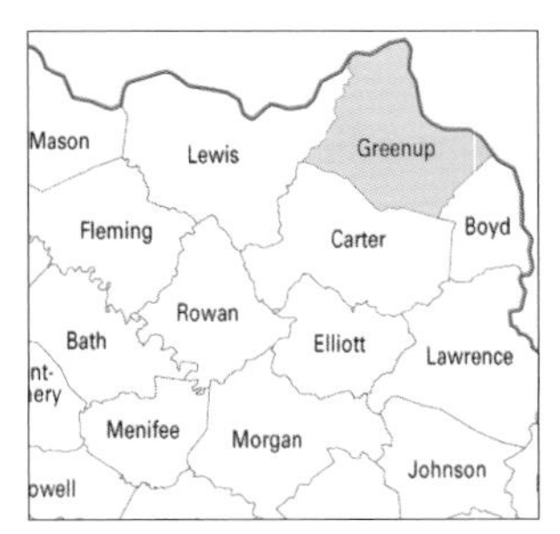

17-45-02

Oldtown Bridge • Greenup County

Description: 192-foot, two-span multiple kingpost truss, built in 1870. *Location*: north of Hopewell on County Road 705 (Frazer Branch Road) over the Little Sandy River, 200 yards off Kentucky Route 1 at Oldtown. *Directions*: from exit 172 on I-64, take Kentucky Route 1 north to Hopewell and continue north on Route 1 for 1.7 miles and turn right on Frazer Branch Road. Bridge is bypassed just ahead on the left. Page 241

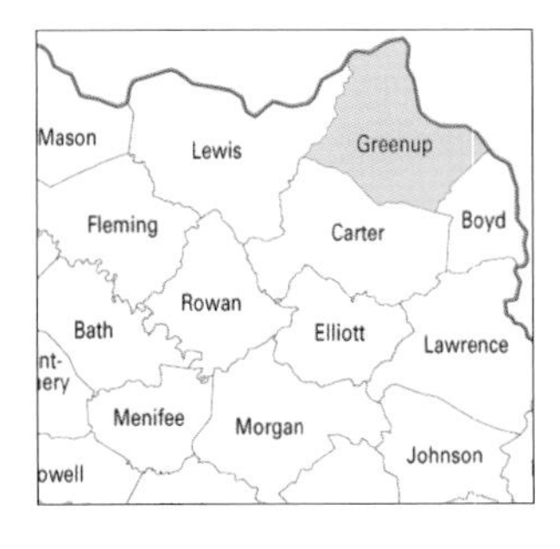

17-68-03

Cabin Creek Bridge • Lewis County

Description: 114-foot multiple kingpost truss with arches, built between 1867 and 1875. *Location*: northwest of Tollesboro on a bypassed section of Kentucky Route 984 over Cabin Creek. *Directions*: from Maysville take Kentucky Route 10 east about 13 miles to Kentucky Route 57 at Tollesboro and then take Kentucky Route 57 north to Kentucky Route 984 and then left on Kentucky Route 984 6.7 miles to the bridge which is on the right. Page 242

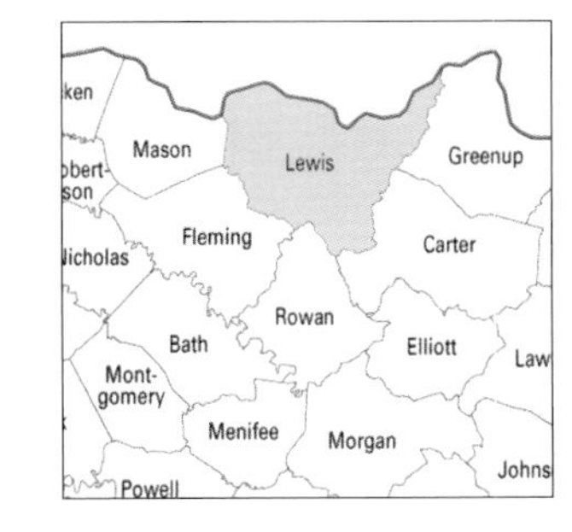

17-81-01

Dover Bridge • Mason County

Description: 63-foot queenpost truss variation, built about 1835. *Location*: on southeast edge of Dover over Lee's Creek on Lee's Creek Road (also known as Tuckahoe Road). The road is not marked, but there is a Kentucky highway marker about the bridge at the intersection. *Directions*: from Maysville, take Kentucky Route 8 west along the Ohio River about 12 miles. .4 miles east of Dover and Kentucky Route 1235, turn south on Lee's Creek/Tuckahoe Road. It is 200 yards or so to the covered bridge. Page 243

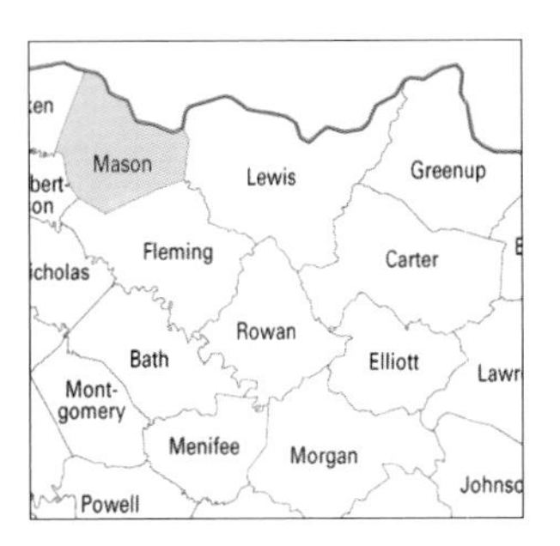

17-81-02

Valley Pike or Bouldin Bridge • Mason County

Description: 23-foot single kingpost truss, built about 1864. *Location*: just off Valley Pike over a tributary of Lees Creek, west of Maysville. *Directions*: from the junction of Kentucky Routes 8 and 435, take Route 435 for 7.3 miles to Valley Pike and turn north on Valley Pike for 1.6 miles to the bridge. Private. Page 244

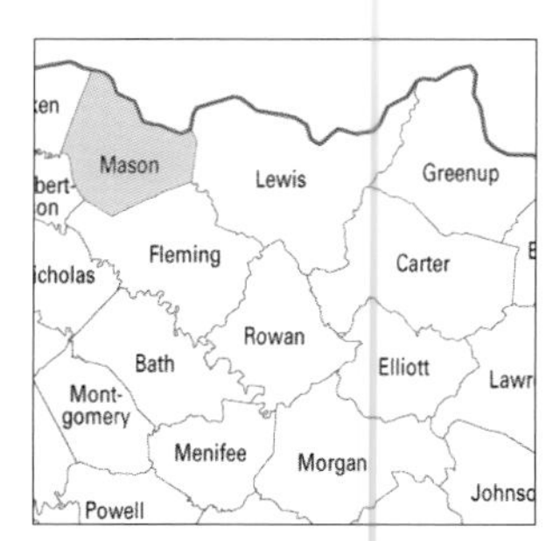

17-101-01

Johnson Creek Bridge • Robertson County

Description: 110-foot two-span Smith truss, built in 1874. *Location*: north of Blue Licks Spring on a bypassed section of Blue Licks Road (Kentucky Route 1029). *Directions*: from Maysville, take US Route 68 about 20 miles south to Blue Licks Springs and turn right on Kentucky Route 165 and go 1.6 miles to Kentucky Route 1029 and then right 2.1 miles to the bridge. Page 245

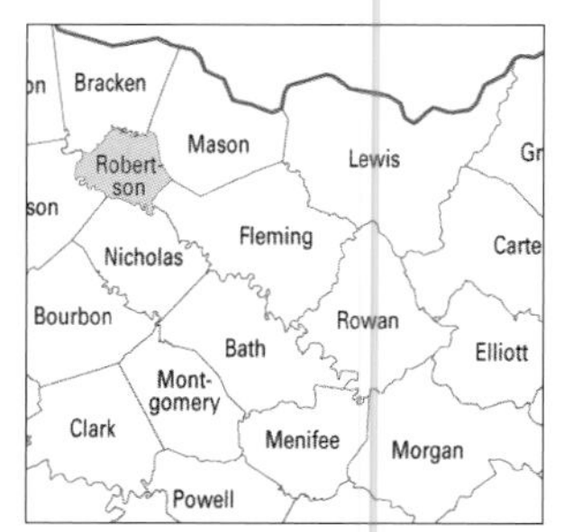

17-115-01

Beech Fork Bridge • Washington County

Description: two-span 211-foot double multiple kingpost truss with arches, built in 1865. *Location*: south of Chaplin and US Route 62 on a bypassed section of Kentucky Route 458 over Beech Fork River. *Directions*: from exit 34 of the Blue Grass Parkway, take Kentucky Route 55 south about five miles to Kentucky Route 458 and turn left on 458 and go 3.5 miles to the bridge. Page 246–247

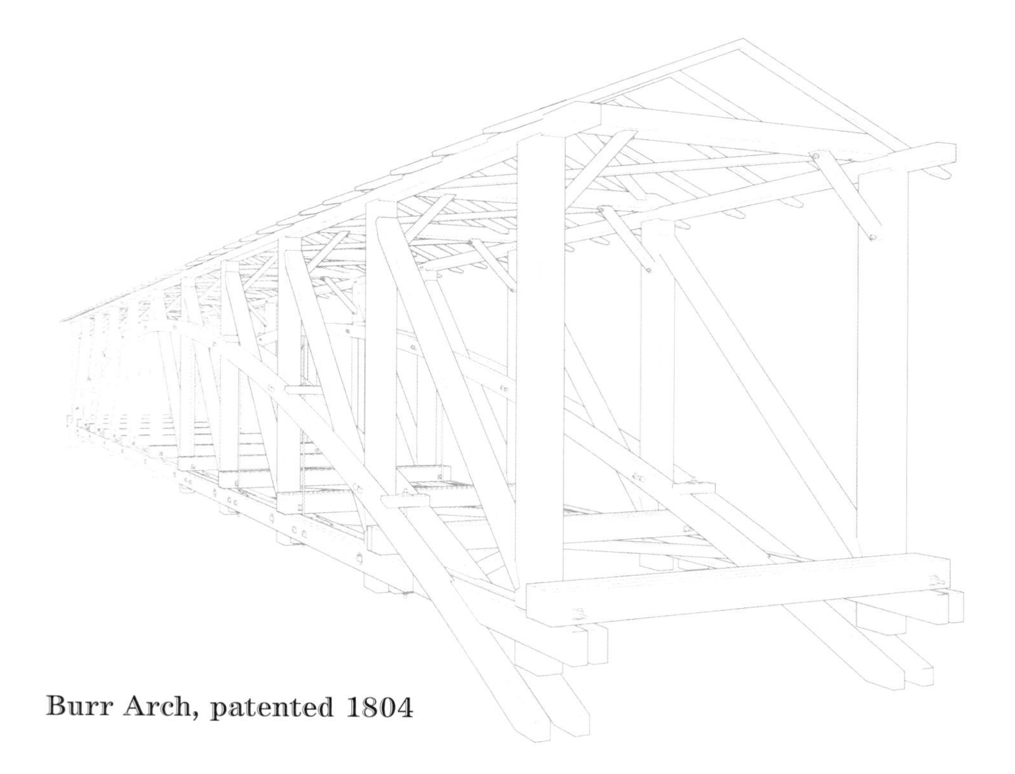

Burr Arch, patented 1804

Philippi Covered Bridge • Barbour County (overleaf)

Today the Philippi Bridge is one of only two remaining structures that display the renowned craftsmanship of Lemuel and Eli Chenoweth. Originally built of yellow poplar in 1852 for the Staunton-Parkersburg Turnpike, it is now the nation's only covered bridge serving a federal highway and is one of a handful of remaining two-lane covered bridges. With a gate at one end, tolls were established based on the number of horses and/or head of livestock that crossed. Military historians remember the bridge for its part in the first land battle of the Civil War. In late May 1861, Confederate troops were disrupting railroad lines in western Virginia and had burned seven rail bridges. During a night rainstorm, they took shelter inside the Philippi Bridge. The next morning they were surprised by Union troops and fled unceremoniously. While there were only three casualties, bullets were reportedly later found lodged in the timbers of the bridge. That night Union troops took advantage of the large bridge for a barracks. The Union victory discouraged secessionist sentiment in the area. Through its long history, the Philippi Bridge has withstood both natural and manmade events. But one accidental fire in 1989 nearly destroyed it entirely. Gasoline flowed onto the bridge as a tanker truck filled the adjacent filling station's tanks. A passing automobile's catalytic converter ignited the fuel and engulfed the entire structure, leaving it severely charred but still standing. Under the expert guidance of Dr. Emory Kemp, a West Virginia University team of restoration specialists carefully restored the bridge to its original appearance for a rededication in September 1991. The West Virginia Forestry Association donated many of the materials for the project.

National Register of Historic Places • Bridge number 48-01-01

Carrollton Covered Bridge • Barbour County
Brothers Emmett and Daniel O'Brien from Beverly, one-time associates of the famous Chenoweth brothers, built the Carrollton Covered Bridge in 1855–1856 as part of the Middle Fork Turnpike. In accepting the bridge, the turnpike superintendent noted that their work had been "executed in a very superior manner" and correctly predicted that it would be "quite permanent and durable."

The superstructure was built from yellow poplar and, with the abutments, cost a total of $4819.26. The wooden rosettes on each gable end are unusual. Several concrete supports and a concrete deck were added in 1962. In 1984 LeStok contractors from Buckhannon, West Virginia, repaired the trusses and siding and installed a new metal roof. A total restoration was completed in 2002 by Hoke Brothers Contracting of Union, West Virginia. National Register of Historic Places • Bridge number 48-01-02

Milton or Mud River Covered Bridge • Cabell County

Following the arrival of the Chesapeake & Ohio Railroad in 1876, the Milton Covered Bridge was built near the site of the present middle school to improve commerce through the rugged river valley that ran along the southern edge of the village. R.H. Baker, the local postmaster, was the builder of this traditional Howe truss. With such a relatively long span, it must have soon shown signs of weakness, for, at an unknown date, a laminated arch of planks was added to strengthen it. Iron rods attached to the arch with iron straps provided additional support for the floor beams and the arches were also bolted to the trusses. This was a common technique for railroad bridges. At the behest of the local Covered Bridge Garden Club, the state completed a major renovation of the bridge in 1971. Nonetheless, because the river regularly flooded, the bridge was felt to be in danger of washing out, so in 1997 it was moved to a new location about a mile to the east and placed on the abutments of a former covered bridge where it received extensive renovations. As the annual October Pumpkin Festival grew in size and popularity, the state decided to again move the bridge, this time to the festival grounds. Abutment stones from the original location were used for the new foundations. National Register of Historic Places • Bridge number 48-06-01

Center Point Covered Bridge • Doddridge County

The stone abutments for the Center Point Bridge were the work of T.W. Ancell and E. Underwood. John Ash and S. H. Smith erected the modest oak superstructure in 1888 for a total contract fee of $130. In 1940 it was removed from the highway system and abandoned. The Doddridge County Historical Society obtained it in 1981. They organized a volunteer restoration effort that included bottom chord repairs, siding replacement, and a new roof. The Righter Company of Columbus, Ohio, completed more extensive renovations in 2002. National Register of Historic Places • Bridge number 48-09-01

Hern's Mill Covered Bridge • Greenbrier County

Erected in 1884 by an unknown builder for $800, the Hern's Mill Bridge provided access to the S.S. Hern Mill. It was also known as the Sink's Mill Covered Bridge. Very low trusses like this were often simply covered with weather boards, but in this case an overhead frame for siding, rafters, and a roof was fabricated to cover the entire structure. A concrete-filled steel pipe was installed at midspan in 1966, and the state put on a new roof in 1982. Grandview Construction of Beckley, West Virginia, completed renovations in 2000. National Register of Historic Places • Bridge number 48-13-01

Hokes Mill Covered Bridge • Greenbrier County

An unknown builder completed the Hokes Mill Bridge between April 1897 and March 1899 for $700. Whomever the builder, he created a craftsman's version of a traditional Long truss. Two thirty-six-inch plate girders were placed inside the trusses in 1980 to carry the roadway. Although Allegheny Restoration and Builders of Morgantown, West Virginia, renovated it in 2001, the structure is now open only to pedestrians. National Register of Historic Places • Bridge number 48-13-02

Fletcher Covered Bridge • Harrison County

Since its construction by Solomon Swiger over a hundred years ago, the Fletcher Covered Bridge has been altered very little. The builder received $7.25 per lineal foot and, with abutments, the entire project cost $1372.46. Swiger's workmanship is noteworthy for its precise joints and connections, especially the elaborate "joggle" splices connecting segments of the lower chord. Work done by Allegheny Restoration and Builders of Morgantown, West Virginia in 2002 included repairs to the abutments, trusses, deck, siding, and roof. National Register of Historic Places • Bridge number 48-17-03

Simpson Creek Covered Bridge • Harrison County

Asa S. Hugill built the Simpson Creek Bridge, including the abutments, near Shinn's Mill in 1881 for $1483. When a flood washed it downstream in July 1888, the bridge was hauled back upstream but repositioned about a half mile from its original site. The following year it was sided and roofed. In the 1970s the state replaced a floor beam, repainted the exterior, and installed interior lighting. Extensive repairs were completed in 1985, but by 2001 Allegheny Restoration and Builders of Morgantown was hired to prepare additional renovations. The bridge is currently open only to pedestrians. National Register of Historic Places • Bridge number 48-17-12

Sarvis Fork Covered Bridge • Jackson County

Sarvis Fork Bridge was originally erected near a ford site on Mill Creek below Ripley. The abutments were completed in the summer of 1886, and R.B. Cunningham received a contract for nine dollars per lineal foot in December 1886 to complete the superstructure. After only four months, and for unknown reasons, all work was ordered stopped. A year later, after locals petitioned the county, the work resumed and was finally finished in 1889. Abandoned in 1924 after a metal bridge was erected nearby, the contracting firm of C.R. Kent, R.R. Hardesty, and E.R. Duke was hired for $1050 to disassemble and relocate it to the current site. The poplar arches are thought to have been a part of that work. R.C. Construction of Cutler, Ohio, completed a rehabilitation in 2000 that has allowed the bridge to remain open to traffic. National Register of Historic Places • Bridge number 48-18-01

Staats Mill Covered Bridge • Jackson County (previous pages)

The Staats Mill Covered Bridge originally stood on the Tug Fork of Big Mill Creek near the Isaac Staats mill and store. Henry F. Hartley, a prominent local contractor, erected the superstructure in 1888 for $903.95. Including abutments and fill, the complete structure cost $1788.35. Despite being constructed nearly six decades after Stephen Long's patent, Hartley followed the design closely, even copying the same double-notch joint shown in Long's 1836 promotional pamphlet on the ends of all the diagonals. Hartley made, however, one important variation in Long's original design: he omitted the wedges that were used to stiffen the trusses. The maintenance headache of keeping these wedges tight had obviously made them unpopular in the intervening years since Long's original patent. In 1971 the state completely rebuilt the floor system with steel. When the bridge was moved three miles to Cedar Lakes in 1983, all the steel was removed and the bridge was returned to its original configuration. National Register of Historic Places • Bridge number 48-18-04

Old Red or Walkersville Covered Bridge • Lewis County

The Lewis County Court originally planned to erect three iron bridges, including the Walkersville Bridge, a short distance south of Walkersville, and contracted for the construction of the abutments. Within a month, the court decided instead that one would be wooden and contracted with John G. Sprigg in December 1902 to build it. The work required three months of labor, and Sprigg was paid $567 for an all-oaken structure that displays excellent craftsmanship. Because the trusswork is so low and the ends of the top truss member are at such inclined angles, it has the appearance of an arch. While the trusses were repaired, a new roof installed, and the siding patched and painted in 1984, by 2002 it was necessary for Allegheny Restoration and Builders of Morgantown, West Virginia to completely renovate it again. National Register of Historic Places • Bridge number 48-21-03

Barrackville Covered Bridge
Marion County

The Barrackville Bridge was a vital link in the Fairmont-Wheeling Turnpike and is now West Virginia's second oldest covered bridge. Built of yellow poplar timbers by the famed Chenoweth brothers, Lemuel and Eli, during two and a half months of the summer of 1853, it originally had no sidewalk or siding. The contract for $12.50 per lineal foot forbade workmen from "insulting or mistreating travelers" and demanded strict temperance. During the Civil War, Confederate General William E. Jones threatened to burn it but was dissuaded by some Southern sympathizers (owners of the local mill) who pointed out that a ford existed nearby. Horizontal shiplap siding, painted white, was applied in 1873. A sidewalk, or "wart," was attached to one side in 1934. Repair work was done in 1951 and 1975. A total restoration in 2000 was completed by Orders Construction of St. Albans, West Virginia. National Register of Historic Places • Bridge number 48-25-02

Dents Run Covered Bridge • Monongalia County

Monongalia County received a bridge petition "for the convenience of the traveling public" at this location over Dents Run in 1863. No action was taken until a second public petition was submitted in March 1889. W.A. Loar was given a $448 contract to build the Dents Run Bridge. He ended up only completing the abutments and subcontracted with William and Joseph Mercer to build the oak superstructure. The finished bridge was accepted in December that same year. The secondary diagonals the Mercers framed into the main diagonals make their design somewhat more elaborate than the typical simple kingpost. In 1972 when a coal company proposed to open a mine nearby and use the bridge for truck traffic, locals demanded that the company instead bypass it with a new concrete and steel span. LeStok contractors from Buckhannon, West Virginia completed a restoration in 1984, but this work had to be renewed in 2004 by Hoke Brothers Contracting of Union, West Virginia. National Register of Historic Places • Bridge number 48-31-03

Laurel Creek Covered Bridge • Monroe County

This modest covered bridge, Laurel Creek Bridge, is the shortest in the state. Lewis Miller built its abutments and Robert Arnott prepared the superstructure in 1911 from oak that had cured for a year. Each truss has three iron rods that support the solitary, central floor beam. Chestnut riven by Lon Wickline was used for the roofing shakes. The total cost, with abutments, was only $365. A steel deck was added in 1976, but Hoke Brothers of Union, West Virginia removed it in 2000 during a renovation. National Register of Historic Places • Bridge number 48-32-01

Indian Creek Covered Bridge • Monroe County

The Indian Creek Bridge, which was built in 1903 for $445, replaced an earlier structure. E.P. and A.P. Smith built the abutments and Ray and Oscar Weikel completed the superstructure. The Weikels were only sixteen and eighteen when they took on the contract, so they were required to get their uncle, who owned the saw mill that supplied their materials, to warranty their work. The two devised their own tackle to hoist the white pine and oak timbers. The bridge was used until 1930. In 1965 it was leased to the county historical society and then acquired by them in 1985. The historical society hired a brother of the original builders to strengthen it. Using hand methods, he fabricated oak shingles to replace the original chestnut and nailed them on, as was customary, during a moonlit night to prevent their curling. This roof was replaced in the spring of 2000 when Hoke Brothers Construction of Union, West Virginia repaired the roof trusses, installed a glu-lam deck and added new siding. The bridge is only open to pedestrians. National Register of Historic Places • Bridge number 48-32-02

Locust Creek Covered Bridge • Pocahontas County (and overleaf)

County voters approved a levy in July 1888 that included $1200 for the Locust Creek Bridge. The contract was let to R.N. Bruce, and he obviously came to some agreement with the Smith Bridge Company of Toledo, Ohio, owners of the patent for the truss (see introduction). This could have included just the plans or may have also included the materials. The bridge, fabricated in hemlock or "dense pine," was completed by mid-November. W.M. Irvine completed extensive repairs in 1904. In 1968 repairs were made to the trusses, floor, and roof. Order Construction Company of St. Albans, West Virginia, repaired truss members, replaced floorbeams, and renewed the roof. It has been bypassed and is open only to pedestrians. National Register of Historic Places • Bridge number 48-38-01

Fish Creek Covered Bridge • Wetzel County

The Fish Creek Bridge is the only remaining covered bridge in a county that once had many. County records indicate that specifications for this bridge were filed in the summer of 1881, but no indication of the builder is given. An overloaded truck destroyed the roof in 1974 and forced the county, who salvaged as much of the old timbers as possible, to prepare a replacement roof. A new deck was installed at the same time. A complete renovation was done by Lone Pine Construction of Bentley, Pennsylvania, in 2001. National Register of Historic Places • Bridge number 48-52-01

48-01-02

Carrollton Covered Bridge • Barbour County

Description: 141-foot Burr truss, built 1855-56. *Location*: in Carrollton over Buckhannon River on County Route 36. *Directions*: US Route 119 south of Philippi about 5.5 miles to Carrollton Road (County Road 36) and turn left; proceed about one-half mile to Carrollton. Page 254–255

48-01-01

Philippi Covered Bridge • Barbour County

Description: 286-foot, two-span Long truss with arches, built 1852. *Location*: in Philippi over Tygart River at the junction of US Route 119 and 250. *Directions*: About forty miles south of Morgantown on US Route 119 in the center of Philippi. Page 251–253

48-06-01

Milton or Mud River Covered Bridge • Cabell County

Description: 108-foot Howe truss with added arch, built 1876. *Location*: in Milton on the grounds of the West Virginia Pumpkin Park. *Directions*: Exit 28 from I-64, south on County Route 13, right (west) on US Route 60, left on Fairgrounds Road (County Road 25-7) and left on One Pumpkin Way. Page 256

48-09-01

Center Point Covered Bridge • Doddridge County

Description: 42-foot Long truss, built 1888. *Location*: over the Pike Fork of McElroy Creek on County Route 10, off County Route 23. *Directions*: north from Salem about 10.2 miles on County Route 23 and turn right (east) onto Pike Fork Road (County Road 10) at Center Point. Page 257

48-13-01

Herns Mill Covered Bridge • Greenbrier County

Description: 54-foot queenpost truss, built 1884. *Location*: over Milligans Creek on County Road 40 north of Lewisburg, off US Route 60. *Directions*: from Lewisburg on US Route 60 west approximately 2.6 miles to Bungers Mill Road (County Road 60/11) and turn left, then turn left onto Herns Mill Road (County Road 40) and proceed one mile. Page 258–259

48-13-02

Hokes Mill Covered Bridge • Greenbrier County

Description: 81.5-foot Long truss, built 1897-99. *Location*: over Second Creek on County Road 62 southwest of Ronceverte. *Directions*: take US Route 219 south from Ronceverte across the Greenbrier River. Proceed approximately 3.6 miles to Hokes Mill Road (County Road 62) and turn right and bear to the left for seven miles to Hokes Mill. Page 260

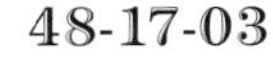
48-17-03

Fletcher Covered Bridge • Harrison County

Description: 58-foot multiple kingpost truss, built in 1891. *Location*: over the Righthand Fork of Ten Mile Creek on County Route 5/29 northwest of Wolf Summit. *Directions*: take US Route 50 west of Wolf Summit to Marshville Exit 5 and turn right (north). Proceed to County Route 5/29 and proceed approximately one-half mile to the bridge. Page 261

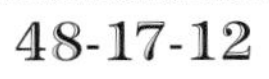
48-17-12

Simpson Creek Covered Bridge • Harrison County

Description: 75-foot multiple kingpost truss, built in 1881. *Location*: over Simpson Creek adjacent to County Route 24-2 northwest of Bridgeport. *Directions*: take Exit 121 from I-79 and take Meadowbrook Road (County Road 24) north towards the Meadowbrook Mall approximately 4 miles. Page 262

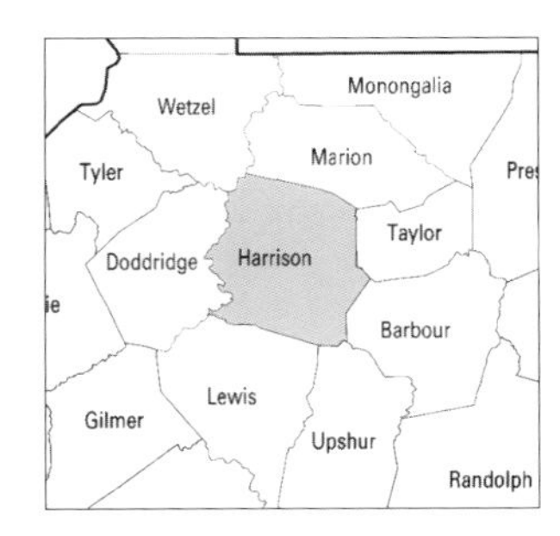

48-18-01

Sarvis Fork Covered Bridge • Jackson County

Description: 101.25-foot Long truss with added arch, built in 1889. *Location*: over Left Fork of Sandy Creek on County Route 21-15 northeast of Sandyville. *Directions*: from Exit 146 from I-77, proceed east on County Route 56 towards Sandyville. Turn left (north) on County Route 21 at New Era and proceed 1.2 miles and turn right on County Route 21-15. Page 263

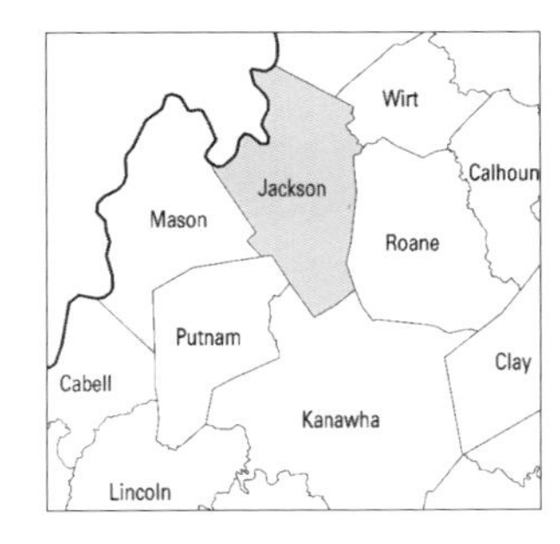

48-18-04

Staats Mill Covered Bridge • Jackson County

Description: 97-foot Long truss, built 1888. *Location*: in Cedar Lakes, the FFA-FHA State Camp, southeast of Ripley. *Directions*: from the center of Ripley on US Route 33, take County Route 21 south to Cedar Lakes Road (County Road 25) and turn left and proceed 1.7 miles to the campgrounds. Bridge is a short distance inside the grounds on the left. Page 264–266

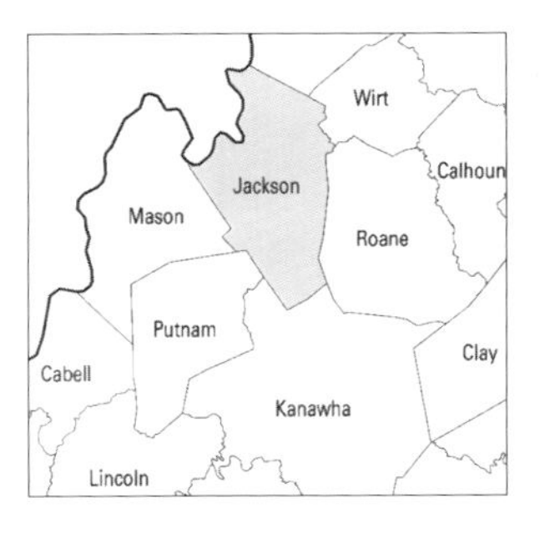

48-21-03

Old Red or Walkersville Covered Bridge • Lewis County

Description: 39-foot queenpost truss, built in 1903. *Location*: over the Right Fork of the West Fork River just off US Route 19, south of Walkersville. *Directions*: from Walkersville proceed south about one mile to Big Run Road (County Road 19-17) and turn right. Page 266–267

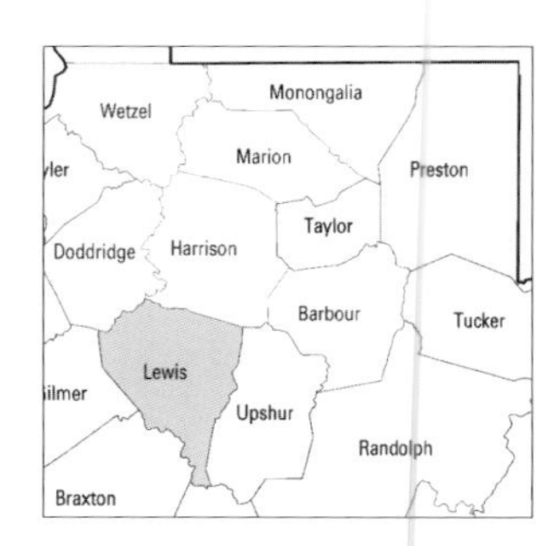

48-25-02

Barrackville Covered Bridge • Marion County

Description: 146-foot Burr truss, built in 1853. *Location*: over Buffalo Creek in the northern edge of Barrackville. *Directions*: from Fairmont, take US Route 250 north to County Route 21 and turn right (north). Proceed through Barrackville to the junction with County Route 250/32. Page 268–269

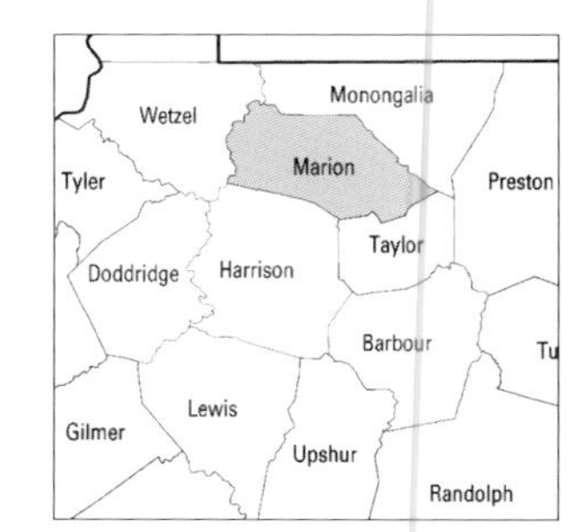

48-31-03

Dents Run Covered Bridge • Monangalia County

Description: 40-foot kingpost truss, built in 1889. *Location*: over Dents Run on County Route 43/3 west of Morgantown. *Directions*: take US Route 19 south from Morgantown to the junction of Sugar Grove Road (County Road 43 where a state historical marker is located) and turn right (north) and proceed .7 miles to County Route 43/3 and turn left (west) onto a gravel road and proceed one mile to the bridge. Page 270

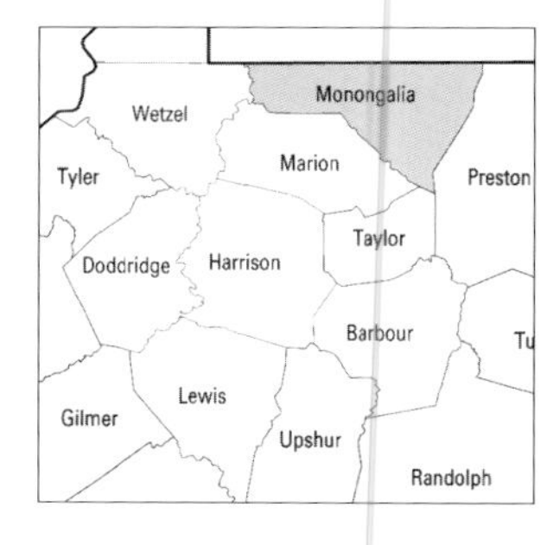

48-32-02

Indian Creek Covered Bridge • Monroe County

Description: 49-foot Long truss, built 1903. *Location*: over Indian Creek near US Route 219, southwest of Union. *Directions*: proceed south on US Route 219 from Union approximately five miles to a point opposite St. John's Church. Page 271

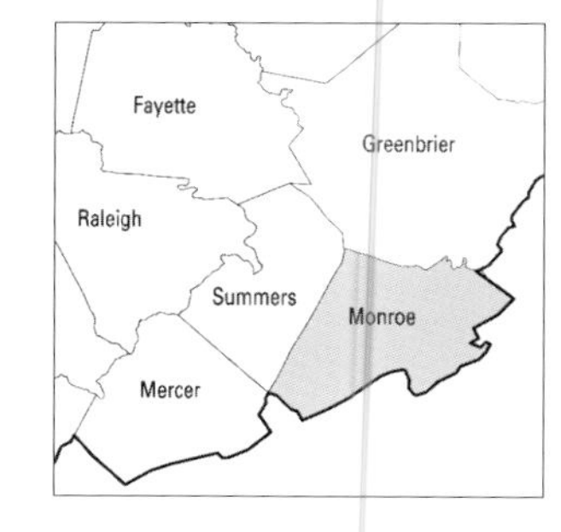

48-32-01

Laurel Creek Covered Bridge • Monroe County

Description: 24.5-foot queenpost truss, built in 1911. *Location*: over Laurel Creek on County Route 219/11 west of Union. *Directions*: from Union take US Route 219 south through Salt Sulphur Springs to Lilleydale Road (County Road 219-7) and turn right (east). Follow it three miles until Lillydale Road forks and take the right fork on Laurel Creek Road (County Road 219-11) and proceed 1.4 miles to bridge. Page 272

48-38-01

Locust Creek Covered Bridge • Pocahontas County

Description: 113.75-foot modified Smith truss, built in 1888. *Location*: over Locust Creek on County Route 31, south of Hillsboro. *Directions*: from US Route 219 in Hillsboro proceed south on County Route 31 approximately 6.3 miles to bridge. Page 273–274

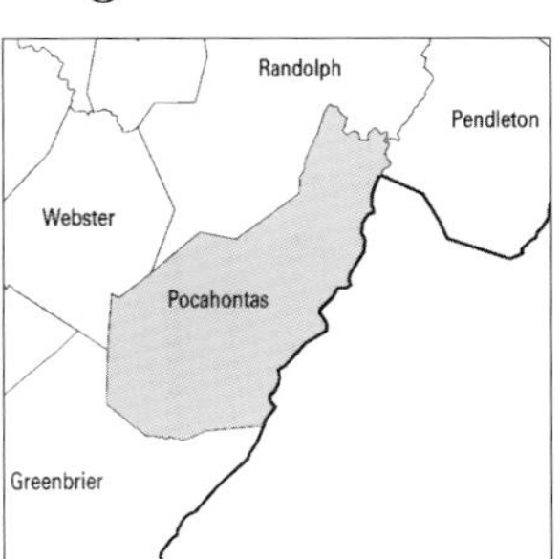

48-52-01

Fish Creek Covered Bridge • Wetzel County

Description: 36-foot kingpost truss, built 1881. *Location*: over Fish Creek, on County Route 13 southeast of Hundred. *Directions*: on US Route 250 in Hundred, proceed east one half mile to County Route 13 and turn right (south). Page 275

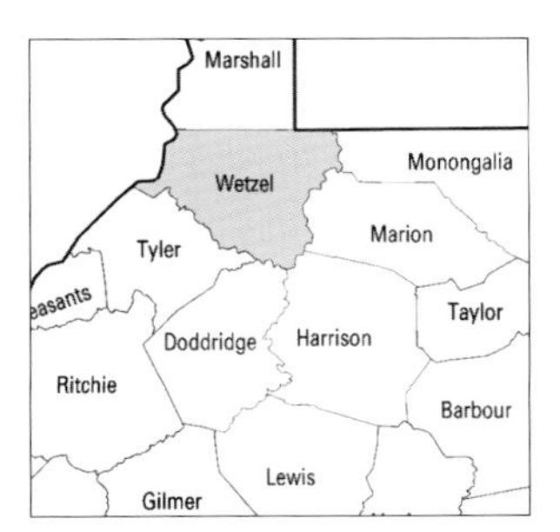

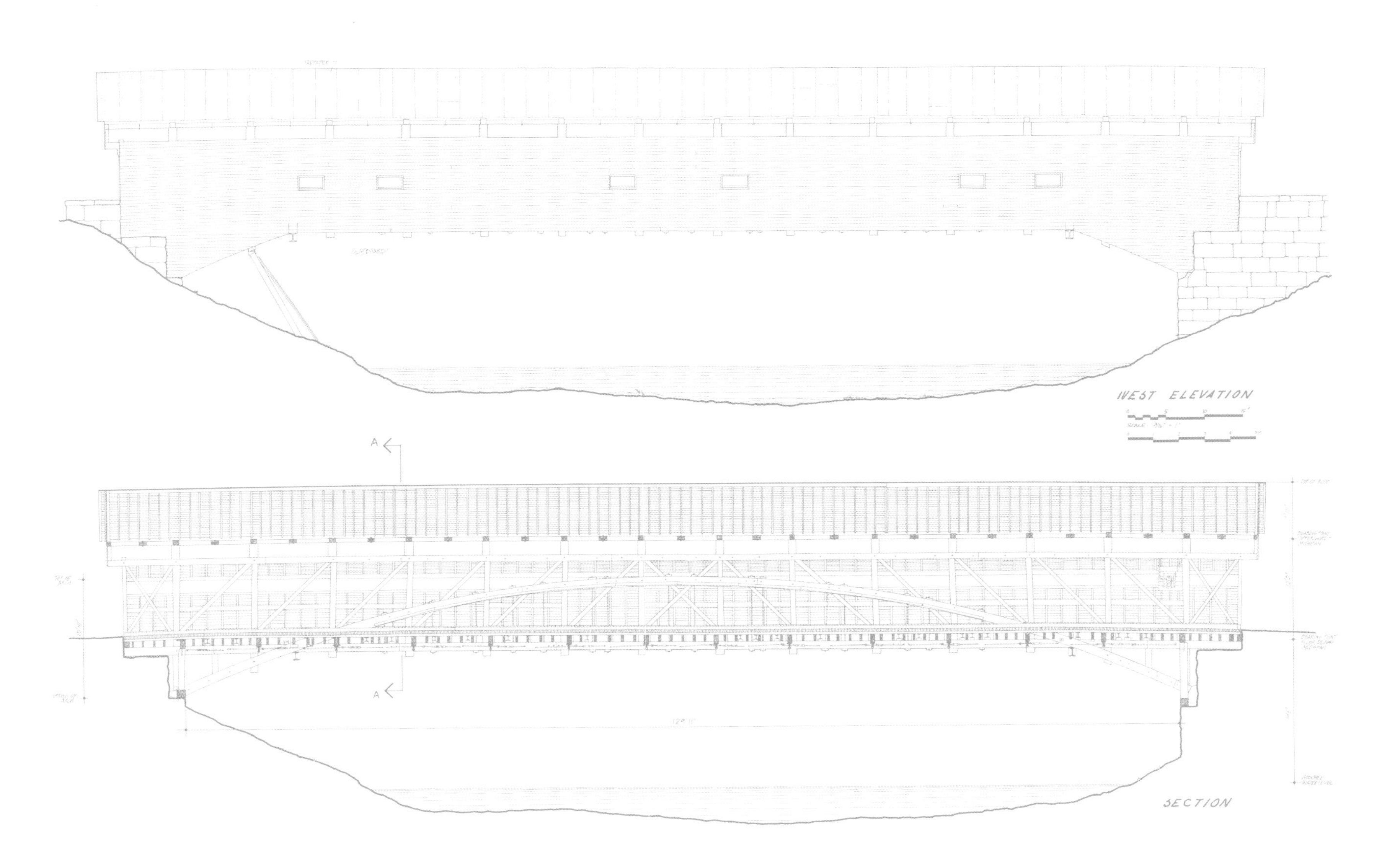

Barrackville Covered Bridge, 1853

Covered Bridge Chronology

(bridges of uncertain date have been omitted; page numbers are for text description)

1829 • Roberts, Burr truss, Preble County, Ohio, 145–146
1831 • Newton Falls, Town lattice, Trumbull County, Ohio, 57
1835 • Dover, queenpost variant, Mason County, Kentucky, 243
1849 • Armstrong, multiple kingpost, Guernsey County, Ohio, 51
1850 • Jediah Hill, queenpost truss, Hamilton County, Ohio, 134
1851 • Mull Road, Town lattice, Sandusky County, Ohio, 164–166
1852 • Philippi, Long truss, Barbour County, West Virginia, 251–253
1853 • Barrackville, Burr truss, Marion County, West Virginia, 268–269
1855 • Carrollton, Burr truss, Barbour County, West Virginia, 254–255
1855 • Harshaville, multiple kingpost, Adams County, Ohio, 113
1855 • Indian Camp, multiple kingpost, Guernsey County, Ohio, 50
1855 • Switzer, Howe truss, Franklin County, Kentucky, 238
1859 • Bowman Mill, multiple kingpost, Perry County, Ohio, 220
1860 • Eldean, Long truss, Miami County, Ohio, 136–137
1863 • Helmick, multiple kingpost, Coshocton County, Ohio, 80–81
1864 • McLeery, multiple kingpost, Fairfield County, Ohio, 191
1864 • Valley Pike, kingpost truss, Mason County, Kentucky, 244
1865 • Beech Fork, multiple kingpost with arch, Washington County, Kentucky, 246–247
1865 • Germantown, suspension truss, Montgomery County, Ohio, 138–139
1867 • Graham Road, Town lattice, Ashtabula County, Ohio, 25
1867 • Hillsboro, multiple kingpost, Fleming County, Kentucky, 235
1867 • Island Run, multiple kingpost, Morgan County, Ohio, 80–81
1867 • Knowlton, multiple kingpost, Monroe County, Ohio, 77
1867 • Mechanicsville Road, Howe truss, Ashtabula County, Ohio, 28–29
1867 • Ringo's Mill, multiple kingpost, Fleming County, Kentucky, 234
1867 • Wiswell Road, Town lattice, Ashtabula County, Ohio, 33
1868 • Black, Long truss, Butler County, Ohio, 124–125
1868 • Culbertson/Treacle, Partridge truss, Union County, Ohio, 171
1868 • Fairfield Pike, Wernweg truss, Butler County, Ohio, 121–123
1868 • Harpersfield, Howe truss, Ashtabula County, Ohio, 30–32
1868 • Middle Road, Howe truss, Ashtabula County, Ohio, 22
1868 • Root Road, Town lattice, Ashtabula County, Ohio, 96–97
1868 • South Denmark Road, Town lattice, Ashtabula County, Ohio, 26
1868 • Upper Darby, Partridge truss, Union County, Ohio, 167–169
1870 • Carillon Park, Warren truss, Montgomery County, Ohio, 140
1870 • Johnson Road, Smith truss, Jackson County, Ohio, 70
1870 • Locust Creek, Smith truss (modified), Pocahontas County, West Virginia, 273–274
1870 • Lynchburg, Long truss, Highland County, Ohio, 135
1870 • Oldtown, multiple kingpost, Greenup County, Kentucky, 241
1870 • Spain Creek, Partridge truss, Union County, Ohio, 170
1871 • Baker, multiple kingpost, Fairfield County, Ohio, 194–195

1871 • Buckeye Furnace, Smith truss, Jackson County, Ohio, 72–73
1871 • Eakin Mill, multiple kingpost, Vinton County, Ohio, 92
1871 • Martinsville, multiple kingpost, Clinton County, Ohio, 127
1871 • McLain, multiple kingpost, Licking County, Ohio, 212
1871 • Shade, multiple kingpost, Fairfield County, Ohio, 190
1872 • Barkhurst Mill, multiple kingpost, Morgan County, Ohio, 78–79
1872 • Byer, Smith truss, Jackson County, Ohio, 71
1873 • Axe Handle, Partridge truss, Union County, Ohio, 172
1873 • Buckskin, Smith truss, Ross County, Ohio, 151
1873 • Dewey Road, Town lattice, Ashtabula County, Ohio, 19
1873 • Parker, Howe truss, Wyandot County, Ohio, 175
1874 • Girl Scout, multiple kingpost, Licking County, Ohio, 209
1874 • Hopewell, multiple kingpost, Perry County, Ohio, 217
1874 • Johnson Creek, Smith truss, Robertson County, Kentucky, 245
1874 • Otway, Smith truss, Scioto County, Ohio, 152–153
1874 • Ponn, multiple kingpost, Vinton County, Ohio, 90–91
1874 • Riverdale Road, Town lattice, Ashtabula County, Ohio, 32
1875 • Adams, multiple kingpost, Morgan County, Ohio, 82
1875 • Bennett Mill, Wheeler truss, Greenup County, Kentucky, 239–240
1875 • Mount Olive, queenpost truss, Vinton County, Ohio, 87
1875 • North Pole, Smith truss, Brown County, Ohio, 119
1875 • Ruffner, Smith truss, Perry County, Ohio, 221–222
1875 • Shaeffer, multiple kingpost, Belmont County, Ohio, 68–69
1875 • Teegarden, multiple kingpost, Columbiana County, Ohio, 42–43
1876 • Bay, multiple kingpost, Vinton County, Ohio, 88–89
1876 • Doyle Road, Town lattice, Ashtabula County, Ohio, 27
1876 • McColly, Howe truss, Logan County, Ohio, 162
1876 • Milton, Howe truss with arch, Cabell County, West Virginia, 256
1876 • Palos, multiple kingpost, Athens County, Ohio, 65
1876 • Rinard, Smith truss, Washington County, Ohio, 104–105
1876 • Salt Creek, Warren truss, Muskingum County, Ohio, 54–55
1876 • Skull Fork, multiple kingpost, Harrison County, Ohio, 52
1877 • Bickham, Howe truss, Logan County, Ohio, 178
1877 • Colville Pike, multiple kingpost, Bourbon County, Kentucky, 231
1877 • Jasper, Warren truss, Montgomery County, Ohio, 141
1877 • McCafferty, Smith truss, Brown County, Ohio, 118
1877 • Scottown, multiple kingpost variant, Lawrence County, Ohio, 74–75
1877 • Stevenson, Smith truss, Greene County, Ohio, 130
1877 • West Engle, Smith truss, Greene County, Ohio, 129
1878 • Harra, Long truss, Washington County, Ohio, 98
1878 • Hills, Howe truss, Washington County, Ohio, 102
1878 • New Hope, Howe truss with arch, Brown County, Ohio, 116–117
1878 • Root, Long truss, Washington County, Ohio, 96–97
1878 • Sells, multiple kingpost, Columbiana County, Ohio, 39
1878 • Stonelick, Howe truss, Clermont County, Ohio, 126

1878 • Swartz, Howe truss, Wyandot County, Ohio, 176–177
1879 • Blackwood, multiple kingpost, Athens County, Ohio, 66–67
1879 • George Miller, Smith truss, Brown County, Ohio, 120
1879 • Hune, Long truss, Washington County, Ohio, 103
1879 • Jacks Hollow, multiple kingpost, Perry County, Ohio, 218–219
1879 • McClellan, multiple kingpost, Columbiana County, Ohio, 40–41
1880 • Kidwell, Howe truss, Athens County, Ohio, 66
1881 • Brown, Smith truss, Brown County, Ohio, 115
1881 • Fish Creek, kingpost, Wetzel County, West Virginia, 275
1881 • Gregg Mill, multiple kingpost, Licking County, Ohio, 210–211
1881 • John Bright, suspension truss, Fairfield County, Ohio, 183–184
1881 • Rosseau, multiple kingpost, Morgan County, Ohio, 79
1881 • Simpson Creek, multiple kingpost, Harrison County, West Virginia, 262
1883 • Ballard Road, Howe truss, Greene County, Ohio, 132–133
1883 • Chambers Road, Childs truss, Delaware County, Ohio, 181
1883 • Charlton Mill, Howe truss, Greene County, Ohio, 131
1883 • Parks, multiple kingpost, Perry County, Ohio, 216
1884 • Cox, queenpost truss, Vinton County, Ohio, 93
1884 • Hern's Mill, queenpost truss, Greenbrier County, West Virginia, 258–259
1885 • Brannon Fork, multiple kingpost, Franklin County, Ohio, 204–205
1886 • Cemetery, Howe truss, Greene County, Ohio, 128
1886 • Foraker, multiple kingpost, Monroe County, Ohio, 76
1886 • Shinn, multiple kingpost with arch, Washington County, Ohio, 94
1887 • Bergstresser, Partridge truss, Franklin County, Ohio, 202–204
1887 • Brubaker, Childs truss, Preble County, Ohio, 147
1887 • Dixon Branch, Childs truss, Preble County, Ohio, 144
1887 • Johnston, Howe truss, Fairfield County, Ohio, 188
1887 • Mink Hollow, multiple kingpost, Fairfield County, Ohio, 198
1887 • Valentine/Green, multiple kingpost, Pickaway County, Ohio, 142
1888 • Bell, multiple kingpost, Washington County, Ohio, 99
1888 • Center Point, Long truss, Doddridge County, West Virginia, 257
1888 • Lockville #2, queenpost truss, Fairfield County, Ohio, 197
1888 • Staats Mill, Long truss, Jackson County, West Virginia, 264–266
1889 • Dents Run, kingpost, Monongalia County, West Virginia, 270
1889 • Sarvis Fork, Long truss with arch, Jackson County, West Virginia, 263
1890 • Kirker, multiple kingpost, Adams County, Ohio, 114
1891 • Fletcher, multiple kingpost, Harrison County, West Virginia, 261
1891 • Hizey, multiple kingpost, Fairfield County, Ohio, 182
1891 • Jon Raab, queenpost truss, Fairfield County, Ohio, 196
1891 • Shryer, multiple kingpost, Fairfield County, Ohio, 192
1894 • Geeting, Childs truss, Preble County, Ohio, 149
1894 • Harshman, Childs truss, Preble County, Ohio, 143
1894 • Henry, multiple kingpost, Washington County, Ohio, 95
1894 • Schwendeman, multiple kingpost, Washington County, Ohio, 101
1895 • Christman, Childs truss, Preble County, Ohio, 148

1895 • Warnke, Childs truss, Preble County, Ohio, 150
1898 • Charles Holliday, multiple kingpost, Fairfield County, Ohio, 193
1898 • Indian Creek, Long truss, Monroe County, West Virginia, 272
1899 • Hokes Mill, Long truss, Greenbrier County, West Virginia, 260
1899 • Roley School, multiple kingpost, Fairfield County, Ohio, 202
1901 • Hanaway, multiple kingpost, Fairfield County, Ohio, 187
1901 • Rock Mill, queenpost truss, Fairfield County, Ohio, 199–201
1902 • Old Red/Walkersville, queenpost truss, Lewis County, West Virginia, 266–267
1904 • Hutchins, multiple kingpost, Fairfield County, Ohio, 185–187
1906 • Zeller-Smith, multiple kingpost, Fairfield County, Ohio, 189
1911 • Laurel Creek, queenpost truss, Monroe County, West Virginia, 271
1914 • Parrish, multiple kingpost, Noble County, Ohio, 85
1915 • Manchester, multiple kingpost, Noble County, Ohio, 84
1920 • Milton Dye, multiple kingpost, Morgan County, Ohio, 83
1947 • Davis Farm, multiple kingpost, Licking County, Ohio, 213
1983 • State Road, Town lattice, Ashtabula County, Ohio, 34
1986 • Caine Road, Pratt truss, Ashtabula County, Ohio, 35
1991 • Canal Greenway, Town lattice, Licking County, Ohio, 214–215
1992 • Memorial, Howe truss, Auglaize County, Ohio, 161
1993 • Fairgrounds, Town lattice, Franklin County, Ohio, 206–207
1995 • Giddings Road, Pratt truss, Ashtabula County, Ohio, 36
1996 • Bluebird Farm, multiple kingpost, Carroll County, Ohio, 38
1997 • Hindman Memorial, Warren truss, Jefferson County, Ohio, 52–53
1998 • Charles Harding Memorial, multiple kingpost, Cuyahoga County, Ohio, 47
1998 • Fletcher, Smith truss, Miami County, Ohio, 138
1999 • Lockport #2, Howe truss, Williams County, Ohio, 173
1999 • Netcher Road, Haupt truss, Ashtabula County, Ohio, 37
2004 • Fairgrounds, Pratt truss, Williams County, Ohio, 174
2004 • Tare Creek, Howe truss, Geauga County, Ohio, 48–49
2007–2008 • "number seventeen," Pratt truss, Ashtabula County
600 foot span length
This is to be the longest covered bridge in the nation.

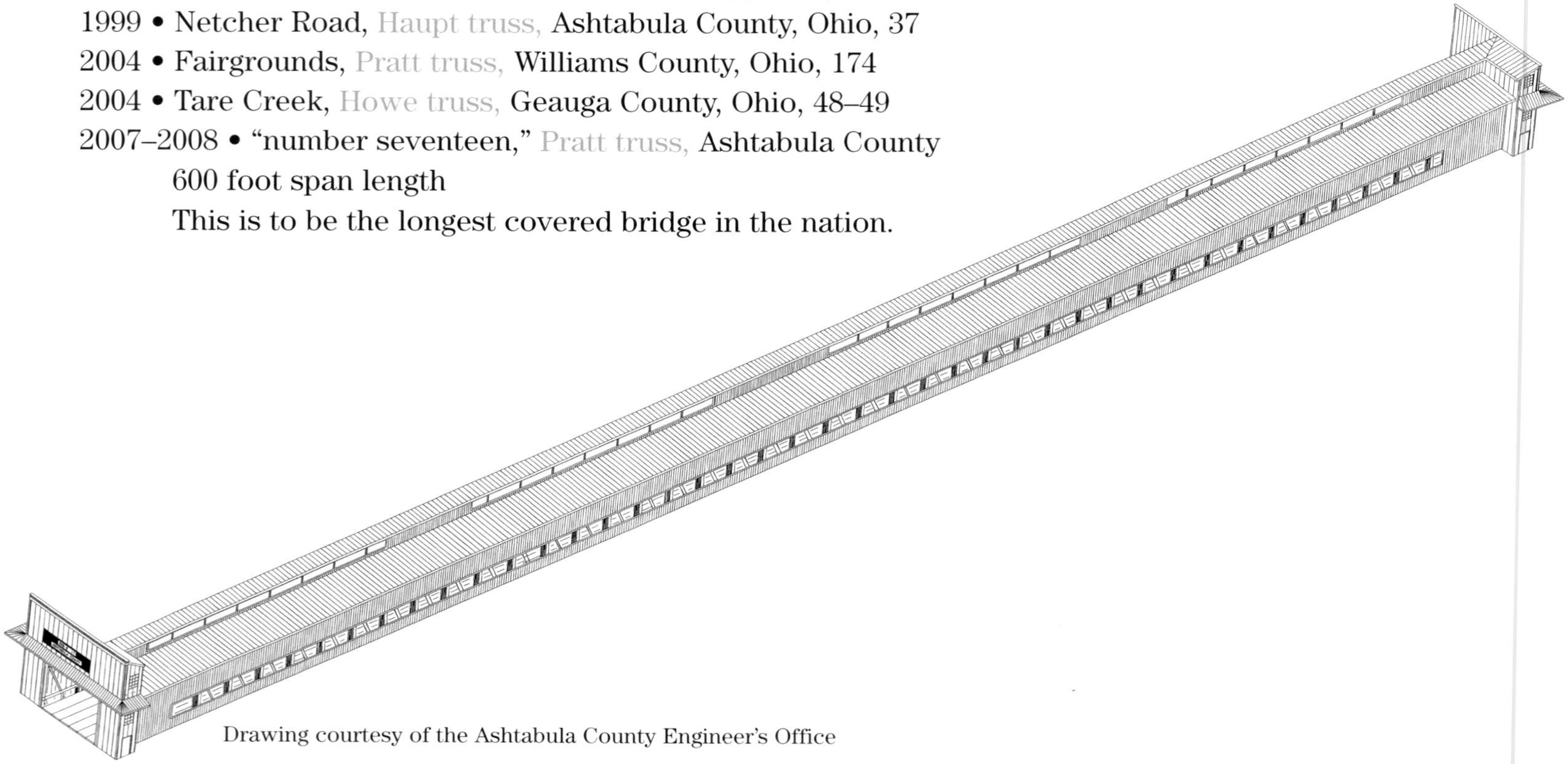

Drawing courtesy of the Ashtabula County Engineer's Office

Index

The first page number (or series of page numbers) refers to the description and photograph, the second page number refers to the directions.

Bridges that are known by multiple names are listed under each name.

Index to *Reflections on Covered Bridges*

Index to the Covered Bridges

The first page number (or series of page numbers) refers to the description and photograph, the second page number refers to the directions.

Bridges that are known by multiple names are listed under each name.

The first page number (or series of page numbers) refers to the description and photograph, the second page number refers to the directions.

Bridges that are known by multiple names are listed under each name.

The first page number (or series of page numbers) refers to the description and photograph, the second page number refers to the directions.

Bridges that are known by multiple names are listed under each name.

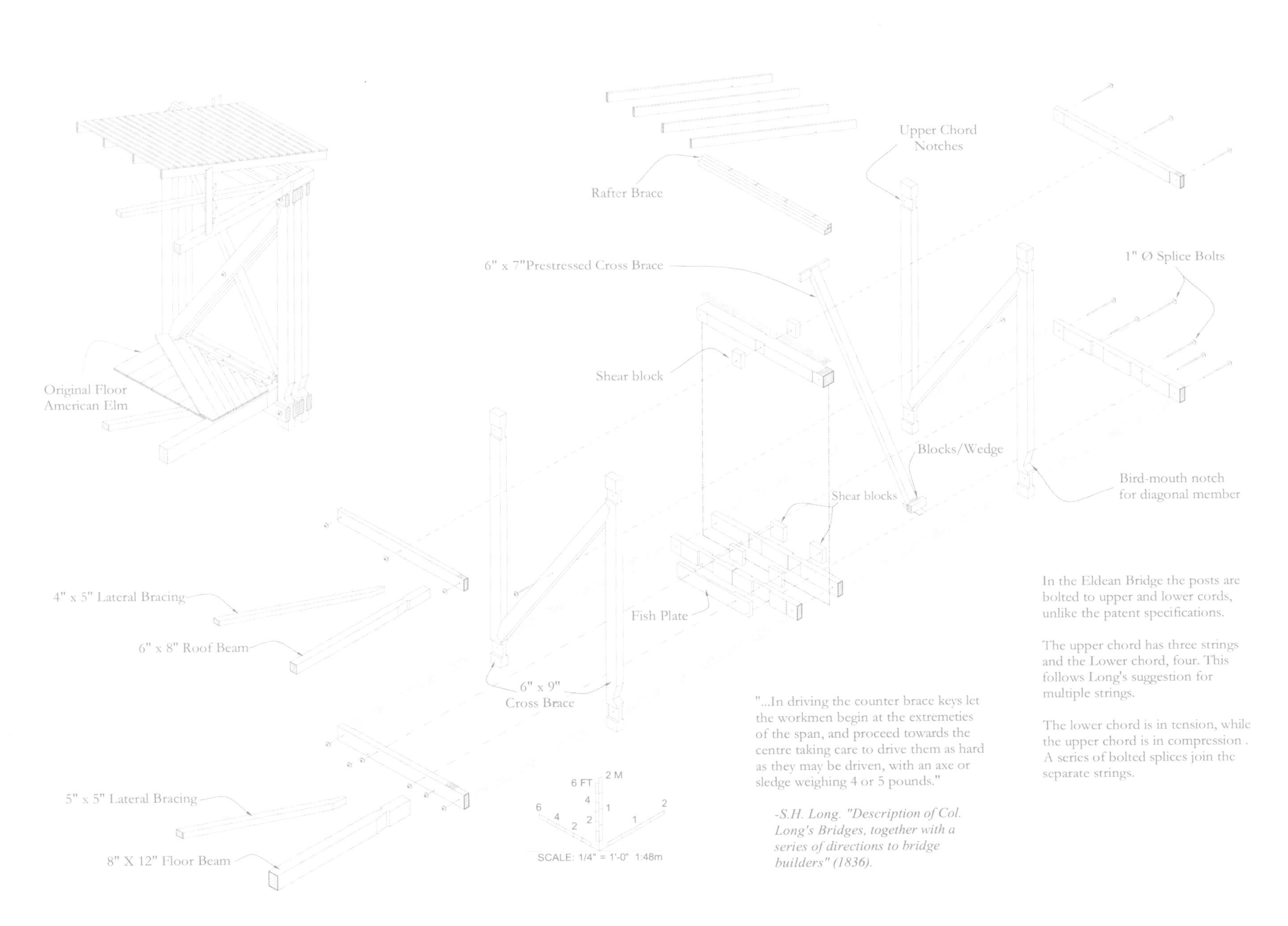

Eldean Covered Bridge, Miami County Ohio, 1860

Ohio Historic Bridge Association

A portion of the proceeds from the sales of this book will be donated to the Ohio Historic Bridge Association. The association was formed in 1960 to save what is now Muskingum County's last covered bridge, the Salt Creek Covered Bridge. Originally called the Southern Ohio Covered Bridge Association, the name was changed in 1993 to reflect the larger interests and preservation concerns of the membership. The group works to research and preserve all types of historic bridges: stone, iron, steel, and concrete, as well as wooden.

The association's quarterly journal, *Bridges and Byways*, keeps readers up-to-date on recent developments affecting the state's historic bridges along with stories relating to their construction and builders. In addition, meetings that feature programs on historic bridges are held in March and November at a central Ohio location. Spring and fall tours of the state's historic bridges are scheduled for the third Sundays of May and September. An annual picnic, held at the Salt Creek Covered Bridge, occurs on the third Sunday of July.

The association publishes a complete traveler's guide, *The Ohio Historic Bridge Guide*. It includes brief descriptions and location information for all the state's covered bridges and some of the more outstanding historic stone, concrete, and metal bridges.

Individual membership categories include life, $250; supporting, $40; contributing, $25; family, $15; individual, $10; and student/senior, $8. Memberships should be sent to Joseph W. Charles, 726 Newark-Granville Road, Granville, Ohio 43023-1451. General correspondence should be sent to the association offices at the Ohio Historical Society, 1982 Velma Avenue, Columbus, Ohio 43211-2497.

Work on the Salt Creek Covered Bridge overseen by the association in 1997–98 exemplifies the possibilities of public/private cooperative projects. As a private, non-profit group, the association combined efforts with private individuals, county agencies, commercial firms, and the Ohio Department of Transportation to renovate this 1876 bridge. Members of the group reinstalled the vertical siding following a contractor's work. They included David Simmons (upper left and moving clockwise), Harry Hill, William Miller, and Joe Charles.

Since early childhood, **Miriam F. Wood** has had a deep interest in covered bridges. Born, raised, and educated in Columbus, Ohio, she graduated with a degree in history from Capital University. Since the early 1950s, Miriam has made an in-depth study of covered bridges and their builders and has gathered a large collection of pictures and information on these bridges. She and her late husband, Richard A. Wood, made many family trips on weekends with their four children to visit and photograph covered bridges.

In 1960, Miriam became a charter member of the Ohio Historic Bridge Association and over the years served that organization in several capacities: as president, corresponding secretary, historian, and editor of *Bridges & Byways*, the quarterly publication of the OHBA. In the 1970s, Miriam nominated over fifty Ohio covered bridges to the National Register of Historic Places for the Ohio Historical Society. In 1989, Miriam served as a consultant to the Ohio Department of Transportation on the preparation of The Second Ohio Historic Bridge Inventory: Evaluation and Preservation Plan. In 1989, the Ohio Historic Preservation Office awarded Miriam with their Public Education and Awareness Award in recognition of her many contributions to the preservation of Ohio's covered bridges.

Miriam is still active with the Ohio Historic Bridge Association as editor of *Bridges & Byways* and as corresponding secretary and historian. She is the author of *The Covered Bridges of Ohio: An Atlas and History* (1993).

Miriam Wood and David Simmons

David A. Simmons is chief editor of *Timeline*, an award-winning illustrated magazine embracing the fields of history, prehistory, and the natural sciences published by the Ohio Historical Society. He is a twenty-year veteran on the *Timeline* staff.

David holds both undergraduate and graduate degrees in American history from Miami University. Before joining the Ohio Historical Society staff, the Darke County native worked with the Environmental Preservation Office in Cincinnati and was executive director of the Preble County Historical Society. He has published articles on a variety of technological history topics, including military architecture, canal construction, and the history of bridge engineering and is the recipient of two writing awards from the Society for Industrial Archeology.

Since 1983, David has been an advisor and contributing writer for the four statewide historic bridge inventories, including evaluation and preservation plans. His extensive research and publishing on the history of Ohio bridge engineering included a regular column, “Historically Speaking,” in the County Engineer’s Association of Ohio quarterly. Since 1985, David has helped plan seven historic bridge conferences, including several international in scope. Among other activities, David is president of the Ohio Historic Bridge Association for whom he oversaw the restoration of the Salt Creek Covered Bridge in Muskingum County, Ohio.

Bill Miller

Bill Miller is a Business Administration graduate of Northern Kentucky University although he considers it a success that he was able to transform his "career" nine years ago from a corporate manager to a full-time photographer. Bill first became fascinated with covered bridges while vacationing in Killington, Vermont. What began as souvenir remembrances of a vacation trip, have now become a calling, having photographed over four hundred covered bridges in twenty states. Recently, Bill has been photographing covered bridges in the Western United States including the Mariposa Covered Bridge (05-22-01, built in 1878) inside Yosemite National Park. Bill's photographic interests also include lighthouses, beach scenes, and historic barns. He was the official photographer for Ohio's Bicentennial celebration in 2003, which culminated in his previous book-length project, *Ohio's Bicentennial Barns*.

Bill drives countless miles and shoots countless rolls of color transparency film, often returning to a bridge site three or four times to capture the image he desires. He uses a Mamiya 645AFD medium format camera and a 35MM Canon EON ELAN IIE. The angle of the light and the weather conditions play a big role in color saturation and balance, and in capturing an image that enhances the natural scene. Bill's secret: patience.

Bill Miller exhibits and sells his photography at many art shows and craft fairs including St. Stephen's Art & Craft Show in Coconut Grove, Florida; the Yellow Daisy Festival in Stone Mountain, Georgia; and the Worthington Art Festival in Worthington, Ohio. Bill is a member of several state and national historical bridge associations.

The combined experience of these contributors in covered bridge wisdom and lore is over 88 years.